Pra... mystery series:

"Quirky . . . intriguing . . . [with] recipes to make your stomach growl."
—*Reader to Reader*

"This debut culinary mystery is a light soufflé of a book (with recipes) that makes a perfect mix for fans of Jenn McKinlay, Leslie Budewitz, or Jessica Beck."
—*Library Journal* on *Meet Your Baker*

"The close-knit group of family and friends, the warm details of baking and running a bakeshop framing the story, and delicious-sounding recipes add up to a satisfying cozy."
—*Booklist* on *A Smoking Bun*

"Clever plots, likable characters, and good food . . . Still hungry? Not to worry, because desserts abound in . . . this delectable series."
—*Mystery Scene* on *A Batter of Life and Death*

"[With] *Meet Your Baker*, Alexander weaves a tasty tale of deceit, family ties, delicious pastries, and murder."
—Edith Maxwell, author of *A Tine to Live, A Tine to Die*

"Sure to satisfy both dedicated foodies and ardent mystery lovers alike."
—Jessie Crockett, author of *Drizzled with Death*

# Killing Me Soufflé

## Ellie Alexander

St. Martin's Paperbacks

This is a work of fiction. All of the characters, organizations, and events portrayed in this novel are either products of the author's imagination or are used fictitiously.

First published in the United States by St. Martin's Paperbacks, an imprint of St. Martin's Publishing Group.

KILLING ME SOUFFLÉ

Copyright © 2025 by Katherine Dyer-Seeley.
Excerpt from *Laying Down the Latte* copyright © 2025 by Katherine Dyer-Seeley.

Town map by Rhys Davies.

All rights reserved.

For information, address St. Martin's Publishing Group, 120 Broadway, New York, NY 10271.

www.stmartins.com

ISBN: 978-1-250-32621-8

Our books may be purchased in bulk for promotional, educational, or business use. Please contact your local bookseller or the Macmillan Corporate and Premium Sales Department at 1-800-221-7945, ext. 5442, or by email at MacmillanSpecialMarkets@macmillan.com.

Printed in the United States of America

St. Martin's Paperbacks edition / March 2025

10  9  8  7  6  5  4  3  2  1

*This book is dedicated to Wendy Ray, who introduced
me to Whaleshead and so much more. May you
live on in these stories.*

# Acknowledgments

A huge shoutout to my crew: Tish Bouvier, Lizzie Bailey, Kat Webb, Flo Cho, Jennifer Lewis, Lily Gill, and Courtny Bradley for your input, suggestions, and help in bringing this story together, with a special thanks to Kat for coming up with what may be the best title of the series! Writing can sometimes feel lonely, but having your support makes me feel like I have my own Torte team cheering me on.

Also, to you for picking up this book, whether you're jumping in at book 20 or have been along for the baking ride since the beginning. Never in my wildest dreams would I have imagined this series would continue to 20 books and more. Thank you for letting me and the team at Torte into your reading world. I'm sending you the biggest bookish hugs.

to Emigrant Lake

Oregon Shakespeare Festival

Lithia Park

The Merry Windsor

Ashland Police

torte

A Rose By Any
Other Name

Puck's Pub

THE GREEN GOBLIN

The Green Goblin

Ashland

to Crater Lake

# Chapter One

They say that moving on is part of life. I knew that to be true, but it didn't mean it was easy. I had carved out a sweet and wonderful world in my hometown of Ashland, Oregon, where my days were filled with baking, laughter, family, and friends. But my little hamlet was changing, and I was changing right along with it.

I breathed in the dewy morning air as I turned onto Siskiyou Boulevard and was greeted by neat rows of antique lampposts lighting my path. Banners for upcoming performances of *Much Ado About Nothing* and *Jane Eyre* at the Oregon Shakespeare Festival fluttered in the light breeze. I passed bungalows and historic Victorian houses with organic gardens fenced in an attempt to keep the deer from grazing on wild summer roses and leafy bunches of kale and arugula. It was a losing battle. Deer outnumbered people by an ever-growing ratio. It wasn't uncommon to watch a mother doe guide her spotted, spindly-legged babies through crosswalks or to bump into herds nestled under flowering Japanese maples in Lithia Park.

Our corner of southern Oregon might not be densely

populated, but what we lacked in numbers, we made up for in creativity. Our community was thriving with artists of every type—musicians, actors, writers, dancers, painters, and (some might even say) bakers. In my mind, there was no question my team at our family bakeshop, Torte, were artists. What my staff could create out of layers of chocolate sponge and buttercream never ceased to amaze me.

The only problem was two of my most talented team members were departing for greener or, perhaps in this case, wetter pastures. My sous chef, Sterling, and lead cake designer, Steph, had been offered an incredible opportunity to manage an ailing restaurant at Whaleshead Resort in a small beach town on the stunning Oregon coast. When they approached me about the possibility of taking the job, I encouraged them to go. Not because I wanted to lose them but because, as a professionally trained pastry chef, I knew this was the nature of our business. Much like grains of sand shifting with the tide and wind, staff often drifted from one establishment to another, picking up new skill sets and experiences and leaving behind their own flavorful imprints on us and the bakeshop. Many other chefs had trained and mentored me in my journey to finding my way back to Ashland. I had made it my mission to do the same for my young staff, and now it was time for them to spread their wings and venture out into the great big restaurant world.

I was truly excited for Sterling and Steph, but I had to admit that lately I had a propensity to break out into tears whenever I thought about how empty Torte felt without them. Of course, in all honesty, I had a tendency to break out in tears pretty much all the time at the moment—blame it on the pregnancy hormones. In a classic twist from the universe, I had learned I was pregnant with twins at the same time Sterling and Steph announced they were leaving. I suppose that's the way things are meant to ebb and flow, much like the spontaneous waterfalls that spring up after heavy rains, tumbling down into tiny rivers and cutting through southern Oregon's unique old-growth forests. People come. People go. Some leaving lasting imprints on our hearts and our lives.

I inhaled deeply, centering myself in the thought as I forced a hard swallow and arrived at the bakeshop. Torte sat on the corner of the plaza like a happy beacon for pastry lovers with its red-and-blue-striped awning and large, inviting windows. The sound of the Lithia bubblers gurgling in the center of the plaza made me smile. Later in the day, tourists would crowd the infamous fountain to taste the uh, let's just say stinky, sulfuric healing waters. Usually, they quickly regretted taking a big swig of the natural spring water, which was infused with the less-than-palatable flavor of rotten eggs.

The thought made my lips pucker. I tried to keep my breakfast down while fumbling through my pockets for the keys. I wasn't surprised by the morning sickness and roller coaster of emotions, but I hadn't expected pregnancy to leave my brain so empty. My organizational skills seemed to be shrinking as my belly expanded.

While I dug through every pocket in my bag, I admired the bakeshop's front window display. Rosa and Steph had outdone themselves once again. Colorful paper-flower bunting was strung across the bright awnings. Pastel cake stands displaying an array of tiered cakes and cupcakes decorated with pale yellow, pink, and green buttercream flowers invited customers in, and whimsical battery-powered flower tea lights flickered like little fireflies.

The plaza was calm at this early hour except for a trail runner, lit up like a Christmas tree with a headlamp and reflective gear. He waved as he jogged toward Lithia Park. The day held the promise of plenty of sunshine, but my day began with the stars. Baker's hours aren't particularly conducive to late-night partying, not that clubbing was my scene. Although, during my years running the pastry kitchen on a boutique cruise ship, the *Amour of the Seas*, my husband Carlos and I spent plenty of nights salsa dancing under the moonlight while cutting through calm, black waters.

When I finally retrieved the keys, I unlocked the front door and flipped on the lights. Inside, the bakeshop was equally still as the plaza at this early hour. I loved the quiet of being the first person to warm the ovens and start yeast rising. Torte was naturally cheery with red and teal walls, corrugated metal siding, a long espresso and pastry counter, cozy booth seating in front of the windows, and an assortment of two- and four-person tables arranged throughout the dining space. Our large chalkboard menu took up a quarter of the far wall. We offered a rotating Shakespeare quote, a tradition started by my parents, and a place for our youngest guests and burgeoning artists to connect with their inner Picasso. Today's quote read "Summer's lease hath all too short a date."

For the moment, summer's lease felt long, but maybe that was because my ankles liked to swell at night, I had multiple new staff members to train, and I needed to pack for our weekend getaway to Whaleshead Resort. Sterling and Steph had invited us to help them celebrate the grand reopening of SeaBreeze Bistro, and there was no chance I would miss it. I couldn't wait to see how they transformed the restaurant and the menu.

SeaBreeze had been through a variety of chefs and managers, none of whom could find a way to revive the failing venture. Whaleshead housed a collection of cabins perched atop a craggy hillside with sweeping views of the Pacific Ocean and the rocky prominences that made southern Oregon's beaches uniquely gorgeous. Most cabins were family owned and well loved. The resort had a casual vibe. It was a place where friends gathered for weekend hikes through the mossy conifer forests, bonfires on the beaches, and misty walks on the shoreline searching for treasures washing ashore. Given the soggy nature of the coastal region and the fact that the area attracted hikers and backpackers, there wasn't anything fancy about the property.

SeaBreeze Bistro was hoping—or betting—Steph and Sterling could bring some fresh, young energy and new menu ideas to the restaurant. It was a huge undertaking for even the most seasoned chef. I had faith they were up to the task, though. I'd been consulting with them and was extremely impressed with their vision. They'd been logging eighteen-hour days prepping for this weekend's relaunch. In addition to giving the menu a "glow-up"— Steph's phrase, not mine—they'd gutted the dining room, given it a fresh coat of paint and deep cleaning, and rearranged the seating. I was tired just thinking about it.

For the moment, I needed to focus on our menu, specifically our daily specials. I did a quick walk-through of the dining room and headed downstairs. A few years ago, we had expanded into the basement space, doubling the size of our kitchen and allowing for a bonus cozy seating area perfect for rainy afternoons curled up with a book and a cappuccino. In the process of renovating, we had also unearthed a wood-fired oven, which had quickly become the centerpiece of our baking.

I brewed a pot of decaf and turned on the bread ovens. Then I lit a bundle of cured applewood in the fireplace. While my coffee brewed, I warmed water, added sugar, and started the yeast rising. Soon the kitchen smelled of woodsmoke and the nutty decaf blend my head barista, Andy, had roasted especially for me. I'm not typically a decaf drinker, but pregnancy meant I had to curtail my caffeine consumption. He had taken me on as his "pity project," trying out a variety of decaffeinated roasts, like my current brew, aptly named Othello's Tragedy.

Andy had begun roasting on his grandmother's kitchen stove as a passion project a few years ago. He had fallen in love with the process and decided to take a break from his collegiate studies to learn everything he could about the craft. His talent was unparalleled, and his beans were so popular that coffee lovers traveled to Ashland just for his roasts. We featured his custom blends at Torte and sold bags of whole beans. Demand was so high Andy was considering upgrading his equipment.

I poured a cup of the rich blend with notes of almonds, cherries, and dark chocolate, and stirred in a splash of heavy cream. The coffee was layered and nuanced with a bright, fruity finish. It reminded me of biting into a chocolate-covered cherry, which gave me inspiration for a dessert. Bing cherries were in season, so I would make a layered chocolate sponge with a Bing cherry compote and chocolate whipped cream, and top it with dark chocolate shavings and fresh, plump cherries.

To start I beat egg whites and vinegar in our electric mixer until they firmed into soft peaks. Then I gradually added in sugar. Next I sifted flour, cocoa powder, instant coffee, cornstarch, baking powder, and salt into another bowl. I whipped the egg yolks with warm water, vanilla, and oil, and incorporated the mixture with the dry ingredients. The final step was to carefully fold the egg whites into the batter to create a light and airy sponge. While they baked, I would make a rich cherry compote and chocolate whipped cream. The cake was always a hit with our regulars, especially because it looked so impressive once it was frosted with the whipped cream and finished with dark chocolate shavings and whole, stemmed cherries.

By the time I had slid the tins into the oven to bake, the back door jingled, and Andy strolled in with a wide grin and a box of new coffee blends. "Morning, boss. I've got the gold here and some new decaf samples for you to try." His cheeks, sprinkled with freckles, were tanned from the summer sun.

I adjusted my ponytail and held my mug in a toast. "I'll never turn down a chance to taste any of your creations, but this one might be my favorite yet."

He scrunched his boyish face into a scowl and adjusted the box, propping it in his left arm so he could shake his finger at me. "Listen up, Jules Capshaw, you say that every time I give you a new roast. *Literally* every time."

"And that's a bad thing?" I countered, placing my lips on the mug and intentionally savoring my next sip like it was the best thing I had ever tasted—because it was.

"It's terrible. You always tell us about how your culinary instructors and mentor chefs pushed you out of your comfort zone and gave you feedback to make your baking stronger and better. You're constantly inflating my coffee ego, and I'm worried it's going to go to my head." He flicked a strand of auburn hair from his eye and tipped his head to the side. Andy was tall and muscular from his time spent playing football at Southern Oregon University.

"First of all, that will never happen because you're one of the most humble and grounded people I know, and second of all, I'm sorry, but you've never made a bad roast. I swear to the coffee gods and goddesses that should you produce a blend that bombs, I will tell you." I made an X over my heart to prove my point.

"Fine. Whatever." He pretended to glower, but his cheeks tinged with a hint of pink at my compliment. "How's the decaf serving you? Are you enjoying Othello's Tragedy, or are you ready for something even more mouthwatering?"

"Ooohhh. What are the new roasts?" I tried to peer into the box, which was neatly packed with brown paper coffee bags, each with tasting notes marked with a black Sharpie and finished with little coffee doodles.

"Not so fast." Andy yanked the box closer to his body. "You'll have to wait and see. I've got some drink specials in mind, but I wanted to see what you're baking first." He paused and stared at the island with concern. "Unless my eyes are deceiving me, that appears to be the remnants of cherries. At least I hope it's cherries, because otherwise it looks like a murder scene."

I rested my coffee on the island and showed him my cherry-stained fingers (one of the cons of working with the

juicy, tart fruit). "Guilty as charged. I'm baking a chocolate cherry torte, thanks to your delicious decaf."

"That's sick." Andy patted the box. "Great minds think
alike. I had a killer idea for a summer latte this morning
that should pair perfectly with your torte. Give me a few
minutes to get the espresso machine fired up, and I'll be
back with something for you to try."

"Great." I grinned. "I'll be ready for it because decaf
doesn't count, right? I can drink it all day long."

He frowned, tugging his eyebrows together. "Uh, I don't
know about that. But I am very happy with this Swiss
Water Process. It removes the nasty chemicals, so in theory, I guess you could drink it all day, but I'm pretty sure
there's a limit even for decaf."

I loved that he was looking out for me. "I'm kidding."

He scowled and studied my face like he was trying to
decide whether I was or wasn't kidding. "Anyway, I want
to remind you that you just swore an oath you'd give me
honest feedback, so I'm going to hold you to it."

I nodded as solemnly as possible while fighting back a
smile. "Understood."

He went upstairs. I set cherries, lemon juice, water,
and sugar on the stove to simmer for my compote. Then
I began mixing our sweet bread dough for cinnamon rolls
and morning buns and then began assembling everything
I needed for our cookie base. We made large batches of
basic cookie dough each day and then added different ingredients. Today I would stick with the cherry theme and
do a cherry, vanilla, and white chocolate cookie, along
with some standard favorites—double chocolate chunk,
oatmeal raisin, walnut and orange spice, and classic peanut butter.

The rest of the team began trickling in. Marty, our bread baker, arrived first, followed by Bethany, Rosa, and Sequoia.

Marty boomed a happy greeting. "Good morning, Jules. What a gorgeous day we're in for." He was in his sixties, with white hair and a matching beard. His energy was that of someone half his age. His easygoing and jovial spirit brightened the kitchen and everyone's mood. Marty had become Torte's surrogate grandfather, sharing his wisdom on scoring designs into sourdough and how to manage life's unexpected turns.

"It's going to be a scorcher," I replied with a nod as I formed cookie balls with an ice-cream scoop and set them on parchment-lined baking sheets.

"You're going to have weather shock when you leave for the coast. I texted Sterling last night, and he said it's overcast and drizzling at Whaleshead, so be sure to pack your rain jacket." Marty washed his hands and tied on our signature fire-engine-red Torte apron.

I loved hearing that the two former colleagues were staying in touch. Not that I was surprised. Marty and Sterling had formed a deep bond over their shared foodie obsessions and grief. Marty lost his wife a few years before he moved to Ashland, and Sterling's mom died young. Loss connected them, and the kitchen healed some of their most tender tears, as it had for me. Having lost my dad when I was in high school, I had come to learn that grief lived on inside of me, morphing and changing like a rising bread dough. Trauma had a way of transforming in the kitchen, and one of the ways I came to connect with my father was by letting him live on in what I was baking. That was the gift of food—the simple smell of his signature lemon bars would transport me back in time to when we were in the kitchen together, his hands dripping with lemon juice, offering me a mini whisk to help him bake. That was my vision for the twins, too. Food was Carlos's and my love language, and I wanted it to be theirs as well.

"Yeah, I heard it's supposed to be drizzly," I said to Marty, returning my thoughts to our upcoming trip. "I love that you and Sterling are texting."

"He's like a grandson to me. I couldn't be prouder of those two." Marty's smile faded. "I have to admit, I'm worried about the restaurant opening."

"Why?" I scooped another ball of cookie dough.

"They're having some issues with their new manager, Erik." Marty grabbed the sourdough starter. He nurtured the starter like it was a baby animal, constantly adjusting its feeding schedule and checking its temperature. "Do you know him?"

I shook my head. "I chatted with him briefly when he hired them. He called for recommendations, and during our conversation, he mentioned the restaurant has been through three different chefs in the last year. Not a good sign, but he seemed to think the problem was with the former chefs' grandiose visions. The past few chefs have tried to make SeaBreeze Bistro into a fine-dining establishment. That doesn't work for the beach crowd looking for comfort food and family-friendly options. He was very clear about wanting young blood, so to speak, and chefs who could reimagine the restaurant."

"That's what I heard as well." Marty scooped flour into the industrial mixer for our rustic ciabatta. "According to Sterling, there's a lot of drama among all of the staff and even some of the guests at the resort. Erik is very demanding, and it sounds downright awful—not for Sterling and Steph, at least not yet—but for the rest of the staff. Sterling was quite upset and is worried that there's going to be backlash during opening weekend."

"Backlash? What kind of backlash?" I didn't like the sound of that. I knew that my young protégés had plenty to worry about when building a brand-new menu and giving the restaurant a facelift.

"He didn't elaborate, but he said Erik has a violent streak." Marty's eyes lost their usual merriment as he attached the dough hook to the mixer. "I hope they're not in over their heads, and I wonder if Erik's behavior explains why the restaurant has gone through so many chefs as of late."

"Yeah, that doesn't sound good," I agreed, checking on my compote, which had simmered into a thick, bubbly sauce.

"It's good you, Carlos, your mom, and Doug will be there." Marty assessed the bubble activity in the starter, which we kept on the counter in order to maintain a temperature of seventy to eighty degrees. "I'm sure they'll appreciate the support. I told Sterling that Bethany and I already had plans to go out the following week. We'll bombard them with Torte support."

Andy came downstairs with a tray of cherry lattes made with his newest roast using pineapple and brown sugar as a base. "This one is especially for you, Jules. I'm calling it a decaf latte with a cherry on top." He dunked a stemmed cherry into one of the drinks. "Because if you have to drink decaf, you need something sweet to top it off, yeah?"

I took one of the cups from him. It looked too pretty to

drink, with chocolate swirls and the fresh cherry bobbing on the creamy pink surface.

"Honest feedback only, please. It's a classic cherry latte minus the fuel, with a touch of rose water, almond, and dark chocolate. I think the fruity roast pulls the flavors together nicely, but hit me with your thoughts." He passed around samples to the rest of the team.

Bethany, our cake designer and brownie baker extraordinaire, took a first big sip. "No notes. No notes." She beamed at Andy with her wide eyes and dimpled cheeks.

She and Andy had been dating, or maybe hanging out was a better description. I knew they enjoyed each other's company, and I knew she had a massive crush on him, but I couldn't tell whether they were content with where things were or ready to get more serious. I didn't care either way, I just wanted my staff to be happy.

That went for my current and former staff. As the morning wore on, I couldn't stop thinking about Steph and Sterling. Hopefully, things would settle down and smooth out once everyone got through the stress of opening weekend. And if worse came to worst (which, for their sakes, I hoped it didn't), they always had a place at Torte.

# Chapter Two

The rest of the day was a whirlwind of activities. Replacing Sterling and Steph, who were invaluable team members, was a daunting task, but as they say, the pastries must "bake on," to borrow a page from my best friend, Lance. He was the artistic director at OSF, as locals refer to the Shakespeare Fest, and a partner in our shared winery, Uva. When I had lamented to him about Steph and Sterling's impending departure, he had tapped the side of my cheek and offered me a pragmatic smile. "Chin up, darling. There are dozens of young pastry ingenues waiting in the wings for their chance to step into the spotlight and shine. Mark my words, you'll have a line around the block with budding, eager-eyed chefs begging for an opportunity to take the pastry stage the moment you list the jobs."

He was right. As soon as we posted the open roles, résumés flooded into the bakeshop. It helped that Southern Oregon University was located on the south end of town, and there were plenty of college students hungry for work and experience. Plus, the benefits of free meals during shifts and deep discounts on food and coffee were an added perk.

We had sorted through the stack of applications and landed on four new candidates. In many ways, the timing was good. My goal was to scale back my own duties a bit once the twins arrived. Expanding our team and having ample time to train them over the summer and into the fall should put me in good shape to take extra leave and delegate some of my responsibilities.

Bethany was eager to take on more projects. She agreed to step into the role of pastry manager. She would oversee our baking efforts, and to my surprise, Marty approached me about managing the kitchen. He had a breadth of experience and a centered energy that made him perfect for the job. I just hadn't expected he would be interested. When he first came to the Rogue Valley after his wife's death, he had planned on retiring but was lured back into the kitchen by the siren call of sourdough. We were all the better for it, and I was thrilled that he was willing to take the lead. Bethany and Marty would make a good team and had been with us long enough to know the bakeshop's quirks, like how the industrial mixer needed a simple hip bump to get it unstuck or why it was imperative to keep a close eye on flatbreads in the wood-fired oven, so they didn't char to a crisp.

I was feeling more solid about our plan. Marty would train our sous chefs, Bethany would supervise the new decorators and bakers, Andy and Sequoia would continue running the espresso bar, and Rosa would oversee the dining room and operations.

Our new staff had varied skill sets, and as hard as it was to swallow the reality that Sterling and Steph were gone, having fresh energy and ideas would likely breathe new life into the bakeshop. I was choosing to embrace the change. What other choice did I have?

We were closing Torte early for an initial meet-and-greet. While Carlos and I were on the coast, our new staff members would spend the weekend shadowing our seasoned employees. When I wasn't running trays of salami and roasted red pepper flatbread or slices of my chocolate cherry torte upstairs, I spent the bulk of the day preparing employment kits, schedules, and paperwork. I wanted everyone to feel welcome and have a clear idea of where to find recipes and supplies and who to ask for help.

By the time we locked the doors for the evening, I had four packets, Torte aprons, and bags of Taming of the Brew, our summer roast, waiting for our arrivals. There was a buzz of nervous anticipation in the kitchen as everyone gathered around the island. Andy had prepared iced coffees, and Marty had arranged a selection of small bites—herbed cheese bread, cold pasta salad with mozzarella, basil, and heirloom tomatoes, and crostini with roasted chicken, honey, and Brie.

"Have you seen my special brownies yet, Jules?" Bethany asked, tugging off her apron and running her fingers through her springy curls. We originally met at Ashland's annual Chocolate Fest, where Bethany debuted her Unbeatable Brownies. Mom and I were so enamored with her baking talent and her infectious optimism that we approached her with an offer for a small percentage of ownership in the bakeshop and an opportunity to expand her brownie empire. It had been a dreamy match. In addition to baking daily brownies, she was an expert cake designer and moonlighted as a photographer—managing our social media with her beautifully stylized food pics and clever posts.

"No, I've been so busy getting everything ready. What surprises do you have in store for our new crew?" I asked, peering over her shoulder to get a better look at the island.

"Check these out." Bethany reached for a platter of brownies that she'd cut into the shape of the Torte logo—a fleur-de-lis pattern with a simple torte cake stand in the center. She had hand-piped the outline of the logo in red and blue buttercream and written *Welcome Team Torte* in an elegant cursive scroll.

"These are so sweet," I said, suddenly feeling ravenous for a brownie. I'm not always great at remembering to eat. I love food, obviously, but during work hours, I usually have dozens of irons in the fire. Pregnancy had put an end to long stretches between meals. Carlos teased me that I was turning into a grazer. Not more than thirty minutes went by before I was desperate for a snack, and chocolate was my weak point.

"Do you want one now?" Bethany asked, handing me the plate and brushing crumbs from her T-shirt, which read DON'T GO BACON MY HEART.

"I can wait," I lied.

She lifted the platter to display her scrumptious sweet bites. "You should probably test them to make sure they're okay."

"Am I that transparent?" I stared at the platter longingly.

"Um, well, you're looking at my brownies like you're a bookish heroine in one of my romances, who's just been swept off her feet by a dashingly handsome man. Why can't the man of my dreams ogle me with dewy eyes like that?" She pushed the plate closer.

"Hey," Andy interrupted. "Who's this man of your dreams?"

"Only about a hundred of my book crushes," Bethany shot back, tossing her hair over her shoulder, and gave me a sly wink before turning her attention back to him. "If you want to keep up, you might want to read a love story or two."

"I thought that coffee was the way to your heart," he said, sounding worried and glancing at Bethany with his wide, eager blue eyes for confirmation.

"Coffee's good, sure. But, you know, give me a burly guy with a book in his hands, and I turn to pure mush." She waited for me to take a brownie and then nonchalantly put the platter back on the island. I could tell she was taking pleasure in making him sweat.

"I like to read . . . I . . . I . . . read," Andy sputtered. "Check my backpack. I'm reading about Costa Rica's history with coffee right now." He waved his arms in defense of himself. "It's a historical look at the political, economic, and social impacts of coffee on the culture. Costa Rica is on the top of my bucket list. I'm dying to go visit the coffee farms and meet with growers. The country produces some of the best coffees in the world—coffees I want to emulate here, but I'm also learning so much about sustainability and how mass producers and climate change are putting the coffee farms at risk."

"I think you're too young for a bucket list, Andrew." Marty clapped him on the back. "Now, an old guy like me, that's another story. My bucket list is practically a tome at this point."

Andy chuckled.

Bethany took out her phone and moved the plates of

food around to get a shot for social. "Coffee history is great and all, but reading a little romance never hurts." She caught my eye and wiggled her eyebrows in mischievous delight.

"Okay, give me a list. I'll do it," Andy challenged her, motioning with his hands again. "Hit up with your romance recs—bring it."

"Maybe we should start a baking book club," Rosa suggested, a small smile tugging at the sides of her apple-shaped cheeks. Her dark eyes twinkled with a touch of joy. I knew she took as much pleasure as I did in the friendly banter amongst our staff. Her naturally calming aura made her someone everyone sought out for advice. "We could match a book and a pastry every month. I think people might really enjoy that."

"Oh my God, I love that idea!" Bethany squealed. "I have the perfect book to kick it off, too. It's called *Batter of the Heart*." She scrolled through her phone to find the cover to show us. "It's a meet-cute between a young baker who is determined to save her grandmother's bakery and a snobby pastry chef who has plans to open a French patisserie in town. But their rivalry turns into an unlikely partnership when they're forced to spend late nights in the kitchen baking for charity. Their midnight pastry sessions spark a romance and some serious heat in the kitchen. It's spicy, but not too spicy. I won't give away any more of the plot, but we could totally bake some of the recipes from the book. You're brilliant, Rosa. We have to do this, right?" Her gaze landed on me for approval.

"I absolutely love it. Mom and I have talked for years about hosting a book club, so I'm a solid yes. And just a reminder for everyone." I paused and looked around the kitchen. "You don't need my permission. You're all taking on more, which I'm so grateful for, and I'm serious about scaling back." My hand instinctively went to my stomach as I thought about how very different the future was going to look. "I want everyone to feel empowered in your roles. If you have an idea like this and the capacity to make it happen, go for it."

"So what I'm hearing is I should book a ticket for Costa Rica?" Andy gave me a lopsided grin.

"*That* we might need to discuss more, but it's not off the table," I replied with a crooked wink. I've never had a good poker face or mastered the ability to wink. What I didn't tell Andy was Carlos and I had already been discussing the possibility of making an excursion to the coffee-growing region. One of Carlos's sous chefs from the *Amour of the Seas* recently moved back to her hometown just outside of San José to take over her family's coffee plantation. She invited us to come stay, tour the farm, and potentially partner on some future blends. I didn't want to get Andy's hopes up until we firmed up our plans, but his bucket list might just have an item crossed off it soon.

The conversation shifted as a knock sounded on the basement door. Marty went to let in our new staff, and within minutes, the nervous energy changed to happy chatter and lots of hugs. I wasn't surprised, but it was lovely to see everyone connect and the instant sense of camaraderie. If day one was any indication, things were going to go smoothly.

I was excited to watch our team start to mesh and confident that our new staff members were in good hands when it came to learning the ropes at Torte. Knowing that put me at ease. Now I could concentrate on my trip to the coast and supporting Sterling and Steph as they stepped into their next chapter.

# Chapter Three

After our little staff party, I returned home to finish packing for the trip to Whaleshead. In the warmer months, I like to walk to work, and today was no exception. The heat peaked earlier, which meant my leisurely stroll through the plaza and along Main Street was relaxing and enjoyable.

The plaza was bustling with activity. Tourists dined at outdoor patio tables at restaurants. A banjo player busked in the center of the square next to the welcome kiosk, covering popular hits in exchange for lunch money. Rather than a hat, he had a QR code propped next to his banjo cases.

The police station, with its blue awnings, window boxes blooming with red and yellow geraniums, and water dishes for thirsty four-legged friends, sat catty-corner from Torte. Posters for summer symphony concerts in Lithia Park and neighborhood night out, and walking maps of Ashland made the station feel more like a little community center.

I waved to friends and familiar faces as I passed London Station, the mercantile in the heart of downtown. Its windows were decorated with a massive tropical flower display made by entwining silk flowers and draping them around the entrance to the store. Summer dresses, wide-brimmed hats, beach towels, and sunbrellas were arranged to make anyone passing by feel like they were in the tropics.

It was funny to think about how far from tropical the southern Oregon coast could be. The coastline was known for its unparalleled natural beauty—majestical coastal cliffs, conifer forests, dramatic sea stacks, hidden coves, and pristine, untouched beaches. What it wasn't known for was sweltering heat or white sand beaches. Locals referred to the region as "Oregon's Banana Belt" due to its temperate climate and abundant sunshine. But daytime temps hovered in the seventies, and a persistent marine layer provided a cooler, refreshing escape.

I continued along, taking in Ashland's one and only "skyscraper," the Ashland Springs Hotel. The historic nine-story European-style boutique hotel dates back to the early 1920s, when Ashland was a draw for its naturally healing mineral waters and Chautauqua lectures. Its cornsilk exterior with creamy accents and garden terrace was a landmark in Ashland and all of the Rogue Valley.

My route home took me through town, past the Carnegie Library, Ashland High School, and eventually the Southern Oregon University (SOU) grounds. There, I turned onto Mountain Avenue and started the steep journey up the forested hillside dotted with madrones and manzanitas.

When Mom and the Professor married a few years ago, she decided to sell the craftsman-style house I'd grown up in, and I jumped at the chance to buy it. Carlos and I had lovingly updated my childhood home to make it our own.

The house was tucked into the forest, with large windows on the backside and an attached deck with captivating views of Grizzly Peak and the flaxen hills to the east. Carlos's latest project was tending to the extensive tiered garden beds he had constructed in our sloped backyard.

I had to take the hill slower than usual since I was sharing my lung capacity with not one but two growing babies. Sweat pooled on my neck as I trudged up the steep slope. Each house in the neighborhood had a large lot with natural landscaping. There were very few fences or manicured lawns. Instead, houses blended into the background, encompassed by redwoods, Douglas firs, and incense cedars.

A text dinged on my phone.

*Saved by the bell.*

I stopped to catch my breath and read the message.

It was from Steph: "You're still coming tomorrow, right?"

"YES!!! Can't wait! On my way home to pack now." I texted back immediately, happy for a reprieve from the climb.

"I wish you were here now. Things are blowing up. It's a disaster."

Steph was the most stoic member of my team. If she was saying things were blowing up, then the fuse had already been lit.

We texted for a few minutes. I tried to calm her down and reassure her reinforcements were on the way.

When I made it to our U-shaped drive, I was out of breath and dripping with sweat. I found Carlos and his son, Ramiro, on the deck sipping hand-squeezed lemonade and engaged in a serious game of Parchís. Ramiro had finished his year at Ashland High School and would return to Spain next month. We were trying to soak up and savor every last minute with him without smothering him. I wasn't sure we were succeeding, and it gave me a new appreciation for how hard it must have been for Mom to let me go when I headed for culinary school in New York shortly after graduating from high school.

"Julieta, you walked home? We would have come for you." Carlos jumped to his feet and greeted me with a long kiss on the cheek. "You look flushed. Sit. Sit."

Ramiro pulled out the custom-designed wooden chair next to him for me. "You came in time to see him lose again. Poor Papa, he thinks he has new tricks up his sleeve, but he is no match for me."

I smiled, wiping dewy sweat from my brow, as I slid into the deck chair and propped a sunflower pillow behind my back. The deck was alive with color. Large tangerine, yellow, and turquoise pots housed hydrangeas and roses. Hummingbird feeders hung from copper posts mounted along the railing. A rock fountain gurgled meditatively, and their board game pieces were scattered on the table.

Carlos and Ramiro's Parchís games were a semi-friendly rivalry. They had taken up the game during the snowy winter months and played nearly every afternoon or evening, depending on Ramiro's school schedule and social and homework load.

Ramiro made a check mark on the bright neon-yellow poster board he created to track their scores and winning totals. "Sorry, Papa, that's another win for me."

Carlos ruffled Ramiro's hair, a proud smile tugging at his lips. "It is unfair. You are too smart. What have they taught you here in American schools? How to usurp your parents' authority?" He winked and poured me a glass of lemonade.

It was exchanges like this that I was going to miss the most. Our big adventures together—moonlight tours on Mount A, hiking around Crater Lake, and white-water rafting on the Rogue River—bonded us closer and left lasting memories, but it was the typical common days that mattered. Ramiro and his friends raiding the refrigerator, sharing omelets and espressos together in the morning, curling up on the couch, and watching movies with a big bowl of Carlos's rosemary and sea salt popcorn and gooey chocolate chip cookies.

"How was the welcome with the new staff?" Carlos asked, massaging my shoulders. "I'm sorry to miss it, but we will have a big dinner when we return from the beach, sí?"

His firm yet gentle touch melted away any lingering tension. "Yeah, for sure. Bethany wants to do a staff Sunday Supper, which I think is a great way to launch our new team officially."

"Good. Good. I will work with Marty on the menu." His soft hands kneaded the knots in my back like they were bread dough. "But the welcome was smooth?"

"I saw Bethany's brownies on social media," Ramiro said, making a star next to his name on the board. "They looked delicious."

"They were. I would have brought some home, but they vanished," I said to him, and then looked up at Carlos. "It went well. Everyone seemed to get along, and Andy's coffee and Bethany's treats broke the ice pretty quickly. I finished the welcome packets and paperwork. Everyone has been paired up with a trainer to shadow for the weekend.

Knock on wood . . ." I paused to knock on the tabletop. "I think we're in good shape."

"Excellent." Carlos balled his hand into a fist and made small circles at the base of my neck to try and release a knot of stress. "You are still tight, mi querida. Are you feeling worried?"

I reached for the lemonade and took a long sip. It was cool and refreshing, infused with tangy Meyer lemons and a touch of fresh basil and honey. "You know me, I'm always worried about something. I feel better now that things are in motion with our new staff, but I am concerned about Sterling and Steph."

I filled them both in on what Marty told me about Whaleshead and my text exchange with Steph.

"This is no good. There is no place for anger in the kitchen." Carlos shook his head in disgust and returned to his seat. "It is good we are going. I will have a word with this Erik if necessary."

I appreciated his rush to defend our friends. Carlos believed food should be produced with love. His philosophy was every dish that left the kitchen was a physical embodiment of the hands that made it. When he was at the helm of the kitchen on the *Amour of the Seas*, there was always music, laughter, and pranks mixed in with meticulously organized choreography and immaculate cleaning protocols. We'd taken that practice to heart at Torte and Uva as well. Commercial kitchens were innately stressful, with staff maneuvering for space amongst open flames and sous chefs wielding butcher knives. There was no need to make it more stressful.

"I'm with you on that," I replied, lifting the cool drink to my forehead. Maybe the walk uphill had been more strenuous than I realized. I hated to admit it, but I was probably going to have to scale back even more. "Trust me, I want to swoop in and save them, but part of running a kitchen is figuring it out on your own. We can be sounding boards for them, listen, and provide insight or reflection, but I think we should steer clear of rescuing them, at least for the short term."

Carlos grimaced, his dark eyes drifting toward Ramiro. "Sí, she is right. This is what she and your mother say about you, too."

"And look at how well I've turned out." Ramiro patted his chest and winked, making the dimples in his olive skin crease.

"You are so very humble, too." Carlo laughed and picked up the game. "Dinner is ready. Everything is packed. Uva and Scoops are in good hands, so I say we enjoy a lovely meal watching the sun paint Grizzly Peak in gold, and then we get an early night of sleep for our trip tomorrow."

"I'll help you with dinner." Ramiro stood and grabbed the poster board. "But first I need to display this on the fridge. Everyone who comes by should know I'm beating you by a mile. I'm sorry to say that I'm the winner, and you are the *loser*." He made an L on his forehead.

Carlos put him in a playful headlock as they went inside.

My thoughts drifted to Sterling and Steph while they went to prepare dinner. It wasn't lip service, I did believe their growth in striking out on their own meant learning how to advocate for themselves. Not that I wouldn't step in and help support them in any way I could, but when I was their age, Mom had let me fail. Another gift I was coming to appreciate on a new level. She was always there to listen and would sometimes ask if I wanted feedback or just needed her ear to process. Usually it was the latter. She would listen without judgment, reflecting back my thoughts and concerns. It couldn't have been easy, but it was what I needed.

My mistakes and blunders made me who I was. In navigating bad bosses, messy gossip, and office politics, I gained confidence in myself as a chef and as a person. I wished I could save Steph and Sterling from any angst and self-doubt. But I couldn't. That much I knew, and that was an important lesson for my future twins, too. As a parent, I might have to watch my kids struggle. How would I find the strength to do so? I was glad I had months ahead to sit with the idea and hopefully learn to embrace it. I had a feeling I was going to need to lean heavily on Mom's listening ear in the days ahead.

# Chapter Four

The next morning, we were up with the sun to hit the road for Whaleshead. Even though the Pacific Ocean was just on the other side of the Siskiyou Mountains from Ashland, the drive took us north and then south (into California briefly) before connecting to Highway 101, which ran all along the coastline from northern Washington to southern California. It was a stunning drive on a two-lane highway that cut through rocky canyons and forests of ancient redwoods. Crystal blue rivers ran parallel to the road, their waters so clear I could see through to their pebbly bottoms.

We passed butterfly gardens and herds of wild elk grazing on lush green grasses. Funky roadside stands selling hand-picked flower bouquets, corn, and fresh eggs popped up every few miles. The curvy highway didn't pair well with my propensity toward morning sickness. I kept the passenger window rolled down and sucked on peppermint candies to keep the nausea at bay.

"How are you doing, mi querida?" Carlos asked, clutching the wheel tight as he navigated around a hairpin turn.

"Okay," I lied, keeping my gaze on the brittle-walled cliffs. Red gravel and debris littered the side of the highway.

Huge steel nets secured boulders the size of the car waiting to tumble down and crush us.

"I can tell when you are lying, Julieta," he scoffed, keeping his eyes on the road.

"Me too," Ramiro added from the backseat, tapping my shoulder to offer me a pack of gum. "Would this help?"

"Thanks." I patted his hand and took a stick. "I'm okay, I promise, but I won't be sad when this phase of pregnancy is over."

"We can stop," Carlos suggested, motioning to a sign for a rest stop in a few miles.

"Nah, I'd rather power through." I unwrapped the gum and used the breathing techniques I'd learned from my yoga class.

"I'll try to get us there as quickly but as safely as possible." Carlos slowed for another turn.

Ramiro kept me distracted with news about his plans for his last year of school in Spain. He would be leaving next month to travel with his mom, stepdad, and sister for a couple of weeks before classes resumed. He would be finishing his "bachillerato" for his final year of high school. The curriculum included a range of subjects to prepare for his university entrance exams. He was also planning two class excursions to round out his educational experience—a winter ski trip in the Pyrenees Mountains and a spring getaway to Greece.

"It's going to be so weird to speak Spanish all the time again. My brain has started to think more in English. I even dream in English now." He ran his fingers through his shaggy hair like he was trying to warm up his brain cells.

"That's the true sign you're fully bilingual," Carlos said, glancing to the backseat with a proud nod.

I was glad to have something other than my churning stomach to focus on, and I was even more thrilled when I caught the first glimpses of the steel blue waters of the Pacific Ocean and a whiff of salty sea air.

We rolled the windows down and let the briny breeze whip through the car as we passed through the small seaside town of Brookings. Kite shops, candy stores, restaurants touting the world's best clam chowder, and art galleries lined each side of the highway. There were signs pointing to beach access, parks, and the wharf. Remnants of the past could be seen in the historic buildings and fishing museum.

Once we made it through town, we continued on to Whaleshead, which was less than nine miles away but would take at least twenty minutes to drive.

"The rocky formations are so cool," Ramiro commented, snapping pictures of the breathtaking scenery on his phone as we drove by the massive prominences that looked like small volcanos jutting up out of the waves. "It's nothing like the beaches in Spain."

"The beaches are also much colder," I warned. Sun was never promised on the Oregon coastline, even in the dead of summer. Misty fog often rolled in over the shoreline, clinging to the cliffs and shrouding everything in a thick, soup-like haze. The beaches were prone to drizzle and biting winds, but on the flip side, they were untouched, rugged, and stretched out for miles and miles, as far as the eye could see.

"It's beautiful today, sí?" Ramiro waved his hand out

the window to mimic the rolling waves. "I can't wait to put my feet in the water. Maybe I'll try surfing too. Is there a shop for rentals?"

"Yes, there are lots of fun shops in town that we can explore, and Whaleshead used to have a small rental shop for kites, surfboards, and boogie boards. I haven't visited in a few years, so we'll have to check it out."

A sign pointing the way to the resort came into view, and my heart skipped a beat in anticipation. It had only been a few weeks since Sterling and Steph left, but I couldn't wait to hug them.

Carlos steered the car up the long driveway framed by redwoods, sequoias, and pines until we reached the turn-around and entrance to the main lodge and dining area. Rust-red cabins with matching decks and hot tubs dotted the cliff and either side of the lodge. A network of path-ways and trails connected the cabins and led down to the beach at least two or three hundred feet below.

Once we pulled in front of the small lodge, we got out and stretched our legs, taking in the magnificent views. Sun sparkled on the smooth waters like glittery gems. Waves broke gently on the shore down below. I could just make out a couple of beachcombers searching for sand dollars and shells and a family building a sandcastle. Otherwise, the beach was empty.

Seagulls squawked overhead, and everything smelled slightly like the sea.

I drank in the fresh air, feeling instantly rejuvenated.

"Ah, I see some color in your cheeks again." Carlos wrapped an arm around my shoulder and smiled at me with relief. "It's good to be out of the car, no?"

"Yes." I bobbed my head in agreement and sucked in another breath of the earthy air. The ocean was always my happy place as a child. My parents didn't get much time off from running and operating the bakeshop, but every summer, they would carve out a week for a getaway and rent a cabin at Whaleshead. Some of my favorite memories were of traipsing through the wooded grounds, searching for fairies, and packing a picnic to tote down to the beach. My dad would bury my toes in the sand while we ate peanut butter and jelly sandwiches on brioche and washed them down with sparkling orange juice. I was flooded with memories of nighttime bonfires, ghost stories about haunted lighthouses, roasting marshmallows, and hunting for whole sand dollars and glass floats.

"Let's go get checked in," I said, motioning to the lodge. It was a large, round building with floor-length windows on every side. SeaBreeze Bistro was on the right side, with a deck that offered outside seating and panoramic views of the coastline and mountains. Hiking and walking paths jutted out in every direction from the lodge, leading visitors to their cabins or down to the beach.

We stepped inside, and a new round of memories resurfaced. The scuffed hardwood floors, worn rugs, and heavy oak furniture hadn't changed since the 1980s. The same was true for the wood-paneled walls and small surf and gift shop attached to the reception area.

A young woman greeted us at the front desk. "Welcome to Whaleshead. I'm Jess. How can I help you?" She was in her midtwenties, with long, glossy hair and sharp features. Dangling gold earrings stretched to her neckline and jangled as she twisted her head. Unlike most residents and guests at the resort, she was dressed quite professionally in a cream pantsuit, heels, and gold necklaces and bracelets.

"I'm Jules, and this is Carlos and Ramiro. We're Stephanie and Sterling's friends, and we're here to help them with the SeaBreeze launch." I extended my hand in greeting.

She looked at it like she didn't know what to do with it. After a second, she finally tapped the tips of my fingers twice and then sprayed her hands with sanitizer, vigorously rubbing them together to create friction. "Do you want to check in first and put your things away in your cabin, or do you want to head straight to the kitchen? I'm sorry to tell you there's no one to help you bring your luggage to your cabin. We're short-staffed, and things are . . ." She sighed and pounded her temples with her fingers. "I don't know what word I'm looking for. Let's just say that we're short-staffed."

"That's no problem. We can get our own luggage." I looked at Carlos. "I vote check in first. What about you?"

"Sí." He nodded in agreement.

"Fine. Fine." Jess typed in her computer, keeping her eyes on the screen. The phone rang. She glanced at it and blanched, her face turning ghostly white. "Um, one moment, please," she said to us, picking up the phone and shielding the receiver with one hand.

It was obvious that she didn't want us to listen to her conversation, so we moved toward the gift and rental shop. Ramiro checked out the surfboards, and Carlos picked up a brochure about bike tours. I perused shelves filled with trinkets from the Oregon coast—polished shells, marionberry candy, canned salmon and tuna, and saltwater taffy in every flavor imaginable, from wild watermelon to cookie dough.

A stone fireplace beckoned in the opposite corner. Its hearth was piled with weathered driftwood, and the mantel held a collection of sea-themed treasures—aged ship lanterns, conch shells, and nautical maps. A collection of seating was arranged in front of the fireplace. Rustic wooden bookcases displayed old travel guides, dated encyclopedias, and mass-market fiction from decades ago.

Jess's desk served as the reception area. Behind her was a small office marked PRIVATE. The doors leading to the restaurant were near the fireplace. Large windows looked out onto the deck and front grounds.

I wasn't trying to eavesdrop, but Jess's tone became more forced and louder. "No. I told you no!" She looked up and met my gaze, frazzled. Then dropped her head and lowered her voice. "It's a no. Like, a thousand times, a no. I can't. I can't now. I have a dozen fires to put out, okay? I'll meet you at the spot later, okay?"

She slammed down the phone and then smoothed her hair like she was trying to soothe herself. "Sorry about that," she called, waving us back over with her fine-tip pen.

A teenager wearing a Whaleshead maintenance shirt hurried past us, lugging an empty bucket and a mop. "Jess, Jess, where is Hoff? He's supposed to be fixing that leak in cabin five, but I can't find him anywhere. Erik is on the warpath. There's a spill in the kitchen, and the fish delivery is late. Erik's going to implode. You better find Hoff."

"Great. Just great." Her nostrils flared as her cheeks pulled in like she'd eaten something sour. Then she seemed to notice that we were still waiting. She plastered on a fake smile and switched her tone, sounding like she was playing a receptionist in a *Saturday Night Live* skit. "Many apologies. Lots of moving parts—leaking cabins, late deliveries, a missing artist, sold-out dinner reservations, an angry boss, my list keeps growing."

Carlos filled out the paperwork she handed us.

"Is there anything we can do?" I asked. If our first introduction was any indication, Sterling and Steph weren't exaggerating about the chaos. Not that I ever thought they were. If anything, they had probably downplayed the situation. "Why is the artist missing?"

"It's typical. Mary Beth is such a flake. Her art is supposed to be up on the walls now." She used her pencil to motion to the walls where blue painter's tape marked spots where paintings should be. "I don't know why Erik agreed to let her display her work tonight. He wanted art for the grand reopening, but there are so many other talented artists in town, and none of them have egos like Mary Beth. She thinks she can do whatever she wants because she's been here forever. She's a freaking dinosaur and so out of touch."

Carlos caught my eye and shrugged. Then he finished the paperwork, and Jess gave us keys, a map of the resort, and directions to our cabin.

"Come on back over whenever you're ready. I'll let Sterling and Steph know you're here." She pointed toward the restaurant with her thumb.

"Thanks, and good luck with everything," I said with a parting smile.

She winced like it hurt to try and fake pleasantries. "See you around."

"This seems very disorganized," Carlos said in a low tone as we returned to the car.

"Agreed." I shot a glance behind us. "It confirms what Sterling told Marty and, I guess, that it's a good thing we're here. Let's unpack and see if they can put us to work."

"Do you care if I go explore the beach after we unpack?" Ramiro asked, gazing at the pathway that cut through the heavily forested hillside. "My friends want to meet for a beach lunch, as long as that's okay. I can also help in the kitchen."

"Not at all," I replied. "You should definitely go have fun. This isn't a working trip for you."

A few of Ramiro's school friends had cabins at the resort and were staying for the weekend. Carlos and I wanted him to enjoy his last bit of time in Oregon.

"Sí. This is your time to be with your friends." He kissed the top of Ramiro's head. "We want you to enjoy yourself, but be smart. The ocean can be dangerous. Pay attention to the signs about the tides and undertow."

"Always, Papa."

Our cabin was located directly across from the lodge and SeaBreeze Bistro. It would make getting back and forth easy. Ramiro and I walked while Carlos pulled the car around.

Each cabin in Whaleshead was perched above the rugged coastline and tucked into the lush landscape. The wooden cabins were painted in three shades of brown—chestnut, sienna, and mahogany. Spacious wood-slat decks with Adirondack chairs and views of the Pacific provided the perfect spot for sipping morning coffee while watching the sunrise or sunset.

Inside, the cabin was filled with coastal décor and cozy touches. Thanks to vaulted windows, the living room was drenched in sun. A small but well-appointed kitchen and dining nook, bathroom, and bedroom took up the remainder of the first floor. Ramiro would sleep in the second-story loft with equally impressive views of the ocean.

It didn't take long to unpack and get organized. Ramiro left with an oversized blue-and-yellow-striped towel and a bag of snacks, promising to see us later at dinner.

I loved that he was getting to experience being a free-range American teen. He had embraced life in America, taking advantage of as many opportunities as possible, from playing on the soccer team to joining student government and backpacking through the Siskiyou Mountains.

That was one of the unique things about living in southern Oregon. I cherished the memories from my childhood. Being adjacent to such wide-open wild spaces meant that Ramiro and his generation of friends spent nearly every waking minute outdoors—hiking through the upper Lithia Park trails, walking to school, kayaking and swimming at Emigrant Lake, and camping on Mount A. So much outdoor time was a rarity in today's digital culture. It was one of the things that made me proudest about having him live in Ashland with us—I hoped his connection with nature would be a gift that would stay with him through his formative years.

I splashed cool water on my face and appraised my appearance. My narrow, high cheekbones had filled out a bit with pregnancy. I pinched my cheeks to give them some extra color, tied my long blond hair into a high ponytail, and stuffed a handful of peppermints into my pockets, just in case.

"Are you ready to see our first baby chefs take their first steps?" Carlos asked with a grin, reaching for my hand. He had smoothed down his dark hair. His skin was naturally tanned from hours spent tending the grapevines at

Uva. I wasn't sure how it was possible, but he seemed to get more handsome with each passing year.

"Let's do this." I looped my fingers through his. We strolled hand in hand along the small path that wrapped around the lodge to the restaurant. Excitement pulsed through my body, not even fueled by caffeine.

As we emerged from the pathway, we were greeted by an awe-inspiring panorama of rugged cliffs and the endless ocean stretching to the horizon. Tiered garden boxes burst with color. Sweet peas, heirloom tomatoes, spinach, arugula, and assorted herbs looked to be thriving in the organic soil. Wooden signposts pointed the way to secluded cabins and the trail that led down to the beach.

"This is gorgeous," Carlos said, gesturing to the unobstructed views on the spacious and inviting deck.

The deck had been scrubbed clean. I could already see Steph's touch in the hanging flower baskets and potted herbs lining the perimeter. Mason jars with bouquets of evergreen branches, driftwood, and bright currants were set in the center of each of the wooden tables, stained red to match the exterior. Lanterns dangled from the rafters, and music wafted from outdoor speakers.

I was about to comment on the décor and cleanliness when the sound of a booming voice interrupted us.

"Get off my back, Erik. I'm not dealing with your crap—now or ever again." A man in his late fifties or early sixties burst out of the double glass doors. "You keep your distance from me, or I swear you'll come to regret it."

He slammed the door so hard that I was shocked the glass didn't shatter.

When he noticed us, he gave his head a half shake and muttered something under his breath as he stormed past.

The infamous Erik Morton swung the restaurant door open again. He wasn't at all what I had expected. He was younger than the other man by a good decade or maybe even two. His skin was sallow like he was seriously low on vitamin D, and his spindly arms reminded me of the knotty pines bending with the wind. "Remember, I can still fire you, Hoff," Erik sputtered, his words evaporating in the sea-kissed air.

Hoff was nearly out of sight but close enough to hear. He turned around and furrowed his bushy eyebrows at Erik, puffing out his chest like he was preparing to fight. "Go ahead and try. I dare you. You fire me, and you're dead."

# Chapter Five

Erik glared off into the distance, keeping one hand on the door like it was holding him up. "I hate that man. He thinks I can't fire him; well, he's sorely mistaken. I run the resort. Not him."

I couldn't tell if he was actually talking to us because his gaze never drifted.

Carlos stepped forward, doing what he does best—smoothing out the situation with his lulling Spanish accent and natural charm. "Ah, good morning. If you're in charge, you must be the manager. Julieta and I are so pleased that you've hired Stephanie and Sterling, two of our very best staff—pleased and envious, of course."

He tore his eyes away from the hillside. "Oh, right. You're the chefs from Cakes, or what's the name of your bakery?" Erik's tone was dismissive, as if he couldn't be bothered wasting his time speaking with us.

"Our bakeshop is *Torte*," I corrected him. "I'm Jules. We spoke on the phone a few weeks ago."

"Yep." Erik nodded, looking bored. He snuck another glance toward the garden beds and trails leading down to the beach. Hoff was long gone, but Erik didn't seem to care. "What can I do for you?"

"We're here to help with the opening." I tried to remain upbeat, but Erik gave off the vibe that he didn't care if I was the President of the United States or the president of the school booster club.

"They already had to call in reinforcements, huh? That's news to me." Erik swiveled his head toward the kitchen. For a minute, I thought he was going to turn around, walk back inside, and verbally lash Sterling and Steph about inviting us. Instead, his condescending smile morphed into a snarl. "I'm not sure whether to thank you. Those two are in over their heads. I was under the impression they were professionally trained, but all they do is whine and complain about the equipment, staffing, and vendors. That's what I get for hiring Gen Z—they don't want to work. They want to be influencers and expect six-figure salaries right out of the gate. No respect. No work ethic."

*How dare he?*

Steph and Sterling were two of the hardest workers I'd ever met.

I seethed internally, my temperature spiking and my heart rate picking up speed. I clutched my fists and pressed my lips tight. "They are professionally trained and two of the most talented chefs in the Rogue Valley." I could hear the defensiveness in my voice, but I didn't care. Erik was insulting me and my former staff.

"You could have fooled me." Erik rolled his eyes. He brushed his hands on his jeans and moved toward the stairs. "Listen, I have bigger fish to fry at the moment— like my fish supplier, who is MIA again. Knock yourself out in the kitchen. I thought there was hope for those two to make a real change, but I have a feeling I'm going to be looking for new chefs by the time the weekend is up."

Carlos made a sound that could only be described as a growl. I'd never heard him utter anything like it, and I pressed my hand on his hip to stop him from going after Erik. Not that I blamed him, but we had to remain professional.

Erik appeared to take pleasure in making people uncomfortable. I heard him let out a little chortle as he passed by us and followed in Hoff's direction.

"This man is odious. Terrible." Carlos ripped a piece of mint from a nearby pot and smashed it in his hand. "These are utter lies about Sterling and Steph—they could work in a Michelin-star restaurant. He should be bending over backward to help them make the opening a success. I do not like this one bit. It's almost as if he's hoping the restaurant will flop."

I didn't like it either. "I know, but remember our earlier conversation. We have to follow their lead. Let's hear what they have to say, and then we can strategize how best to support them."

"Sí, you're right and always wise, but I could also take him in a fight. A stiff breeze would knock him off his feet." Carlos dropped the sprig of mint and pretended to swing a punch. Never in our years together had he ever resorted to violence. I knew there was no chance he was serious, and I didn't blame him for wanting to take a swing at Erik. I wouldn't have minded swatting the superior grin from his face, either.

Steph appeared at the doors wearing a pale green apron with the SeaBreeze logo embroidered in the center. "Jules, Carlos, I thought we heard your voices." She practically

leapt into my arms and hugged me tight. Effusive shows
of affection weren't normal for Steph. I returned the hug
and waited for her to release her grasp first. When she
did, she brushed a tear from her eyes, smudging her violet
shadow.

"We're so happy to be here and so excited for you," I
said, feeling like a proud parent.

"Thanks." She gulped, swallowing her emotions. "Sorry
to be so needy. It's good to see familiar faces." Steph was tall
and thin, with dark hair cut into a blunt, angular shoulder-
length bob that was streaked with violet highlights. Her eye
shadow and makeup matched her moody color palette.

I reached for her arm. "Obviously, we've heard a
little about what's been going on from you and Sterling,
and we just had the . . ." I searched for the right word.
"Pleasure? Of meeting Erik."

"He's a nightmare." Steph tucked her hair behind her
ears and shook her head. "Talk about terrible bosses. Sterling and I both knew how great we had it at Torte, but we
had no idea that Erik's management style was going to
be aggressive and borderline tyrannical. I guess I should
have clued in during the interview process. He was intense,
but interviewing is always hard. I thought part of it was
me. I was awkward and trying to make a good impression,
but I never imagined he'd be so awful."

"Has he been bad to you?" Carlos rounded his shoulders in a show of protection.

"No. Not really. I mean, nothing we can't handle. It's
the rest of the staff, mainly, at least for now. I think that's
because he doesn't know us well enough. He treats everyone else like they're his personal servants. The other staff

have been here for years. He's a serious control freak but a hot mess. It doesn't add up. It would make sense if he were über-organized, but he's not. He's always behind on vendor payments and is constantly missing in action. I don't know where he goes, but he'll be MIA for hours." She brushed a smudge of purple mascara from her eye and stared behind us like she was checking to see if anyone was listening. "Let's go inside. Sterling is hyped to see you, and then we can both fill you in more. It would be good to get your perspectives." She held the door open for us.

Carlos and I shared a look as we followed her inside.

The interior of the SeaBreeze Bistro had a distinctly nautical theme with old ship anchors, huge pieces of driftwood, buoys, rope, and floating glass balls. There was an assortment of large and small tables, most arranged so that every seat had an ocean view. The same bouquets from outside, along with larger floral displays, gave the room a pop of needed color. The walls were painted in a soft shade of pistachio that matched Steph's apron. Menus at each of the place settings appeared to be new. I couldn't wait to see the final menu Sterling and Steph had come up with for their reimagining.

I could tell immediately she had designed the new logo. SeaBreeze was written in an elegant script. The word "Sea" was highlighted in a gradient of blue to reflect the ocean, while "Breeze" was depicted in a light shade of green to evoke the rustling coastal winds. Beneath the name was a subtle wave motif and a sketch of the cliffside.

"It's campy," Steph said, watching my face. "Campy is kind of in right now. We think we can work with the cheesy beach vibe. It's like putting lipstick on a pig, isn't that the saying? You know, go all in on the kitsch factor."

"I hear kitsch is in again." I tried to wink unsuccessfully.

"I hope so. The one thing I can say is that it's spotless," Steph continued. "We scrubbed every inch of floorboard and trim and every table and chair. The paint is new, and we moved all of the furniture so that each table has a view."

"I like it," Carlos replied, stopping to admire a hand-carved stone statue of a whale. "Is the menu a beach vibe, as the kids say?"

Steph's stoic face split into a wide grin. "I'm sorry, but uh, no. That's not what the kids say. No one is catching any vibes, Carlos. Fish maybe. But vibes, no."

His sheepish expression let me know he was kidding. It was his way of putting Steph at ease.

"The kitchen is through here." She directed us through a door at the back of the restaurant. "It's weird after working in an open kitchen for such a long time. I thought I might like the privacy, but I kind of miss having customers peer in to see what we're doing. Sterling even talked to Hoff, the head of maintenance, about the possibility of knocking out this wall to give guests a view. What do you think?"

"I love it." Carlos nodded his head in enthusiastic approval. "Is it possible?"

"Hoff thinks so." Steph knocked on the wall. "He has to check, but he doesn't think the wall is load-bearing, so it might be able to come down."

Sterling dropped his spatula the minute he noticed

us and hurried to hug me. "Thanks so much for coming, Jules. It means the world to me and Steph." His ice-blue eyes were filled with emotion as he pulled away from me. He looked like he had matured even more in the last few weeks.

"As if you could keep us away." I punched him playfully in the arm. The stainless-steel countertops and workstations reflected like mirrors on the gray epoxy floors.

His dark hair fell over one eye. He pushed it away and smiled, but it didn't reach his eyes. "Yeah, well, it's awesome to see you both. It's been a busy and stressful couple of weeks, and it still doesn't feel real that we're opening in less than six hours."

"We are here to alleviate that stress," Carlos said, clasping him on the back in a half hug and then motioning to the stove. "Remember what we taught you. You infuse your emotions into the food. The food will feel it and suffer if you're tense."

"I know. I keep trying to remind myself of that, but it's not working." Sterling sighed and ran his fingers through his wavy hair, revealing the hummingbird tattoo on his forearm. "I figured I would be feeling some level of nerves with our first restaurant opening, you know, first-day jitters, but dealing with Erik is piling on the stress."

"Do you want to talk about it? Or the better question is, do you have time to talk about it?" I studied the kitchen. Along one wall, rows of stainless-steel counters provided ample workspace for precision dicing, chopping, and assembling dishes. Above the counters, open shelving displayed pots and utensils, practically arranged for easy access. The island was clearly Steph's domain with industrial mixers, bright overhead lighting for meticulous piping work, and canisters with an assortment of spatulas and palette knives.

Their prep work looked solid. Sauces and soups simmered on the industrial stove, and the grill hummed with sizzling corn on the cob. Vegetables, fruit, and herbs were cut, chopped, and organized in mise-en-place containers. Pastries and cakes waited to be finished at Steph's workstation. The kitchen was dated, as was the equipment, but it was tidy and spotless. I'd worked with less. The mark of any good chef was being able to use the tools at hand. Despite the aging appliances, I knew that Steph and Sterling would be able to produce high-quality, delicious meals for their guests.

"It would really help to talk it through with you," Sterling replied, looking at Steph for confirmation. "We can work and talk, right?"

"Yeah." She washed her hands in the sink and gestured to the neat rows of cupcakes on the island. "I wouldn't mind an extra hand piping while we talk."

I patted my heart. "You're speaking my language. Hit me with a piping bag."

"What's simmering?" Carlos walked to the stove and lifted the lid on one of the pots. "May I taste?"

"Please." Sterling showed him to the spoons and waited with bated breath. "It's my take on an Italian tomato sauce, with tomatoes from the garden, basil, onion, garlic, and a touch of fresh lemon and cream to bring out the brightness. I plan on serving it with handmade pasta and meatballs. It's nothing fancy, but it's a true taste of the resort. I want the focus to be on the herbs and tomatoes, so I kept it simple."

"Aww, a classic Sunday sauce, as they say in Italy. Divine. Perfection. No notes." Carlos pressed his fingers to his lips and blew a kiss in the air. "You have arrived, Chef."

A proud blush spread across Sterling's cheeks. "Thanks, Chef. That's high praise from you."

Steph gave me a piping bag filled with seafoam green buttercream.

"What's your vision?" I tapped the shell piping tip and then placed my finger on my temple like I was a mind reader. "I'm guessing shells?"

"Exactly. You're too good, Jules. A real prophet." She rolled her eyes and reached for her sketchbook to show me her design. "We're leaning into the beach theme, like I said. I want to do a trio of sand, shells, and the sea."

"What flavors are these?" I asked, picking up what appeared to be a vanilla cupcake.

"That's an animal cracker. These are s'mores." She pointed to the tray of chocolate cupcakes. "And these are some of my personal favorites. I went with food memories from what we would eat at the beach when I was a kid. I know I had a vagabond lifestyle, so maybe they won't translate to everyone, but like you taught me, I'm putting myself in the dish."

Steph's childhood was anything but typical. She grew up in a camper van, traveling across the country with her parents, who were circus performers. It wasn't a traditional lifestyle, which was something she struggled to come to terms with. We'd had lengthy discussions about how she used to wish she'd had a "normal" upbringing, or at least the perceived idea of normal—a house with a white picket fence, a dog, and parents who drove a minivan instead of a caravan. As Steph sunk deeper into herself, she came to realize that the creativity, spontaneity, and adventure in her childhood shaped her artistry and had given her a completely different lens on the world.

I studied the last tray. The cupcakes were golden yellow and looked like they had chunks of fruit. "Something tropical? Pineapple and coconut?"

"Close. Fire-roasted bananas with a chocolate center. I'm going to finish those and the s'mores with marshmallow buttercream. Did you ever make banana boats when you were younger?"

"Banana boats!" I clasped my hands over my mouth in excitement. "That's brilliant. Yes—that's one of my favorite beach memories, too."

"What is a banana boat?" Carlos asked, dipping a clean spoon into Sterling's cheese sauce.

"You slice a banana in half and fill it with chocolate and marshmallows. Then you wrap it in tinfoil and roast it over the fire," Steph explained.

"I will never understand America's obsession with food over fire, but I must admit it is the best." He gave Steph a cheeky grin. "How soon can I taste them?"

"You know, we should make the real thing with Ramiro while we're here," I said. "We can light a big bonfire one night. It's a beach tradition."

"Maybe after we get through dinner service or Monday night," Sterling suggested. "That can be our reward and something to look forward to."

"It's a date. I'll get a bundle of firewood and the supplies for banana boats and s'mores." I twisted the shell tip and angled the edge on the rim of a cupcake.

"What is the menu for tonight?" Carlos asked, tying on an apron.

"We're doing comfort classics," Sterling replied. "Spaghetti and meatballs, a retro grilled cheese with chicken corn chowder, fish and chips, fresh salmon pasta, shrimp linguini, coconut calamari, and a beach burger."

"Ambitious but manageable." Carlos clapped Sterling on the back. "Put me to work, Chef."

"Well, there's one glaring problem. At the moment, we have no fish. As in zero, zilch. We're waiting for the delivery, but I'm not convinced we're going to get it," Sterling said, glancing toward the dining room as if he was hopeful that his supplier would walk through the doors. "Erik and Travis, our local fish supplier who owns a small private fishing operation, Catch of the Day, apparently had a falling-out. Travis is threatening to withhold our order. I don't know if it's financial, like maybe Erik is late on payments, or if something else is going on, but regardless, we were supposed to have fish on-site two hours ago, and there's still no sign of him. It's going to be a lame menu without any fish. After all, you can see and smell the ocean from here." He nodded toward the dining room.

"Tell us more about Erik. What's his deal?" I asked, dotting the cupcake with a shell pattern.

"Where do I even start? He's our version of Richard Lord," Steph said with a sneer. "He may be worse, honestly. At least you can ignore Richard, but Erik's our boss. He's abrasive and authoritarian. There are tons of rumors swirling about his mismanagement of resort funds, which is why Sterling and I suspect the fish delivery is on hold."

"This is no good," Carlos said. He motioned to a stack of onions. "Should I begin chopping these?"

"Yeah, thanks. Those are for the corn chowder." Sterling handed Carlos a sharp knife and made room for him at the counter. "I called and texted Travis, hoping that we could cut Erik out of the conversation, but he hasn't responded. He might be out on his boat. We've been racking our brains to come up with plan B. A beach restaurant without any fish on the menu is going to be pretty unimpressive."

"What about the local market?" I suggested. "We could head into town and purchase at least enough fish for a couple of dishes."

"We thought about that." Steph scooped fluffy marshmallow buttercream into a piping bag. "The only problem is that we don't have any funds of our own. We're responsible for putting together a food budget, but Erik insists that all payments go through him. It's such a pain, and neither of us want to use our own money to pay for products because there's no guarantee he'll reimburse us."

That was odd. It was common for chefs to have company credit cards, checks, and lines of credit for food, materials, and supplies.

"No. Do not use your personal funds," Carlos cautioned. "Is there anyone else you can speak with about the situation?"

Sterling shook his head. "Hoff, the head of maintenance, has been here the longest, but he and Erik hate each other. Jess, who runs the front desk, told us the rumor about Erik mismanaging funds. Aside from us, there are a few housekeepers, waitstaff, and maintenance crew.

Erik is the most senior staff member and is in charge of everything, so you can see our dilemma, right?"

"Sí." Carlos tucked a dish towel into his apron. "This is a problem."

"A huge problem," Steph repeated with emphasis. "Our boss is a criminal, and there's nothing we can do about it."

# Chapter Six

I felt terrible for Steph and Sterling, but there wasn't time to lament about their unfortunate circumstances. Every table for the grand reopening was booked. In a few short hours, the restaurant would be buzzing with hungry guests. We needed to come up with solutions and an alternate menu—now.

"What do you have in terms of supplies?" I asked, setting my piping bag down and moving toward the walk-in.

"Sí, let's work the problem," Carlos agreed, following me.

Sterling matched our urgency, hurrying to grab his spiral-bound notebook containing recipes and sketches for future recipes. "We're solid on dessert and bread. The pasta with meatballs, grilled cheese and soup, and burgers are all a go." He flipped through the notebook. "It's just that we have four fish dishes to replace. And we don't have a lot of time to prep."

"What if you did a simple lemon butter and herb pasta in place of the shrimp linguini?" Carlos suggested, picking up a basket of Meyer lemons.

"Yeah, that's good." Sterling made a note. "We have

some local smoked elk sausages. I was thinking I could make a bean and rice stew with them."

"And maybe a bruschetta with tomatoes and herbs from the garden," Steph suggested.

Sterling wrote the ideas down.

"See? This is coming together. You've got this," I said, hoping my face looked enthusiastic. It was no small feat to completely shift a menu hours before service, but if anyone could pull it off, I knew it was our team.

Before Sterling had a chance to respond, the kitchen door burst open, and a guy in his early thirties wearing waders and waterproof overalls came in, carrying a large box of fish. His gray sweatshirt had an intricate illustration of a fishing boat sailing on choppy waters and was lettered with the words CATCH OF THE DAY.

"Travis. You're here." Sterling sighed with relief. "I don't think I've ever been so happy to see someone."

"I wouldn't get too excited—this might be the last time you see me." Travis hoisted the box with both of his muscular arms. He had a gray towel with the Catch of the Day logo draped over his shoulder. "Where do you want this?"

"No, really, man, you have no idea how glad we are to see you. We were worried fish was going to be off the menu tonight," Sterling said, pushing aside ramekins and his notebook. "Put it right here."

Travis complied. "It was going to be off the menu, but Jess called and begged me to help you out tonight. Let me be clear: this is a one-time favor for *you*, not for Erik, and if I don't get payment tonight, it won't happen again."

"We appreciate it," Sterling said sincerely, picking up a freshly caught salmon and holding it to the light. "You saved our bacon. Dinner's on us tonight if you want to come to the opening party."

"Maybe I will." Travis cracked his knuckles. "That way, I can force Erik to pay up."

The sound of voices made him stop. A woman I didn't recognize entered the kitchen with Hoff on her heels.

"Where is he?" Hoff demanded, dumping his toolbox on the floor.

"Who?" Sterling asked, placing the fish back on ice.

"Erik," Hoff barked. "We saw Travis and figured Erik has to show his face for once and pay him."

"I haven't seen him for a while," Sterling replied, running his finger over the salmon's pink, shiny scales.

"He's probably hiding out because he knows everyone is looking for him," Hoff said.

"I was supposed to meet with him thirty minutes ago," the woman said, tapping her wrist. "This is very unprofessional." She was petite with wiry, tight curls stuffed into a bun and a leather-bound notebook tucked her arm.

"Unprofessional?" Hoff huffed. "Unprofessional is Erik's middle name."

"You're sure he's not here?" the woman asked Sterling, looking at him with an angled chin and narrow eyes as if she thought he was lying.

"I promise he's not here," Sterling retorted, spreading his arms wide to prove he wasn't hiding anyone. "It's just us."

"Are you the new chefs?" She stepped forward, pressing down the front of her blouse and making a quick appraisal of the kitchen. She was a bit older than me. I'd have put her in her forties, maybe even fifties. She wore a pair of skinny jeans, ankle boots, and a low-cut blouse. Her light hair was tied in a severe bun, which made her features appear sharp and stern.

"Yeah, I'm Sterling." Sterling waved with his free hand. "And Steph is the pastry chef."

Steph bobbed her head in a hello but didn't speak.

"You two are quite young," the woman observed with skepticism. "Erik said he was desperate, but I didn't realize he was this desperate."

That was unnecessary.

Just because Sterling and Steph were in their mid-twenties didn't mean they weren't qualified to run a kitchen.

Carlos immediately jumped in, forgetting everything about our earlier conversation. "I will have you know these are two of the best-trained chefs in all of southern Oregon."

The woman stepped back and waved her hands in front of her. "Apologies. Apologies. I meant no offense. I'm sure you've heard that Erik has blown through a number of chefs. He can't keep anyone on staff, so it's no surprise he's trying to take a more youthful approach. Good luck to you," she said to Sterling with a patronizing smile. "Maybe you'll finally break the SeaBreeze curse."

That didn't make her insult any better. I wasn't a fan of her cloying smile or attempt to brush off her rude comment.

"I'm Lucy Clarke, by the way. Local real estate agent and developer. I've heard there's going to be a brand-new menu this evening, and I, for one, am thrilled that you're doing something other than frozen fish and chips and hot dogs. The food here has been abysmal. Costco muffins for Sunday breakfast? No wonder Erik can't keep a chef. Unfortunately, I'm afraid it's going to take much more than your pretty cupcakes to salvage this place. I do love that you're giving it your full attention—ah, the naïvety of youth. The logo is cute, and I like your color aesthetic. If you only knew what you're really getting into." She paused and checked behind her. "It's a shame to see you put so much effort into it, though."

"Why?" Sterling asked, his brows scrunched together in distrust.

"You're in a sinking ship without a life raft, honey." Lucy patted her chest twice, like it pained her to continue. "Haven't you heard? The Whaleshead owners are finally ready to sell. The restaurant and cabins will soon be under new ownership."

"What?" Steph dropped her piping bag.

"I'm so sorry you haven't heard. I do hate to be the bearer of bad news," Lucy said with a condescending smile.

It was apparent that she absolutely enjoyed being the bearer of this news.

"We've been in talks for months." She adjusted her leather notebook. "Since the resort is owner controlled, we need a majority of the ownership to vote in favor of the sale. Everyone has finally reached their limit with Erik. They've lost all trust. The vote is in two days, and I'm very confident that everyone is going to vote to sell."

"What does that mean for SeaBreeze Bistro?" Steph asked.

"Oh, I'm sorry, dear. It will likely be torn down. We have a much bolder vision for the resort. High-end condos, upgraded amenities, and a fine-dining restaurant."

Steph's face turned white.

Sterling glanced at me and mouthed, "What?"

"Like I said, though, I'll be eager to try your cuisine this evening. Perhaps there will be an opportunity for you to get hired on under new management." She twisted her watch. "Look at the time, I need to find Erik. Lovely meeting you."

With that, she turned on her heels and strolled out of the kitchen.

"I need to go fix a cabin," Hoff said, trudging after her with heavy steps. "If you see Erik, tell him I need to talk to him ASAP, and that's not a request—it's an order."

After they both left, Sterling hung his head and placed his chin in his hands. "I can't believe this. Whaleshead is getting sold. How could Erik have failed to mention that when we interviewed? Shouldn't that have been the first thing he told us? I never would have agreed to this job if I knew the restaurant was up for sale."

"It's terrible and unprofessional." Carlos squeezed his shoulder in a show of solidarity. "But this isn't the end. We don't know about the sale yet, and like she said, maybe she will hire you. It sounds like working for Erik isn't a good match, anyway. Maybe this will be an even better opportunity for you both."

Steph muttered something under her breath.

"Carlos is right. There's no point in dwelling on it," I said, trying to sound chipper. "On the plus side, the fish is here, so we don't have to tweak the menu. Let's get through your first night of service, and then we'll deal with everything else."

"I'm so glad you're both here." Sterling ran his fingers through his hair and stood taller. "You're right. I know you kindly offered that should we ever be in need of a job, we might still have a spot at Torte. I didn't think we'd need to call in that favor quite so fast, but . . . maybe we're heading back to Ashland quicker than we imagined."

"Always. You always have jobs with us." I met both of their eyes and placed my hand over my heart. "There's no question. Ever. You always have a place at Torte, but let's not go there yet, okay? Let's get dinner out and not worry about anything else for the time being."

Steph rubbed her lips together and nodded like she was fighting back tears.

"Listen, this is how it goes in commercial kitchens." I looked at Carlos for confirmation.

"Sí. I went through three owners at my first job, each with a different vision."

"Yeah," I agreed. "You have to learn to roll with whatever the tide brings in for you, to borrow an ocean analogy. This is a setback that is completely out of your control, so my best advice is to home in on what you *can* control."

"Thanks, Jules."

I hoped my pep talk helped. What I didn't tell them was I was equally worried about their future. Restaurant sales, transfers, and renovations were messy at best. The odds that Sterling and Steph would be able to retain their roles were small. But dwelling on the negative wasn't going to help them or get dinner prep finished, so the only thing we could do for the moment was to dive deep into making tonight's grand reopening the best meal the guests had ever tasted.

# Chapter Seven

We spent the next hour decorating cupcakes and dicing veggies for a rich and hearty chicken corn chowder. Sterling blasted a beach-themed playlist with vintage oldies from the Beach Boys and Bob Marley. Listening to music during prep created a lively and energetic atmosphere. It was something both Carlos and I encouraged. However, once the restaurant was open and dinner service was in full swing, we would kill the music. Having background noise while calling out orders and making sure dishes are delivered hot is too distracting.

I finished the last of the shell cupcakes with a sprinkling of luster dust and brushed my hands on my apron. "I hope I did justice to your vision," I said to Steph, placing the final cupcake on a tiered stand.

"They're even better. Thanks so much, Jules." Her voice caught. "I really appreciate you being here and jumping in. I don't know what we would have done without you, especially with the drama surrounding Erik and the future of Whaleshead."

"It's my pleasure." I checked around us. Carlos was

filleting fish while Sterling rolled meatballs by hand. "What else can I do?"

"Would you mind picking some tomatoes and fresh herbs for the salad?" Steph nodded to the other side of the counter. "There are shears in the top drawer, and the garden boxes are just down below the deck."

"I'm on it." I gave her a salute and went outside.

On the deck, the buttery sun kissed my shoulders. I drank in the salty sea air and the quiet stillness of the afternoon. The skies were calm and clear, although the weather forecast was calling for a storm to blow in tomorrow. I allowed myself to be enveloped by nature—the cry of seagulls and the small breeze rustling through the trees.

Bees hummed on clumps of wild lavender and blackberry vines as I took the short path to the garden boxes. They were located on the hillside just below the deck. The narrow path continued past the beds and connected with the main trail that led down to the beach.

I snipped bunches of mint, rosemary, and thyme, enjoying the sound of the waves cresting below and seagulls circling overhead.

I filled a basket with herbs and tomatoes plucked straight from the vine and started to retrace my steps back to the kitchen, but the sound of a scream halted me in my tracks.

I stopped in midstride and glanced in the direction of the scream.

*Or was it the wind?*

*Or the seagulls?*

I froze and listened intently, every cell in my body on high alert.

*Nothing.*

I tucked the basket over my arm and took another step when a second wail reverberated off the evergreens. No, that was definitely a scream.

I dropped the basket and jogged in the direction of the sound. It was coming from the trail farther ahead.

"Hello? Hello?" I called as I scanned the jagged cliffside.

There was no sign of anyone on the trail. I could see at least a few hundred feet in front of me. The pathway hugged the edge of the sheer drop-off before it curved and began a gentler slope down to the coast.

I'm not particularly afraid of heights, and there was plenty of space on the trail for two people to walk side by side, but I was conscientious about my footing. Pregnancy had made me a bit unstable and clumsy, and I didn't want to risk falling. I stuck to the middle of the path and continued to search for anyone in distress.

There was no railing or barrier on the trail for protection. My mind drifted to worst-case scenarios. I hope someone hadn't fallen.

*Maybe I'd imagined it.*

*I hadn't been sleeping well—could I be hallucinating?*

Another thought entered my mind. What if it was just kids playing around? That was probably the most likely explanation. Sound carried easily on the coastline, catching the wind like a kite.

For all I knew, it could be Ramiro and his friends returning on the trail.

As I wandered farther, the sound of crashing waves grew louder.

*You're being overly dramatic, Jules.*

I sighed.

This was silly. There was still plenty to do before Sterling and Steph opened the doors at five. I needed to get out of my head and concentrate on making sure everything went smoothly tonight.

Mom would blame my overactive imagination on Dad. "You are so your father's daughter, Juliet," she would tease. "He would spend half the day with his head in the clouds, making up stories and daydreaming about new recipes."

She meant it as a compliment. They had been a good match. Much like Carlos and me, they balanced each other out. She was the practical one in their relationship, firmly planting her feet on the ground while Dad tended to flit like a hummingbird, darting between his many interests and the ever-running narrative in his head.

I couldn't help but continue to check the cliffside. My body shuddered at the thought of slipping. The rocky face was unstable, with massive boulders and loose rocks that looked like a stiff breeze that would send them tumbling a hundred feet to the ocean below.

Around the next bend, a bench carved from driftwood invited weary hikers to pause and take in the majestic views.

A couple carrying a large picnic basket and blanket approached me on the trail.

"Good afternoon." They greeted me with a smile. "Are you heading to the beach? It's a stunner today."

I pointed behind me. "No, I just came from the restaurant."

"Just so you know, the return trip is all uphill. It will get your blood pumping, that's for sure," the young woman noted with a scowl. "Hey, did you hear screaming a minute or so ago?" she asked, studying my face like she was trying to assess whether I was in danger. "We thought we saw someone running in the woods near the trail after we heard the scream. We're worried that someone had an accident, but there's no sign of anyone around."

A touch of relief mixed with a sinking dread washed over me. At least I hadn't imagined the screams, but that wasn't exactly good news. Who was screaming? And why? "I heard that too. In fact, that's why I hurried down here. I was concerned that someone had fallen. As you can see, there's no railing on this side of the trail, and it's a steep drop-off."

"Right, we'll be extra careful." The woman peered around me. "Were you with that other guy?"

"Other guy?" I asked, furrowing my brow.

"I think he must be maintenance for the resort. He was running in the other direction. We thought maybe there was an emergency. I'm terrified of tsunamis, but there's no siren warning."

Maintenance. Were they referring to Hoff?

I shook my head. "No, I haven't seen anyone else on the trail."

"And you haven't heard a tsunami warning?" the woman asked, chewing on her bottom lip.

"No. I've spent many summers here in Whaleshead and have heard the test sirens enough to know that you wouldn't miss it."

She smiled. "Okay, thanks. That's a relief because I was ready to run to our cabin and pack up our car."

"I think you're fine," I assured her.

They waved and continued past me on a small trail that led to a collection of cabins.

I turned to head back up the hill.

As I passed the bench, I noticed a gray towel wadded up in the corner. Someone must have forgotten it.

I grabbed it to take to lost and found, but when I did, I noticed something else—something much worse.

I sucked the salty tang of the sea air in through my nose and grabbed the edge of the bench for support.

*Just take a quick glance, Jules.*

*You could be wrong.*

I stood on my toes to look over the ledge.

Sprawled out below me was Erik's lifeless body.

# Chapter Eight

Erik had fallen off the cliff and landed thirty or forty feet below on a rocky overhang. His body looked like a mangled pretzel, and his head was twisted at an unnatural angle. The worst part was that his eyes were wide open and staring up at me with a glossy, lifeless gaze.

"Erik, Erik, are you okay?" I called, knowing he wasn't. I couldn't help it. Instinct kicked in. "I'm going to get help."

I raced back to the restaurant as fast as I could, tucking the towel under my arm, and tapping into my former cross-country-running days.

Panic bubbled up inside. I thought I might be sick.

*Keep it together, Jules.*

I focused on the scenery to keep the panic at bay, noting how my feet crunched on the dry pine needles and concentrating on my footing.

I ran around the last bend and spotted Hoff and Lucy, who were huddled next to the garden boxes, like they were holding a secret meeting.

"Erik fell," I blurted out, motioning behind me. "He's in bad shape."

"Fell where?" Hoff pulled away from Lucy like she was suddenly contagious.

"He's on the side of the cliff. I can't reach him. I don't know how anyone is going to reach him. They're probably going to have to rappel down to get him." My voice was wobbly as I tried to catch my breath and not go into a full panic attack.

*This couldn't be happening.*

*Not now.*

*Not tonight.*

Poor Steph and Sterling. They had worked so hard.

And also poor Erik. He may not have been the nicest boss, but seeing him sprawled on the overhang like that made me want to vomit. This time, I didn't think it had anything to do with my pregnancy hormones.

"I'll go," Hoff said, brushing past me with authority. "You stay here."

"We need to call the police," I said, wishing I hadn't left my phone inside. Every minute counted. If there was any chance that Erik was still alive, the sooner rescuers could get to him, the better the odds of his survival.

"I have my phone. I can call," Lucy said, unzipping her purse and reaching for her phone.

Hoff took off, thundering past the garden boxes in a full sprint.

"Here, you speak with them. You saw what happened, didn't you?" Lucy thrust her phone in my face, appraising me like I was somehow responsible for Hoff's death. "Let's move onto the deck."

I answered the dispatcher's questions to the best of my abilities.

Lucy picked up the leather notebook she'd had with her

earlier and stared over the railing like she might be able to see something. We couldn't. The trail curved in the opposite direction.

After I passed on every detail I could share, the operator told me help was on the way and to stay put until the professionals arrived.

"What did they say?" Lucy asked when I gave her back her phone.

"That under no circumstances should we attempt to make a rescue. They're sending a special team that's trained for this kind of situation."

"I'll go tell Hoff." She tossed her purse and notebook on an empty table.

*Why was she in such a hurry to leave?*

"Uh, okay, I need to let everyone in the kitchen know, and then I'll come join you. The operator said witnesses should stick around until the police and first responders arrive."

"I'm not a witness. You are." Again, the accusation in her tone was undeniable.

I unfolded the towel I'd found on the bench and gasped—it belonged to Travis. The Catch of the Day logo was immediately evident. I'd seen Travis with the towel when he delivered the fish. When had Travis been down by the bench? Or maybe he had a partnership with Whaleshead and gave the resort free towels to share with guests in exchange for advertising?

That didn't feel quite right, but I wasn't going to let the towel out of my sight until the police showed up.

I retrieved the basket I'd abandoned earlier and clutched it as tight as I could, hoping it might quell the shaking. Reality was starting to sink in.

Had Erik fallen?

Or had someone pushed him?

Was that the scream I'd heard?

My knees buckled at the thought. I grabbed the railing to try and steady myself. The world began to spin. Tiny bright dots shrouded my vision.

*Am I going to pass out?*

*Breathe, Jules.*

*Breathe.*

I took a second to inhale deeply through my nose and then slowly release my breath. It was a tool I'd learned years ago to help center myself. Usually, a few rounds of centered breathing did the trick, but not now. My heartbeat thudded against my chest. Blood rushed to my head and spread across my cheeks.

I needed to sit down.

I limped to the door and opened it. "Carlos, are you here?" I called weakly. My voice sounded distant, as if it were coming from somewhere far away.

Carlos rushed from the kitchen. "Julieta, what is it? Are you okay?"

Steph and Sterling followed close behind him.

I shook my head and sunk into the closest chair, placing the towel on my lap. "It's Erik."

"Erik?" Carlos dropped to his knees and scanned my body for any signs of injury. "I don't understand. Are you hurt?"

"No, I'm fine." I massaged my temples and continued to suck air in through my nose. "Well, I'm not fine emotionally. Sorry. I know I'm not making sense. I'm trying not to lose it."

"Sí, it is okay. We are here with you. Relax. Breathe."

He massaged my knee. "Sterling, can you get her some water?"

Sterling nodded and vanished into the kitchen.

"Good, yes. That's it. Nice and slow. In and out." Carlos's tone was smooth and silky as he breathed with me. It brought me an instant sense of relief.

He was right. I was fine. But Erik wasn't. I needed to concentrate on doing what I could to save him.

"I was picking herbs and tomatoes when I heard a scream," I said, taking a gulp of air.

Steph stood next to the table, looking at me with wide eyes. "A scream?"

I nodded. "I thought I was imagining it, or maybe it was the wind or kids, but I went down the trail a little way to check it out, and that's when I spotted Erik's body."

"His body?" Steph asked, scrunching her forehead and squinting like the sun was too bright. It streamed in through the windows, creating patterns on the floor.

"He'd fallen." I swallowed hard, trying to loosen the knot swelling in my throat. "He must be a good thirty or more feet down the cliff. The only thing that stopped him from falling all the way to the beach was an overhang. But it looks bad. I don't think he could have survived the fall."

"You think he's dead?" Sterling asked, handing me a glass of water.

I managed to nod. Another wave of nausea flooded my body as the image of Erik's mangled limbs popped back into my head.

Sirens wailed in the distance.

The police were on their way.

That was a glimmer of good news.

I cradled the water glass and took a timid sip.

"It sounds like the police are close." Carlos encouraged me to drink. "Try some more water—it will help. Do you want something sweet?"

"I'm making a batch of concha bread." Steph glanced at her phone. "According to my timer, they'll be hot right from the oven in about five minutes."

"That just might tempt me." I took another sip of the cold water.

*Think about bread, Jules.*

*Bread.*

*Anything other than the image of Erik's broken body.*

The Mexican sweet bread was a personal favorite. Concha, or pan dulce, was named for its round shape and crispy topping resembling a seashell. The crunchy streusel was made with butter, sugar, flour, flavorings, and food coloring and then scored before baking to give each soft and pillowy brioche roll a colorful design.

"I have lemon, strawberry, vanilla, and chocolate if that helps sway you." Steph gave me a rare grin. It was almost like she knew I was trying to block out Erik's death with thoughts of pastry.

"I'll see how the water stays down first." I held my drink tighter.

"I can't believe Erik fell," Sterling said, pacing in front of the window. The tables glowed with a sweet warmth. Peachy light spilled inside, warming the dining space and giving it a homier feel.

My pulse felt slower, and my heart had stopped pounding.

"I'm not sure if he fell," I replied, allowing the visions to take shape again. I could handle it. I was in control now and surrounded by people who loved me. "I mean, he fell, but I'm wondering if he was pushed."

"Why?" Sterling stopped at a table to adjust the place setting, repositioning a fork so that it was aligned with the other silverware.

"It's the angle of the fall that's bugging me." I sat up straighter. My head felt clearer. The water and taking a minute to sit must have helped clear the sticky stress from my brain. "If he fell, wouldn't he have landed face-down? Like, if he were looking over the side of the cliff or had stopped to take a picture or even tripped, it would make sense that he would have landed on his stomach, right?"

Everyone nodded in agreement.

"But he didn't. He landed on his back. Face-up." My body quivered at the memory. "His eyes were staring at the sky. I know it sounds ridiculous, but he looked terrified, like he didn't know what was coming. I think he was pushed off the cliff."

Sterling paced again, pushing chairs into each table and fiddling with the napkins and place settings. "That theory makes sense, although I guess there's a chance he could have tripped and fallen backward or turned over before he died."

"True. True," I acknowledged with a quick nod. "Obviously, the police and first responders will have to confirm."

"You didn't see anyone nearby, though?" Steph asked as the timer on her phone went off.

"There was a young couple heading back from their cabin after a picnic on the beach. They said they had heard screams, too, but they took off on a smaller trail before I found him. Otherwise, there was no one around except for

Hoff and Lucy, who were outside near the gardens." I considered the timing. I'd been a good quarter of a mile down the trail. Either of them could have pushed Erik and then run up the path to the restaurant. I made a mental note to make sure to tell the police about the young couple. They could be the key, especially because they had mentioned seeing someone wearing a maintenance shirt fleeing the scene.

Had they witnessed Hoff running away right after he killed Erik?

# Chapter Nine

Steph left to take the conchas out of the oven. Red and blue flashing lights and the piercing sound of sirens broke our conversation.

"It looks like the cavalry has arrived." Sterling glanced out the windows, untied his apron, and set it on the back of a chair. "I don't know who's in charge now, so I guess I should probably speak with them. Or find Jess."

I was proud of him for stepping up. "I'll come with you."

Maybe that wasn't such a good idea.

The room started to spin again. I held on to the table for support and reminded myself to keep breathing.

"We'll stay here and keep an eye on the kitchen," Carlos said, gently helping me to my feet. "Let us know what they say about dinner tonight."

"Okay." I was glad to have professionals on the scene, although I wished Mom and the Professor were here. They were coming for dinner, but I didn't know when. She had texted me earlier to coordinate meeting for dinner, but I hadn't heard from her since.

Everything outside was a blur of activity. First responders carrying ropes, backpacks, and a backboard gathered at the base of the trail. Uniformed officers shouted orders, and an older woman wearing jeans, hiking boots, and a Curry County Sheriff half-zip sweatshirt approached us.

"I'm Detective Mars." She tapped the emblem on her sweatshirt. "Someone called in an accident."

"That was me." I raised my hand, my fingers trembling again. "I'm Jules Capshaw."

"Where's the victim?" She didn't waste any time with introductions or other questions.

"Down the trail about a quarter of a mile." I motioned in that direction with the towel.

"Go ahead, team. We'll be right behind you." She stepped out of the way and directed the rescue team to proceed. Then she turned to me. "Can you walk with me?"

"Of course." I wasn't eager to see the condition Erik was in, but if there was even the slightest chance he was still alive, I had to do everything I could to help. "You should take this," I said, handing her the towel. "I found it on the bench where he fell. I think it belongs to Travis, a local fisher. This is his logo."

"I'm familiar with Catch of the Day." She tucked the towel under her arm. A look I couldn't quite decipher passed across her face.

Did she know him because he was a local, or did he have a criminal record?

"Can you give me a rundown of what you witnessed?" Detective Mars asked as she ushered me forward.

I kept a good pace while watching my footing and explained everything that had transpired.

"Do you have an approximate time you heard the first scream?" she asked, taking notes on her phone as we made our way down the trail.

"It was probably around three or just shortly after. I checked the time right before I came outside to pick the herbs and tomatoes," I explained, pointing behind us to the garden boxes.

"Did you notice anything out of the ordinary?" Her tone was kind yet reserved. It was clear that she was all business, which was understandable.

"You'll see in a minute, but the angle of his fall seems wrong to me." I didn't want to get ahead of my self or try to insert my personal opinion into her investigation.

"Can you expand on that?" She maintained eye contact as she waited for my response. It was obvious that she had responded to similar calls. Her attire was the first giveaway. Her sturdy hiking boots made it easy for her to manage the trail's incline. A fanny pack with a two-way radio, flashlight, and multitool was secured around her waist.

"He landed face-up," I said, hoping I was moving fast enough for the rest of her crew. "I also bumped into a couple on their way back from the beach. They heard the screams too, and mentioned seeing someone wearing a Whaleshead maintenance jacket running down the trail toward the beach."

"Are you able to describe them?" Her pragmatic approach put me at ease.

It was good to feel like I was helping, even in the smallest way. I had information she needed. Information that could be essential to her investigation.

I gave her a brief description of the couple as Hoff came into view. He was standing in front of the bench precariously close to the ledge, peering over the cliff.

"Hey, over here. Over here." He waved wildly like he

was worried we were going to continue on without stopping. "He's right down there." Hoff stabbed his finger
toward Erik.

The emergency responders strapped into harnesses and
ropes and rappeled down the hillside.

"They left that way." I pointed to the wooden sign
tucked into the tree line. "I noticed a towel on the bench. I
figured someone probably forgot it and was going to grab
it to bring it back to the lodge for lost and found, and
that's when I realized he had fallen."

She typed with her thumbs, keeping the towel secured
under her arm.

The first responders worked at a dizzying pace to gear
up. They stretched red and black climbing ropes around
the base of two trees and secured their belay lines. I was
impressed by their speed.

"Let's step over here," Detective Mars suggested, using
her phone to point toward the trailhead.

I scooted as far away from the bench as possible. Not
only did I want to stay out of the way of the rescue crew,
but there was also no reason to subject myself to seeing
Erik's body again.

A small crowd began to gather around us as vacation-
ers coming to and from the beach took notice of the
police activity.

"I need everyone to stay back," Detective Mars com-
manded, motioning for people to steer clear of the scene.
She handed the towel off to one of her officers. "Bag this
and add it to evidence."

"Can I be of assistance?" I heard a familiar voice
behind us and turned to see the Professor and Mom coming toward us.

The Professor wore khaki shorts and a whale-print short-sleeve shirt. Mom's yellow-and-pink-striped halter dress and cardigan accented her petite frame. They looked like they belonged on a cruise ship. It was a strange juxtaposition to see them dressed in casual beachwear strolling up to a crime scene.

The lead paramedic called out orders as two team members launched themselves over the side of the cliff.

I raced to hug Mom while the Professor introduced himself to Detective Mars.

"I'm so glad you're here." I buried my face in her shoulder.

"What happened, honey?" She squeezed my waist tight. "Doug and I pulled into the resort and saw the police vehicles. You know I'm not prone to panic, but I will admit my heart stopped momentarily, thinking that something could have happened to you, Carlos, or Ramiro."

"We're all fine," I said, pulling away. "I'm sorry to scare you. It's Erik, the resort manager."

"He fell?" Her eyes immediately drifted to the jagged hillside. "From there? That can't be good."

"Yeah." I filled her in on finding him. "But I'm not sure he fell."

"Oh dear, that's terrible." She wrapped her arms around her cardigan and rubbed her shoulders. Then she gave me her best mom look, studying my face for any signs of stress. "How are you doing?"

"I'm fine," I lied. "I'm just trying to avoid seeing his body again. I'm sure he's dead, but I guess there's always hope."

The corners of her mouth sunk into a frown. "Perhaps."

"Yeah, it looks bad, doesn't it?"

Her walnut eyes filled with concern. "I don't know. But I'm confident you've done everything you can, and now the authorities are here, and they can take over."

"Exactly."

Detective Mars's radio crackled. The team hollered commands in a perfectly choreographed rhythm. Rescuers on belay at the top of the cliff carefully loosened slack on the ropes as their teammates reached the overhang.

The Professor and Detective Mars huddled together, whispering. I wondered if that meant they'd received confirmation from the recovery team below that Erik was indeed deceased.

"How are Steph and Sterling?" Mom asked. I knew she was trying to distract me, and I was grateful for it.

"Good. They have everything under control. I'm so impressed, especially because when we arrived, we learned that things had been quite stressful for them. Erik has been challenging to work with."

She wrinkled her brow. "Really?"

I told her about the fish deliveries, his treatment of the staff, and their lack of autonomy when it came to spending in the kitchen.

"What's going on?" A woman interrupted our conversation, pushing Mom and me apart to try and get a better view. She was close to Mom's age, with long gray hair tied into braids. Her flowing paisley gown fluttered in the breeze.

"There's been an accident," I replied.

"A tourist? I've told Erik a thousand times he needs to install a railing. This trail is so dangerous. I see parents letting their toddlers run free all the time. It's a death trap if you ask me." She twisted her hand in dismissive disgust.

"He's going to have a lawsuit on his hands. That's just what the resort needs right now."

I was afraid she was right—at least about that part of her speculation.

"Who is it? A tourist? Did they fall?" She tried to get closer, but a police officer held her back. "What an idiot. Who would stand close enough to the ledge to fall?"

"Someone did fall," I replied, unsure if I should tell her it was Erik. She clearly knew him. "Are you a resident at the resort?"

"A resident? No. I'm Mary Beth Wells." She said it like I was supposed to recognize her name.

Mary Beth—the missing artist Jess had mentioned earlier.

"Do you work for the resort?" I asked, slightly confused.

She tossed her shawl over her shoulders. "No, I'm an artist. I have a gallery here on-site, and the restaurant is showing my work this evening. In fact, I'm late. I'm supposed to meet with Erik and the new chefs to discuss plans."

"Oh, I saw that they were preparing for your showing. I'm looking forward to seeing your work," I said. "I'm Jules Capshaw, and this is my mom, Helen. We're here to help Sterling and Steph with the reopening."

"Are you from Ashland, too? Erik's been bragging all over town about how he scored some great new chefs."

"He's right. Sterling and Steph have worked for us for years, and they're the best of the best. You're in for a real treat." I couldn't conceal the pride in my voice.

"It's going to take more than skill to keep the SeaBreeze afloat," Mary Beth said with a dismissive flick of her wrist. "Erik's doing his best to run this entire resort into the ground. He's succeeding, if you ask me. Of course, no one asks me. If they did, we wouldn't be in this position, would we?"

I figured her question was rhetorical.

"I take it you know him well," I prompted, hoping she might offer more insight into Erik's management style.

"I wish I could say I didn't, but unfortunately, yes, I know him well. He makes it impossible not to know him. He inserts himself into places he has no business being— like my art, for example. I told him yesterday I would stab him with one of my sharp-tip pens or smack him over the side of the head with a paint bucket if he didn't stay in his own lane. Erik likes to believe that he alone is the most important and integral piece of the resort, but that's false. He's the reason this ship is sinking, and I'm done letting him get away with it. I'll be glad to speak with your former staff about how we can take him out, because let me warn you, if Erik is left to his own devices, there'll be nothing left of this resort. Nothing."

Those were strong words.

I tried to get a read on Mary Beth. She was passionate, which lined up with her artistic streak and creativity, but could that passion had gone too far?

"People, I need everyone to move back. Please move off the trail so that we can bring up the stretcher," Detective Mars said, motioning for us to make room.

A new flurry of activity and calls broke out as the crew hoisted the stretcher up the cliff.

Mary Beth gasped as the first responders lifted the backboard over the ledge. "Oh my God! It's Erik. He looks dead. Very dead."

"I'm so sorry." I reached out to try and console her, but she swatted my hand away.

"Don't be sorry, dear," she scoffed. "This is a cause for celebration."

# Chapter Ten

Mom nudged my waist.

"Erik is dead." Mary Beth cackled like a villain from a cartoon. "What sweet justice. Talk about karma. Erik has wreaked havoc on everyone's lives, and now the universe has caught up with him."

That was a dark response.

I wouldn't wish Richard Lord, my least favorite person in Ashland, dead, nor would I relish his demise. Mary Beth's reaction was a glaring red flag.

Where had she come from, anyway? She had seemingly appeared out of nowhere. Had she been nearby the entire time?

The Professor assisted Detective Mars in keeping the bystanders at bay as the rescue climbers carted Erik's body up the trail to the waiting ambulance.

"I hope this doesn't push back the party tonight," Mary Beth said with a long sigh. "I have a number of prominent clients who I've invited. It would be a shame to have to postpone the evening."

More of a shame than Erik's accident?

Was she being serious? Could this be her reaction to

trauma? I understood everyone processed grief and shock differently. I wanted to give her the benefit of the doubt, but she was making it difficult.

"My husband is a detective." Mom gestured to the Professor. "Their job is to secure the scene, interview witnesses, and begin piecing together a timeline of events leading up to the accident. This is the most crucial time in any investigation, so I doubt that they'll rush it. Whether or not the restaurant opens on time is entirely dependent on how quickly and easily they're able to make assessments and take statements."

I could tell that she was holding back from the way her cheeks pinched in and her slight frown.

"Why would an investigation be necessary?" Mary Beth pulled her neck inward like a turtle shrinking into its shell. "That seems like a waste of time and resources for an idiot hiker who slipped and fell off the trail."

"Was Erik a hiker?" I asked.

"It's a figure of speech. You know what I mean." She flicked at the air like she was swatting at an imaginary fly.

I had no idea what she meant. She was a walking contradiction. At this point, I wasn't sure I believed anything she was saying. I didn't want to jump to conclusions, but she certainly was acting suspiciously and had no problem making it clear that she and Erik hadn't gotten along, to say the very least.

"Were you at the beach?" I asked, hoping my question came across as innocent. "My stepson is down there with his friends, and I wondered if you heard the commotion down there. Did you hear Erik screaming before he fell?"

She gaped at me like I was speaking a different language and tossed her hand in that direction. "The beach is a mile downhill. How could anyone possibly hear the commotion from that far away?"

I noticed she didn't answer my question. "I remember the trek from visiting Whaleshead when I was younger. The walk down is a breeze, but the hike back up always gets the blood pumping."

She flicked at a swarm of gnats. "I wouldn't know. I don't take that route any longer. My knees don't do hills."

"Were you coming from the lodge or the trail?" I pointed above and behind us.

"Why does it matter?" A brief flash of irritation washed across her face, but she recovered quickly. "If you must know, I was coming from my gallery, on the far side of the property. This side trail connects to it." She gestured to the sign. "It's just around the next bend and very private. Fortunately there are only a handful of cabins on this side of the resort. I could not handle the constant chatter of kids and families if I had a spot near the lodge. Speaking of the lodge, I'm supposed to be setting up now. In fact, I think I'll have a word with the detective and see if I can be excused to go prepare for the event."

She moved closer to Detective Mars and the Professor and barged into their conversation.

I found it odd she didn't have any canvases or supplies with her if she was setting up for an art show.

"She's something," Mom said under her breath. "I don't know if I've ever heard someone react like that to a tragedy."

I watched as the Professor served as traffic control, steering bystanders past the recovery scene. The rescue crew lifted the backboard and prepared to transport the body to the ambulance waiting near the lodge.

"I was thinking the same thing. Even if she and Erik didn't get along, you would assume she would have an ounce of empathy."

Mom blew out air like she was in a yoga class. "It's worrisome that she couldn't at least fake it."

We scooted into the shade as the team maneuvered the backboard up the trail. Detective Mars roped off the bench and placed TRAIL CLOSED signs on both sides of the pathway. Her crew placed yellow evidence markers on the bench and around the edge of the path.

"The timing of her showing up is also interesting. She could have pushed him and then scurried off to the side trail to make it look like she was coming to the lodge." Theories started taking shape in my mind. Once they took hold, it was hard to think about anything else.

Mom patted my arm. "I can see your mind is already spinning, Juliet."

"I know. I'll try to let it go. It's good the Professor is here. That makes me feel better." Detective Mars struck me as professional and highly competent. Between her and the Professor, I felt like we were in good hands.

Mom gave me a knowing smile. "You have plenty to think about without worrying over Erik's accident."

"If it was an accident," I interjected, raising my eyebrows and tipping my chin to the side.

She smiled and shook her head. "It's too late, isn't it? You're already invested."

"I wish I could lie to you, but I suppose since I found him, I feel tethered to him. I would like to know what happened, whether the Professor thinks it was simply an accident or whether they're opening a formal investigation."

I didn't have to wait long, because as if reading my mind, he excused himself from Detective Mars and Mary Beth and strolled over to join us.

"Juliet, I'm sorry the weekend has taken such a horrific turn." His tone was solemn. He folded his hands together and pressed them to his chin. "According to Detective Mars, you were first on the scene, correct?"

"Yeah." I nodded and then explained everything that had happened. When I finished, I couldn't hold back from asking whether Erik was dead. "Are they transporting him to the hospital? Is there a chance he'll survive his injuries?"

The Professor pursed his lips. "Unfortunately, no. They are transporting him, but there are no signs of life, and the impact of the fall was fatal."

I gasped, sucking in a gulp of air. I already assumed as much, but hearing it confirmed gave me pause.

Mom looped her fingers through mine and squeezed them tight.

I leaned my head on her shoulder. "I figured, but you never know."

"That's why we always respond immediately." The Professor pulled a Moleskine notebook from his shirt pocket. He never went anywhere, even on vacation, without his trusty journal. "Are you feeling up to giving me the specifics? Detective Mars has asked me to assist in her investigation. She's short-staffed, so I told her I would gladly provide any support I can."

"Of course."

"Would you be more comfortable if we proceed to the

restaurant? Detective Mars and I agreed to divide and conquer when it comes to witness statements. She'll be asking everyone to gather on the deck so we can preserve the crime scene. We need to allow the police space to take photos and document the area."

"Sure." I released Mom's hand and fell into step with her and the Professor. "Do you think it was an accident, or was he pushed?"

A sad frown tugged on his lips. "Indeed, I do." He glanced toward the ocean. "I'm reminded of this passage: 'Time, whose millioned accidents creep in 'twixt vows, and change decrees of kings, tan sacred beauty, blunt the sharpest intents, divert strong minds to the course of altering things.'"

The Professor was a walking treasure trove of Shakespeare quotes and facts. I had to read between the lines to catch his meaning.

He stretched his arm toward the forest. "To be among such beauty and calm and yet to have a life cut short."

We made it to the deck, and he directed us to a table. I sat down, happy to be off my feet for a minute and far away from the scene of the crime.

"Do you think someone made it look like he fell?" I asked before he could even get to his questions.

He raised one eyebrow. "It appears that way, although I will say they didn't think it through with the utmost consideration."

"Because he fell face-up?" I was suddenly thirsty again. My throat felt dry and scratchy like sandpaper.

"Undoubtedly." He flipped his notebook to a blank page. "If you could be so kind as to walk me through everything."

I replayed the afternoon minute by minute, making sure

to include what I'd witnessed prior to Erik's fall as well. Going over the details cemented them in my mind, and it made me feel good to at least be able to provide the Professor and Detective Mars with a tangible timeline and other witnesses to track down.

"The couple who passed me on the way back to the beach were probably the closest to the scene. They heard him scream, but they took the trail back to their cabin, so they wouldn't have seen his body," I said to the Professor. Then, I described the young couple. "I found a towel that belongs to Travis, the local fish vendor, on the bench. Lucy and Hoff were over near the garden beds when I ran back to get help, and Mary Beth claims she came from her gallery, which is down the same trail. You can probably ask the couple if they saw her."

He wrote everything down in detail. "Your word choice is important. You say Mary Beth 'claims' to have come from her gallery. Can you elaborate?"

I looked at Mom. She nodded in encouragement. "You'll be able to get a better sense of her personality when you interview her, but she made it crystal clear that she's not a fan of Erik's."

"She was almost giddy about his death," Mom added, pulling her cardigan around her shoulders. The creamy color brought out the golden flecks in her eyes.

The Professor frowned and jotted something in his notebook. "Where exactly is her gallery?"

"I'm not sure. She mentioned that there's a trail not far from where Erik fell that connects to the other side of the resort. I didn't remember an art gallery from our stays when I was in school." I looked at Mom. "Did we ever visit the gallery?"

Mom tapped her forehead. "There wasn't a gallery, but there was a community gathering space. They used to show movies and have game nights there. That's on the other side of the lodge. I wonder if that space has been converted?"

"We'll take a look," the Professor said, closing his notebook. "I'll let you get back to preparations for tonight."

"Wait, is the dinner still on?" I was pleasantly surprised to hear he was considering having the meal go on as planned.

"Yes, Detective Mars intends to close the trail to foot traffic, but the restaurant shouldn't be affected by that. She also believes this evening will be an opportunity for us to observe the guests and staff. People can be much more revealing when they're not being officially interrogated. We'll both be on hand for the duration of dinner service. I explained your willingness to help, and she agrees that if you're willing to be another set of eyes and ears for us, it would be most appreciated."

"I'll do whatever I can," I agreed.

"Excellent. Let's check in as the evening progresses, and please come find me sooner if you observe anything unusual." He closed his notebook and offered me a pained smile.

I felt terrible for him. This was supposed to be a getaway weekend for him and Mom, and now he was roped into a murder investigation.

"I will." Having a task was helpful. It would give me something to focus on in addition to serving meals and making sure everything in the kitchen was running smoothly.

Mom stayed with the Professor while I returned to the

restaurant. I wasn't sure who had pushed Erik off the side of the cliff yet, but I intended to do anything and everything in my power to figure out who had decided to take such drastic measures and why.

# Chapter Eleven

Sterling paced in front of the stove, lifting the lid on his saucepot and then returning it like a chef without a plan. "Jules, what do we do? Go ahead with dinner? Cancel? Everything feels wrong, you know?"

"Yeah. It's a terrible situation, but I was just talking to the Professor, and he and Detective Mars want dinner to proceed. They're going to hang out in the dining room and continue their inquiries. They're cordoning off the trail so no one can disturb the crime scene. Guests will be arriving soon, so let's dig in and do everything we can to serve a memorable meal."

"Should we say something?" Steph asked, adding pearlized sugar beads to the cupcakes with a pair of tweezers. "I mean, we can't pretend like nothing happened. It's going to be fairly obvious when guests arrive and see cop cars everywhere. And it will feel weird if we pretend like everything's cool. Erik was a jerk, but the man is dead . . ." She didn't finish her thought.

She didn't need to. We were all thinking the same thing.

"I think it would be a good idea to acknowledge what happened. People are going to wonder, like you said, especially when they see the police vehicles parked in front of the lodge. I would keep the details to a minimum. Explain that there's been an accident and take a moment to honor Erik's memory, but then leave the rest to the Professor and Detective Mars. I suspect that's one of the reasons they plan to stick around tonight. But ultimately, this is your event. You two are in charge, and if you don't want to go ahead with service, I completely understand, as will the Professor."

Steph and Sterling looked at each other. She shrugged, rolling her shoulders back. He gave her a half nod like he was in perfect synch with whatever she was thinking. Then Steph turned to me. "No, we're good. Let's do this."

"Yeah, concentrating on dinner will take my mind off Erik and what in the world we're going to do about the restaurant moving forward." Sterling lifted the lid from the pot of tomato sauce, and the aroma of basil, onions, and garlic enveloped the kitchen.

"I'm not sure I'm going to be able to concentrate on much when your sauce is smelling this good." I wafted the scent to my nostrils and breathed it in.

Sterling rolled his eyes. "I see right through you. You're trying to make us feel better."

"It's true, I confess." I threw my hands up. "But I'm trying to make myself feel better, too, and there's nothing like a slowly simmered sauce to do the trick."

Carlos came in balancing an armful of plates. "Jess said these arrived and you might need extras."

"That's a win," Sterling said, stirring the sauce. "Can you put them over by the bread? We were short on salad and dessert plates. I guess it's a sign of how great reservations are for tonight. There weren't enough plates to get through each course, and we don't have time to wash and dry them between the main course and dessert. No one wants a hot dessert plate with melted buttercream."

"No, this would be bad." Carlos scowled. "Jess also said she's still looking for Hoff to fix the cabin."

"When I saw him last, he was down on the trail." My eyes drifted to his toolbox, which was still sitting on the floor.

"Jess asked to please send him to cabin eight immediately. The owners are very upset that they don't have running water, and he was supposed to fix it hours ago." Carlos stacked the dessert plates next to the baskets of bread waiting to be delivered to tables. "Should I take these out?"

"Yes, thanks. There are also ramekins of herbed and honey butter that are ready to go," Sterling said, and nodded to the island.

"I'll take those," I offered. Dinner started in less than thirty minutes. Carlos and I set baskets of bread and the herb-infused butter on each table. We filled water pitchers and made sure every place setting was sparkling.

I lit the votive candles, and Carlos dimmed the overhead lights, giving the dining room a romantic ambiance. The sunset would be spectacular in a couple of hours, but for the moment, the natural fading evening light made the tone all the more atmospheric. Each of their special touches made the space feel uniquely like Steph and Sterling—the menus with Steph's gorgeous calligraphy, the flow of tables, the flower arrangements, and the seascape paintings on the walls.

Fortunately, it appeared Detective Mars and the Professor had completed their initial round of interviews. The deck was clear and waiting for guests.

"Should I turn on the outdoor heaters?" Carlos asked.

"Probably. There's a bit of breeze, and as soon as the sun sinks, it will get chilly. I'm betting people who booked outdoor tables will come prepared for the elements. This is the Oregon coast, after all."

He went to light the heaters, and I took one final turn through the dining room. Despite the horrific afternoon, everything was serene inside. Sterling must have turned on the speakers because light piano music drifted through the room. The Professor's suggestion of going ahead with dinner felt even more right. Having a touch of normalcy was important.

A voice interrupted my thoughts. "Excuse me, are we seating people yet?" Lucy Clarke peered into the restaurant. "There's a line out here that wraps around to the fireplace in the lobby, and no sign of a host or hostess. We're floundering out here, and people are starting to get restless."

"Give me a minute." I wasn't sure how many staff the resort employed. Sterling had mentioned there would be servers but I hadn't heard about a maître d. "What's the status on opening the doors?" I asked Steph, returning to the kitchen. "Do you have anyone to help seat guests?"

"Jess was supposed to step in," Steph replied, twisting her lips and frowning. "I went to confirm with her while you were out picking herbs—before everything imploded—and she wasn't at the front desk. I haven't seen her for hours. Not that that's anything new. She's always taking off for long stretches. She just vanishes without telling anyone where she's going. I don't know what her deal is; she's so flaky."

"Really? I got the opposite impression from her when we checked in."

"It's all fake. Compensating for her terrible work ethic. It's for show. She dresses like this is a bougie resort, and she acts like she's so important and busy, but I have no idea what she does. She's rarely at the desk. She disappears for hours and then pretends like everything's fine." Steph arranged chocolate, strawberry, lemon, and vanilla conchas on the counter.

"I can go find her," I said. "Carlos must have just seen her because she gave him the plates. If she's not at the desk, I'll jump in and get people seated."

"Thanks, Jules."

Carlos had finished lighting the heaters, and I decided to ask him about the missing staff. "Have you seen anyone for front-of-house?"

"No, I was just going to check with Jess. You saw her at the desk a while ago, right?"

"Not at the desk, no." He peered outside. "She was coming from one of the cabins on the other side of the resort. I bumped into her, and she asked if I would mind taking the plates."

I wondered what that meant in terms of Erik's death timeline. Why did Jess keep leaving her post? If she had been gone for a long period like Steph suggested, that would have given her enough time to push him and get back to the other side of the resort.

I sighed. I didn't have time to dwell on it.

"Don't worry about finding her. We can seat people." Carlos smoothed down his shirt. "It will be a nice touch and a way to welcome everyone."

"Good point." I hoped I didn't look too disheveled. I hadn't had a chance to change or check my appearance since finding Erik, but this was casual dining, not a Michelin-star restaurant, and Carlos and I were in our sweet spot when it came to making customers feel at home. It would be like going back to our early roots when we would host private dinners on the *Amour of the Sea*.

Lucy was at the front of the line, shifting from side to side like she needed to use the restroom. "Well, are you going to seat us? My reservation was for five p.m., and it's fifteen minutes after," she snapped.

She hadn't exaggerated about the line. It was a fantastic turnout. The queue snaked from the fireplace, around Jess's desk, to the gift and surf shop.

"I'm sure you'll understand that with everything that happened this afternoon, we had a slight setback, but yes, your table is ready. This way." I led her into the dining room.

"You're right." She tucked a curl that had fallen loose back into her bun. "I apologize for being short with you. It's not your fault. It's so distressing to know that Erik's dead. I'm trying to wrap my head around it all and figure out what's next."

"It's okay," I replied sincerely. "Sterling and Steph are in the same position."

"Tell them not to worry. As long as tonight lives up to the hype, I'm sure they'll have long-term positions at the resort." She waved me closer and gave me a conspiratorial smile. "Don't let this get out, but I can probably guarantee them positions. I'll be taking the lead with restaurant renovations and can put in a good word."

*Why the sudden shift?*

Earlier, she had practically told them to start looking for new jobs.

"You mentioned the possibility of upgrading the property. Does Erik's death change that?"

She took off her quarter-sleeve cardigan and wrapped it on the back of her chair. "This is going to sound terrible, and I'm concerned that the police have already pegged me as a potential suspect."

I was intrigued by her statement for a number of reasons, but mainly because the Professor had made it sound like they weren't announcing that Erik's death wasn't an accident. Had that changed?

"Why?" I asked, waiting for her to sit.

"In many ways, Erik was our biggest blockade to pushing the sale through. The vast majority of property owners are interested in selling. They know management has failed to follow through on their contractual obligations. Cabins are in desperate need of new roofs, upgraded plumbing, electric, and general maintenance. The same goes for the grounds and this place." She paused and swept her hand around the room. "Look at how dated this is. It's like stepping back in time, but not in a good way. Erik was negligent in his duties at best. You can't skimp on repairs in a climate like this. The weather takes a massive toll on the cabins. I don't know if you noticed water damage or other issues in the cabin you're renting, but our estimates show that nearly eighty percent of the units are grossly overdue for major overhauls."

Her perspective lined up with everything Steph and Sterling had shared, as well as what I'd witnessed today with Hoff being needed for immediate repairs.

"The detectives asked me dozens of questions about my

negotiations, and I explained to them that the deal was basically done," she continued, seemingly unaware I had anywhere else to be. "They hinted that I could have killed him to get him out of the way—literally and metaphorically. That's utter rubbish. Why would I need Erik out of the way when I already have the support of staff and homeowners?"

I wasn't sure if it was a rhetorical question.

"It doesn't matter anyway, because I have a rock-solid alibi during the time of his death." She folded her fingers and inspected her notebook.

How did she know when he died? The Professor had still been determining that when we spoke less than an hour ago.

I kept my tone neutral. "I wasn't aware the police are already sharing that information with the public."

"Well, they're not officially. I'm simply speaking based on my whereabouts. I was at an afternoon council meeting in downtown Brookings. There's no possible way I could have pushed Erik. I was a good twenty-minute drive away when he fell."

But I had seen her with Hoff right after I spotted his body.

She must have realized this, too, because she poured herself a glass of water as if trying to buy herself a minute. "You saw me arriving as well. We can be each other's alibis."

I didn't mention I didn't need an alibi. The Professor would take my statement into account and proceed accordingly, but I couldn't imagine he would consider me a top suspect.

"I got here right before the emergency responders arrived. You saw me. That's when I arrived, I swear." Lucy stumbled on her words. "I came directly from my council meeting."

I wasn't sure I was buying anything she was saying. It felt too scripted and perfect. Not to mention, was it typical to have city council meetings on a Saturday afternoon?

It was no surprise the Professor and Detective Mars had had additional questions for her. There were too many holes in her story.

"Anyway, I'm as shaken up over Erik's death as anyone. It's a real blow. I hope they'll be able to tell us definitively whether he fell or whether someone else had a hand in his death, but I'm quite relieved I attended the council meeting this afternoon. I almost skipped it. That would have been a disaster. Then I'd really be scrambling to come up with an alibi." She placed her napkin over her lap and picked up the menu. "I shouldn't keep you, but feel free to tell the police you saw me arriving at the restaurant. I'll do the same for you."

I gave her a noncommittal nod and went to seat the next group of diners.

Lucy was working overtime to convince me of her innocence and that Erik had nothing to do with the sale of the resort. Why?

I had seen her before we began prepping for dinner and then again right after Erik's fall. Could she have left during that window, attended a council meeting, and returned all within the stretch of a couple of hours? Potentially. But could she also be lying?

My answer to that question was a resounding yes.

# Chapter Twelve

Carlos and I seated the first wave of guests, and to my utter delight and surprise, two familiar faces were among the crowd—Lance and his partner, Arlo.

"Hello, darling. Did you miss me?" He sashayed over to me and kissed both my cheeks as if he were Parisian.

"Lance, what you doing here?" I couldn't believe they had come. Lance was hardly a vault when it came to keeping secrets. He hadn't said a word about joining us for the weekend.

"Arlo and I wouldn't miss our little debutants' debut for anything, now, would we?" He nudged Arlo with his elbow. "And let's be honest, no party is a party without yours truly."

I chuckled. "Seriously, I can't believe you're here. I would have reserved seats at our table for you." I glanced at a six-person round table next to the windows.

"Please. You wouldn't expect me to sit with the commoners." He lifted his arched brows and gave me his signature devilish grin. "Arrangements have been made."

I shouldn't have doubted him. Lance didn't miss a detail, not even with his immaculate style. Instead of his usual tailored suits, he was dressed for the beachy occasion in navy dockers, a dark blue jacket, and a matching navy polka-dot dress shirt. His soft leather slip-on shoes and a simple white pocket square rounded out his look.

He offered me one hand and Arlo the other. "Shall we?"

When I caught Arlo's eye, he gave me a look that said, *Don't bother asking questions.* Arlo was tall, dark, and handsome, with a muscular build and a gentle sweetness. They complemented each other well.

"You made it." Mom stood to greet them with long hugs. "I was about to text you to make sure you hadn't changed your mind or gotten caught up with an issue at OSF, but there's been a lot going on."

"Shhh, Helen." Lance pressed a finger to his lips. "Don't give away our secrets. Juliet can't know the methods to my madness."

"I'm pretty sure I already do." I sucked in my cheeks and gave him my best side eye.

He pulled out my chair with a flourish. "Sit, darling. Rest your weary feet. We don't want your dainty ankles to swell."

"I can swat him for you," Arlo said, swiping his hand in the air.

"Don't worry. I can handle this one." I attempted to glower at Lance. It didn't work.

He tipped his head back and cackled. "Oh, darling. You're too much. As if this face could ever harbor such hatred."

"I'd watch out if I were you. Pregnant women aren't to be trusted." I rubbed my belly. "I'm raging with hormones right now." I furrowed my brow.

That only made him laugh more. Once he recovered,

he crossed one leg over the other and strummed his fingers together. "Enough of the teasing. Let's get to the good stuff. We heard there's been an accident. That perhaps is not an accident."

Carlos finished seating the last guest and joined us, holding bottles of wine and sparkling water. "Drinks, everyone?"

"Please." Lance lifted his glass for Carlos to fill. "Juliet is just filling us in on everything we missed."

"Sí, it's very sad." Carlos poured deep burgundy wine into everyone else's glass and then filled mine with bubbly water.

"Do tell, was it an accident?" Lance swirled his drink like a professional sommelier.

"No." I took a small sip of the effervescent water. It had a hint of lemon mixed in with the tiny bubbles. "We think he was pushed, and it seems like the Professor agrees. Right, Mom?"

She tucked her bobbed hair behind her ears and moved her reading glasses to the tip of her nose so she could read the menu. "Unfortunately, yes. He and the lead detective, Ms. Mars, agree that Erik was most likely pushed. The fall doesn't appear to be natural."

"What a way to go." Lance shuddered and turned to me. "And rumor has it that you found him?"

"Yeah. I was picking herbs when I heard the screams." It still didn't seem possible Erik was dead. I wondered if Whaleshead would have to reconsider putting up fencing or some sort of barricade along the path to the beach to prevent future incidents.

Carlos placed his hand on my knee in a show of solidarity.

"Any leads? Suspects?" Lance's eager eyes darted around the room like he expected someone to stand up and confess.

"Not officially." I reached for my sparkling water and let my eyes drift toward Lucy's table. A group of people I didn't recognize had joined her. They were reviewing paperwork and taking photos of the dining room as if they were scoping it out for demolition. She couldn't be trying to push the sale through now, could she? That seemed in poor taste, to say the least.

"The problem is that Erik had a number of people at the resort who were unhappy with him," I said, pulling my eyes away from Lucy. I wished we were sitting closer so I could get a better look at the paperwork.

"Excellent." Lance raised his glass in a toast. "It's fortuitous that I'm here, then, isn't it? The game is afoot. There's no time like the present moment to start a list of key players."

Arlo sliced the bread and passed it around the table.

I slathered a piece with garlic and basil butter. "I can't believe I'm going to say this, but I agree. It's been helpful to talk through everything and keep the details crisp in my mind."

Mom opted for the honey and sea salt butter. "It's true. Doug always says the first few hours after a murder are the most critical. He often says that human memory is subject to rapid decay. The reason he interviews witnesses immediately is to capture those memories while they're fresh and the most accurate."

"Yes, I read a fascinating study a few months ago about witnesses' memories being quickly contaminated by speaking with other witnesses and listening to media reports," Lance said, tapping Arlo's sleeve. Arlo was more casually dressed in jeans, a long-sleeved shirt, and a puffy vest. "Do you remember that? We were prepping for rehearsals of *Perfect Crime*, which, if I do say so myself, is going to be a megahit when it opens. I wish we had space in a bigger theater for it."

"Where is it being staged?" I asked. OSF had four stages on its campus. The outdoor Elizabethan (or Lizzie, as Lance affectionately called it) was the flagship stage. Additionally, there were two indoor theaters with varying seating capacities—the Bowmer and the Thomas—and "the bricks," an outdoor courtyard for preshow entertainment.

"The Thomas. It's going to be an intimate revival of the off-Broadway production, but early reviews have been stellar, and the cast is absolutely phenomenal. I know we'll extend shows and offer additional matinees. I recommend you get your tickets now."

"You haven't done a mystery in recent years," Mom commented, helping herself to a second slice of bread.

"It's true. I felt like it was time for a bit of murder and mayhem. It's not that our guy Will Shakes doesn't give us ample material to work with, but this set is going to hyper-focus on a tiny New York apartment. I want to set it in a gritty city. Give it some depth and angst. It's more of a psychological thriller." He rubbed his hands together and sucked in his cheeks in a villainous grin.

When Lance took over at the helm of OSF, he committed to working his way through the entire Shakespearean canon. The company produced multiple shows of Shakespeare's works each season, but it additionally staged new plays, modern musicals, and one-person shows. There was something for everyone, from the most die-hard Shakespeare aficionados to families looking for sing-along fun.

"What Lance isn't telling you is that he went way down the rabbit hole to direct this show. I'm honestly surprised you didn't fire the lead and take on the role yourself," Arlo said with a smile. Arlo managed the financial side of the theater, and I didn't envy him. Keeping Lance's grandiose visions in check and within budget had to be an ongoing challenge.

"If I weren't so busy with my side projects like the Fair Verona Players, I might have. Don't tempt me. We're in previews now. There's still time," he threatened. Then he set his wineglass on the table and clapped twice to get our attention. "People, people, let's focus. We have a murder to solve. Juliet, tell us your thoughts on suspects."

Our waiter came to take our order, buying me an extra minute to collect my thoughts. I opted for the pasta, while Carlos went for the fish.

I stole another glance in Lucy's direction while the rest of the table put in their dinner requests. Lucy handed the man seated next to her a pen and appeared to be encouraging him to sign the papers in front of him.

*Is she actually closing the deal?*

*Here?*

*Tonight?*

"Ramiro will be here shortly. What should I order for him?" Carlos studied the menu.

"One of everything?" Mom suggested.

"Helen, you're not far off. I'll get him the heartiest meal on the menu," Carlos replied, deciding on the burger. "With extra fries, please."

Once our waiter was out of earshot, Lance impatiently circled his hands. "Come on, darling, give us the low-down."

I reviewed what I'd heard and seen for a third time. "Hoff and Erik were arguing before he fell. Hoff certainly has the physical strength to have done it. He was near the scene of the crime and then seems to have been missing for long stretches."

"That's something." Lance snapped once and tossed his index finger in the air like a lightbulb had gone off in his head.

"Maybe. Disappearing for periods of time seems to be the norm around here." I told them about Jess vanishing from the front desk and how Lucy claimed to have been at the council meeting when Erik was killed.

"Doug will easily be able to confirm that detail," Mom added. "Council meetings are on public record. If she's lying about that, she picked the wrong alibi."

Lance pretended to drop his napkin and then pick it up in order to get a good look at her. "Or she's not the sharpest tool in the shed."

"She doesn't strike me like that." I savored a bite of the thick bread. It was soft and tender on the inside, with a hint of tang from the sourdough. The crust was flaky, and the garlic and herb butter made my taste buds sing. "She presents as very professional and capable."

"And she wants to take over the resort," Carlos said. "That must give her a motive, yes?"

"It will be interesting to hear what the Professor has to say about that," I replied. "She was adamant that the sale was happening with or without Erik, and—don't look—but I've been keeping an eye on her table. She's been passing around paperwork for everyone to review. Do you think she could be trying to close the deal as we speak?"

"Oh, brazen." Lance blew on his fingers.

"Or she could be lying," Arlo added, twisting his head to the side in a pensive gaze. "Maybe the sale isn't as solid as it seems. She could be trying to convince everyone it's a done deal and scrambling to make something happen. Scrambling, as in pushing the person trying to block the sale off a cliff."

"Without a doubt," I said to him in agreement. "I'm with you, too, Mom—her alibi is shaky at best. If she was at the council meeting, why would she need me to vouch for her? It doesn't add up."

"Could it be that easy?" Lance asked. "Do we already have our killer?"

"It's way too soon," I said. "There's also Travis. He's the local fisher. He provides the resort with all of its fish, but he wasn't going to deliver today because apparently Erik's been late on payments. I found his towel on the bench, which seems strange. He ended up delivering the fish as a favor to Jess and Sterling and Steph. He has a towel just like the one I found with him then. How did it end up on the trail? I was hoping he might show up tonight. Sterling offered him a free dinner in thanks for coming through with the fish, but I don't see him. I wonder if he's avoiding the resort because he wants to distance himself from Erik as much as possible."

"Good question." Mom jumped in. "And don't forget about Mary Beth."

"Ohhh, another player enters the stage." Lance reached

for the wine bottle in the center of the table to top off his glass. "Who, pray tell, is Mary Beth?"

"She's a local artist showing her work here." I motioned to Mary Beth's painting hanging behind him. It depicted a sunny summer afternoon during the annual kite festival. There was no denying her talent. I could almost feel the wind with the way she'd captured the colorful kites bobbing and darting above the tranquil coastline.

"We spoke with her while they were retrieving Erik's body," Mom said. "I can't recall a conversation more unsettling. She was practically giddy about his death. It was disturbing."

"A scorned lover, perhaps?" Lance suggested. "Could she and Erik have had a falling-out that led to another kind of fall?"

I shook my head. "I don't think so. I got the impression her anger was directed at his business practices or lack thereof. She was fuming. Mom's right. It was a bizarre response. Even if they didn't get along, I can't imagine taking any pleasure in someone's death."

"Don't forget Jess," Carlos said, raising his wineglass to his lips. "She has been missing a lot, sí?"

"True. Steph said she vanishes for hours. I don't know why, but she was away from her desk when Erik fell. There seemed to be a lot of animosity between them. She could have snuck away from the reception area and pushed him in the time she was gone."

Our salads arrived. We took a brief pause from the murder conversation to savor the fresh greens, bright heirloom tomatoes, roasted red peppers, toasted pistachios, and house-made garlic croutons. The salad was tossed with a citrus herb vinaigrette.

"This is divine," Lance said through a mouthful of salad. "Kudos to our burgeoning chefs. I do hope they'll make an appearance at some point this evening to take a bow."

There was no chance that Steph or Sterling would take a bow, but the odds were good they would at least come out to thank everyone for attending the reopening, especially since we had discussed saying a few words about Erik and taking a moment to honor his memory.

The kitchen door swung open. Hoff stormed out, carrying his toolbox over his shoulder, like a scene from an '80s movie in which the main character tries to win the love of his life by serenading her with a boom box.

Lucy tried to catch his arm as he walked by, but he brushed her off and stomped toward the exit. His heavy footsteps thudded, breaking the easygoing atmosphere of dinner. The Professor stopped him at the door. I hadn't seen the Professor show up, and his appearance was like a magic trick.

I couldn't hear what they were saying, but it was clear that the Professor was asking Hoff not to leave.

Detective Mars entered the room behind the Professor. She marched to the center of the room, right in front of the windows, and whistled through two fingers to get our attention. "Excuse the interruption."

The room quieted. "I'm Detective Mars, and as I'm sure you're well aware, there was a fall at the resort earlier today. We've already spoken to many of you, but we'll be coming by each table to ask further questions. I know some of you are homeowners and guests here. We're particularly interested in hearing from you if you saw anything between the hours of two thirty and four thirty this afternoon. We'd be very grateful if you could share that with us, especially if you saw Erik Morton, the manager of Whaleshead, during that timeframe."

People mumbled in hushed tones around us.

"Is Erik all right?" someone at a table nearby asked.

Another person nearby shook their head and gasped. "I saw Erik earlier today. He was surveying the property like usual. It can't be him."

"I'm afraid it was him," Detective Mars replied in a matter-of-fact tone. Then she addressed the room again, speaking loud enough for everyone to hear her. "Erik Morton is dead, and we believe he was murdered."

I guessed that answered the question about whether they were going to keep the cause of death under wraps. Was that because they believed his killer was in the room?

# Chapter Thirteen

"Someone's feisty. She's not holding back, and I'm here for it," Lance said, leaning so close to my ear that I could smell his expensive cologne. "She's furious that this lovely oceanside resort has been tarnished by murder. That, or she's fuming she has to work extra hours on the weekend. Either way, I don't blame her."

I shushed him so I could hear what Detective Mars was saying.

"Please, continue to enjoy your dinner. We'll do our best not to intrude, but we will need to ask some questions and take everyone's statements. I'd like to remind you not to leave the resort until you've had a chance to speak with one of us. Is that understood?" She paused and waited for everyone to nod in agreement.

I was impressed by her ability to hold everyone's attention. She didn't come across as harsh or demanding, but it was instantly clear that she was in charge.

"Excellent." She placed her hands on her hips and surveyed the room table by table, making firm eye contact with nearly every dinner guest. "My team, as well as my esteemed colleague from Ashland, appreciate your assistance."

She ended her brief speech with a nod to the Professor, then she pulled Hoff to the side to speak with him individually. Where had he been? I hadn't seen him for hours. He was at the scene when the first responders recovered Erik's body, but he wasn't at the lodge or in the vicinity for dinner, unless I'd missed him.

I tried not to stare, but I couldn't help but wonder if Detective Mars was equally curious about his whereabouts. Hoff looked like talking to her was the equivalent of getting a root canal. He moved his bulky frame awkwardly as she peppered him with questions. She wisely blocked his escape route. Smart move. Because he looked ready to take off in a sprint at any second.

"Everyone, if we could take another minute of your time." Sterling's voice pulled my attention in the other direction. He and Steph stood in front of the kitchen doors, wearing their matching pistachio aprons and nervous smiles. "Welcome to the new SeaBreeze Bistro."

Timid applause broke out.

Sterling squared his shoulders, bolstered by the show of support. "Thank you. Steph and I are very excited to share our updated menu and vision for the restaurant with you. Before we serve the main courses, we want to acknowledge Erik Morton. Erik gave us a shot and hired two unknowns to revamp the restaurant. If we could all take a minute of silence to honor his memory and pay our respects." He bowed his head and stared at the floor.

A hush fell over the dining room. I closed my eyes and held Erik in my heart.

"Thank you," Sterling said, calling everyone back to attention. "Erik was enthusiastic about tonight, and we feel like one of the best ways to recognize him is to share a meal in his memory."

I knew this wasn't the speech Sterling had intended to give, but I was incredibly touched by his maturity and ability to handle the breadth of the moment.

Steph stood by his side like a statue. "We're dedicating tonight's menu to Erik."

"Hear, hear." Lance raised his glass.

Diners around us responded in kind.

Glasses clinked, and people applauded again, this time with more gusto. "To Erik."

"To Erik," Sterling echoed. "Dinner will be out soon. We hope you enjoy it and that you'll swing by during the rest of your stay to try some of our other offerings. We're making picnic boxes for the beach, which you can order in advance or pick up to take with you on your adventures. We'll also be hosting a traditional brunch tomorrow morning, and Steph, our pastry chef, will be serving special happy hour desserts and snacks in the lounge." He paused and glanced at her with dewy eyes. "Rumor has it that tomorrow's brunch will feature chocolate soufflés among other things."

Ooohs and aaahs broke out.

"That's brave," I said to our table. "I hadn't heard that she's going to tackle soufflés."

"That's our girl." Mom beamed at Steph with pride.

"Thank you for your time and your support. Sit back and enjoy the rest of the evening. We'll be eager to hear your thoughts and suggestions. Please fill out the comment cards on the back of your menus and let us know if there's anything we can do to make your time here at Whaleshead more enjoyable." Sterling pressed his hands together in gratitude and slipped back into the kitchen.

"They're ridiculously adorable." Lance reached for his wine again.

Arlo held up the comment cards Steph had designed. They were printed on thick cream cardstock with the SeaBreeze logo and pistachio green lettering. Questions ranging from rating favorite dishes on the menu to future requests were printed on the front. The back contained a thank-you note to guests, a few paragraphs about Steph's and Sterling's backgrounds, and their favorite quote by Cesar Chavez: "The people who give you their food give you their heart."

"How sweet is this?" Arlo pressed the card to his chest.

"I feel like a proud papa," Carlos said, patting both of his shoulders. "Our chefs are all grown up and out in the world."

Ramiro showed up breathless and dusted in sand as our food arrived.

"You're just in time," Mom said, scooting her chair to make room for him. "We considered ordering you one of everything on the menu."

Ramiro kissed her cheek, making my heart swell. "I wish you had. I'm starving." He brushed sand from his hoodie and popped three fries into his mouth. "We hiked the beach for miles, and then, on the way back, we had to take a long route on the main road because the trail was closed. I heard that there was a fall?" He looked at Carlos for confirmation.

"Sí." Carlos unfolded his napkin and smoothed it over his lap. "A man fell to his death."

Ramiro nearly choked on his fry. "What? When? How? They fell here?"

Carlos explained what had happened. I was glad for the reprieve. I'd told the story plenty of times, and I was suddenly ravenous. I twisted the spaghetti noodles slathered in Sterling's rich sauce and sprinkled with fresh Parmesan around my fork while Carlos finished filling Ramiro in.

The pasta was cooked al dente, just slightly chewy yet tender. My mouth practically sang with delight as I savored the tangy tomato sauce and bit into the flavorful meatball packed with fresh herbs and sourdough breadcrumbs. It was tender and juicy and literally melted in my mouth. Spaghetti and meatballs often get overlooked for fancier and more involved dishes, but every chef knows that good pasta is hard to achieve.

Carlos had taught Sterling well. I could tell that he had undercooked the noodles and finished them in the sauce to give them their signature al dente texture. There's nothing worse than a soggy, limp noodle or a dry, overcooked meatball.

"How is it?" Carlos asked.

I held up my finger. "No words. No words. I can't speak. It's too good."

"Haven't you been warned never to interrupt a pregnant woman while she's eating?" Mom teased.

"Same goes for a hungry teenager," Ramiro said, taking a huge bite of his juicy burger.

Carlos chuckled. We passed around plates and took tastes of everyone's meals.

"They've outdone themselves," Mom said, savoring her

corn chowder. "I know I'm biased, but there's not a miss on the entire menu."

"Agreed." Lance stabbed a buttery shrimp with his fork. "I'm not biased, and I have high standards when it comes to fine dining."

"Do not let him get away with these lies." Arlo wagged a scolding finger at Lance. "You are most certainly biased. During the entire drive out here, the only thing you talked about was Steph and Sterling, how talented they are, and how this is just the first of many future restaurant openings for them. You were absolutely gushing."

"I don't recall gushing," Lance scoffed. His angular cheeks tinged with a touch of pink. "Come to think of it, I most certainly don't gush. It's beneath me."

"I'm happy to gush," Mom bantered. "This is a gushworthy moment."

The conversation flowed as we enjoyed the meal. Ramiro regaled us with stories of treasure hunting on the beach and finding secret caves. I polished off my entire plate of meatballs and had a second helping of bread. My stomach rumbled in happy thanks. It felt good to set Erik's murder aside for a moment and be completely present.

The feeling eroded when the Professor joined our table. "Good evening, all. I'm sorry not to be dining with you. Everything smells divine. I trust that the food is as exquisite as expected?"

"Can you stop for a bite?" Mom asked, looking up at him with tender concern.

"Alas, duty calls. But not to worry about me. I'll find time to eat." He smiled at Mom, but his eyes held a sadness I recognized. He had been moving closer and closer to retirement in recent years. My dear friend from high school, Thomas, and his wife, Kerry, had taken on larger roles—leading the charge into investigations in town. The good news was that Ashland wasn't exactly teeming with seasoned criminals. Police work was about engaging with the community and connecting people to the support and services they needed.

The Professor took every case that came across his desk to heart, becoming personally involved in seeking the truth and finding justice. It was a skill that made him highly sought after and endeared him to the community. But it also took a toll on him emotionally. Since marrying Mom, he had made a conscientious effort to scale back and let Thomas and Kerry flourish in their roles.

Being brought into a murder investigation probably hadn't been on his weekend agenda, but there was no chance that he wouldn't use his skills and insights to assist Detective Mars.

"Do you have any leads, or is it too early?" Lance didn't hesitate to get straight to the point. "Detective Mars isn't messing around. She's all business, and I, for one, quite like it."

The Professor massaged his gray-and-auburn-speckled beard with his index finger and thumb. "She believes the best path forward is one of directness and honesty, and I'm inclined to agree with her. She has a very impressive track record. I told her I'm happy to assist with anything she needs, but I'll defer to her to direct the investigation."

"Yeah, we were surprised that she announced to everyone that Erik's death was a murder," I said, dabbing the sauce on the edge of my plate with a hunk of bread.

"As was I, but I believe her philosophy is to put as much

pressure on the killer as possible—make them acutely aware that we're watching and listening." He took a fry from Ramiro. "Thank you, don't mind if I do."

"Not a bad plan," Lance said, tilting his head from side to side like he was considering the strategy.

"Detective Mars seemed interested in speaking with Hoff," I said to the Professor.

"She did." He munched on the fry but declined Ramiro's offer of more. "He wasn't pleased with our questions and didn't appreciate being detained because he has a backlog of projects, but he was able to provide us with a timeline and an alibi."

"He has an alibi?" I was curious if he and Lucy had decided to pair up. Since I'd seen them together right after the murder and she'd been so eager to establish that fact, it made sense that she would have had the same conversation with Hoff.

The Professor paused to check his notes. "According to his statement, he was making repairs in cabin eight."

"That's his alibi?" I asked, letting my mouth hang open. "I'm not sure about that."

"Really? Do you know something that contradicts his statement?" The Professor paused and looked at me with new interest, lowering his voice slightly.

Guests enjoyed their dinners around us. The music, background chatter, and clinking plates and silverware were telltale signs that dinner service was going well. I was pleased for Steph and Sterling. After everything they'd been through, at least the meal was going according to plan.

"Maybe." I replayed the events quickly. "I didn't see him during the actual murder. I bumped into him and

Lucy outside on the deck when I ran back to get help, so I can't speak to where he was, specifically when Erik was pushed. They were both acting strangely. They were huddled together. I don't know what they were talking about, but Hoff jumped away from her when I showed up like he didn't want to be seen talking to her. I could be reading into that, but there is potentially a *big hole* in his story."

"Big hole?" The Professor's eyes widened. He removed his pen from his pocket and waited for me to say more.

"It's his toolbox. It was bugging me earlier," I said, glancing toward the kitchen. "He brought it into the kitchen before I found Erik. He was supposed to fix the cabin then, but he left it on the floor. It was still there when I returned. In fact, it was still there when we opened the doors and started seating people. He had it with him when Detective Mars stopped him at the door."

"Is that so?" The Professor made a note.

"Yes. I'm one hundred percent sure it's been in the kitchen since two thirty or three this afternoon, so here's my question. How could he have been fixing the water in cabin eight without any of his tools?"

A smile tugged at the side of the Professor's lips. "An excellent question, Juliet. An excellent question indeed."

# Chapter Fourteen

The Professor made another note before moving on to the next table.

"Jules, you're a genius," Arlo said, grinning widely and bowing to me. "Talk about noticing the small details."

"I don't think I'm a genius," I said, brushing off his compliment. "The toolbox was obvious. I thought it was strange at the time that he left it behind. How can you fix a water leak without any tools? Now that he's claiming that he was fixing the water in cabin eight when Erik was killed, I'm even more suspicious. I saw him—sans toolbox—shortly before I found Erik. Then I saw him again right after I discovered Erik's body. How could he have fixed the leak that fast?"

"Maybe he's a magician," Ramiro said, dipping his last fry in ketchup. "He waves a magic wand, and the pipes fix themselves."

"That's the only explanation that makes sense," I replied, taking a long sip of my bubbly water. "Because no other maintenance worker would leave their tools behind, right?"

Mom offered Ramiro the rest of her grilled cheese. "I can't finish this half. Would you like it?"

"Sí. Thank you." Ramiro bobbed his head and snatched it from her like he was worried she was going to change her mind. Then he scanned the table. "I'll take any leftovers in case anyone else can't finish."

He was a bottomless pit. Where did the food go? It disappeared in his long, lanky arms.

Arlo slid his plate across the table. "I'm waving the white flag. This is all yours."

"Yes." Ramiro clutched his fist in the air like he'd won a prize.

"We can order you more." Mom smiled and patted Ramiro's arm, then she turned to me. "I'm sure Doug will explore this further, but you're right, honey, I would be very interested to hear from the owners of cabin eight to know whether they can confirm Hoff's presence. Has their water been fixed? Did they see him in their cabin?"

"Exactly," I said, finishing my sparkling water.

Our waiter took our plates and our dessert orders.

"You're thinking what I'm thinking, right?" Lance scooted his chair closer and whispered while everyone was distracted.

"Uh, I don't like the sound of this."

Lance had a habit of roping me in to situations that were less than optimal.

"We'll have a little tête-à-tête with the inhabitants of cabin eight." He drummed his index fingers on his knees in rhythm to the words "tête-à-tête."

"And how exactly do you propose we do so?"

"Details, darling. Details." He dabbed his chin with the

edge of his napkin. "I say we excuse ourselves for a few minutes."

"Now?" I glanced around the table. "I think everyone will easily guess what we're up to if we just take off. It will be pretty obvious."

"Nonsense. Trust me, I have a plan." He patted his breast pocket and raised his eyebrows with a devilish delight.

*Oh no, I really don't like this.*

*I recognize that look, and it means Lance is up to no good.*

He stood up as if preparing to make a grand entrance on the stage. "My esteemed friends, would you please excuse me and Juliet for the briefest of moments? I need her assistance with a very special matter. We have a little something for our chefs this evening. But do not fret—we'll be back to get our just 'desserts.'"

Mom caught my eye and winked.

Carlos's gaze was much more skeptical. "I can help you," he offered, starting to push his chair back.

"Don't worry, your lovely wife will be in these very capable hands." Lance wiggled his bony fingers and then reached for my arm. "Back in a flash, ta-ta."

He practically yanked me away from the table.

"Subtle."

"My middle name is Subtle."

I couldn't contain a laugh. "Where exactly are we going?"

"To cabin eight, of course."

"What are the odds that the owners are even there? For all we know, they're in the dining room," I said, gesturing behind us.

"There's one way to find out." He looped his arm through mine like he was escorting me to a ball. "Shall we?"

I didn't bother to protest. The truth was I wanted to know whether Hoff was lying, and there was no dissuading Lance once he was on a mission like this.

We passed through the lobby on our way to the cabin and found Jess and Mary Beth rearranging paintings. Jess had changed out of her dress skirt and blouse and was wearing a pair of faded jeans, a T-shirt, and sandals. Where had she been all night? Like Hoff, she had been a bit of an enigma, flitting around the resort and rarely at her desk.

I was about to say hello when Mary Beth noticed us.

"Oh, dear, don't sneak up on people like that." She startled and dropped her hammer on the floor. It landed on the hardwood with a heavy thud. She clutched her stomach and glared at us. "You can't just waltz in here and scare us like that."

"Scare you? Isn't this a public lobby?" Lance countered. "Many apologies, but we're simply passing through."

Mary Beth readjusted her sheer paisley gown, tightening the belt around her waist into a firm knot.

"Maybe if you'd been on time earlier, we would have had this set up and ready to go before dinner," Jess said to Mary Beth, holding her finger to mark a spot on the wall.

"Don't take that tone with me, young lady. You're one to talk." She shot Jess a warning look, wagging her finger in her face. "I know what you've been up to, and I'm quite sure you don't want me to discuss it, do you? Because rumors around here have a tendency to blow up quickly. I bet you'd hate for word to get out about your little antics."

Jess kept her eyes glued to the spot on the wall as if she

were personally responsible for holding the entire wall in place.

"That's what I thought." Mary Beth's satisfied smile was unsettling.

What was she hinting at?

What did she know that Jess didn't want her to reveal?

Perhaps where Jess had been during Erik's murder?

I couldn't get a good read on Jess. She cleared her throat and lasered her eyes on the floor.

"You're doing a showing this evening?" Lance asked innocently, dropping my arm and appraising Mary Beth's art.

"Yes, but this mess with Erik delayed everything." Mary Beth bent to pick up the hammer and then pounded a nail into the wall.

I cringed, hoping she wouldn't smash Jess's finger in the process. Jess yelped and yanked her finger out of the way at the last second.

"You got me." She sucked the tip of her finger and waved her hand like she was trying to shake off the pain.

"Oops." Mary Beth hit the nail harder.

Was she taking out her pent-up rage and aggression on the nail?

"Hand me that piece." She directed Lance to a stack of paintings propped against the baseboard.

Lance obliged. He picked up the first canvas, taking a moment to appreciate it before handing it over to her.

We watched as she centered the oil painting. It was a large piece— at least four feet long by two or three feet wide. Again, I had to admit that her talent was undeniable. The brushstrokes were fluid, blending seamlessly with the landscape.

"I see like any good artist, you take inspiration from your surroundings," Lance said.

She swiveled her head toward him. "Why do you say that?"

"This cliffside." Lance pointed to the painting. "The vantage point is from here at the resort, isn't it?"

She tilted the edge of the canvas to bring the bottom parallel. "I paint the southern Oregon coast, so many of my pieces have views like this."

"But this is here at Whaleshead," Lance insisted.

I took a closer look at the painting and realized why he was pressing the issue. Not only was the painting done at Whaleshead, but it was also from the specific place where Erik had fallen. I recognized the jagged cliffside, the sweeping views of the ocean, the wispy white clouds hanging in the sky, the waves rumbling onto the shore, and most importantly—the bench where Erik had been killed.

Mary Beth hadn't sat at the bench to paint, but instead, she had painted the bench into the scene. It was almost like she had staked out the spot.

"Yes, of course it's at the resort. I'm the artist-in-residence here. This is what I do." She was noncommittal. "There's not a bad viewpoint at Whaleshead, but this spot is iconic. I've painted it at least a dozen times. It's the way of the artist; you find a muse and inspiration, and you come back to it again and again in hopes of capturing its essence in a new and profound way, watching the landscape shift with changing seasons and moods. We develop a deep connection to our subject matter. It's the only way you can truly appreciate the nuances and intricacies of a place."

I felt the same about pastry. I often returned to the same

recipe, not only because repetition is the key to mastery but also because with each bake, I would refine my technique, incorporate seasonal ingredients, and revisit my artistry through presentation.

The desk phone rang. Jess went to answer it while Mary Beth unwrapped her next painting.

"Beautiful work," Lance said to Mary Beth, taking my hand again. "I'll be eager to see everything in its entirety once you finish setting up." He gave her a two-finger wave as we made our exit.

Once we were outside, he stopped. "Well, that was illuminating."

"She basically painted the murder scene."

It couldn't be that easy, could it? If Mary Beth had killed him, it wouldn't be wise for her to display that particular painting unless she was taunting us.

"I find it fascinating that out of all the pieces she opted to display, that's the one she hung front and center." Lance inhaled through his nose and then blew out his breath in three short whistles. "I wonder what the Professor will say. It cannot be a coincidence that she chose that viewpoint."

"I guess it's possible," I said, playing the devil's advocate. "I mean, she made a fair point—that the bench and that view are iconic."

Lance cleared his throat and narrowed his brows. "I'll say it's iconic—or perhaps a tad *ironic*. It's where her nemesis fell to his death. Something you yourself said she took great pleasure in."

It was hard to argue with that.

"She's gloating. She's showing us what she did—she's the killer, Jules."

"I don't know if we can take that leap."

"Oh, I've already leaped." He proceeded to prance in the air. "She's a mastermind, and she must be convinced that she's above the law. The only problem for her is she likely never considered our resident detective would be on the case."

I wasn't ready to declare Mary Beth the killer yet, but I agreed with Lance. Everything about her behavior, from her reaction to hearing about Erik's death to her choice of paintings to feature, was suspicious.

# Chapter Fifteen

"Onward to cabin eight," Lance said, dragging me behind him and using the flashlight app on his phone to guide us. Solar lights lined the path from the lodge to the cabins, but having extra illumination was helpful, especially with my clumsy feet these days.

"What do you think Mary Beth meant about knowing what Jess has been up to?" I asked. The sun sunk on the horizon, kissing the ocean with a symphony of pinks and oranges. Dusk filtered in through the trees, bringing with it a cool evening breeze. I breathed in the heady scent of late-blooming jasmine and climbing roses.

A chill came over my body as we turned toward the second grouping of cabins not far from mine.

I wished I had a jacket with me.

Fortunately, cabin eight was just around the first bend.

"What are we going to say?" I asked Lance, stalling as we made it to the front door. "We're not with the police. We don't have any authority in the case."

"Police. Who needs police when you're with moi?" He flicked his hair as if modeling for a runway show. "Come on, there's no time to dally."

The cabin needed attention. Old terra-cotta pots and bird feeders looked like they might sink into the saggy porch boards. The wood trim and decking showed signs of rotting, and a thin layer of moss made the steps slippery.

"Oh, ye of little faith." He made a dismissive sound under his breath. "As always, follow my lead." He rapped softly on the cabin door.

It took a minute for anyone to answer. I heard shuffling footsteps approaching the door. Then an older woman in her seventies opened the door a crack. She was dressed in a faded pink bathrobe with curlers in her silvery hair. It looked like she was ready for bed.

I felt terrible knocking this late. Although, technically, it wasn't that late—when we'd left the dining room, it had been close to eight thirty.

"Good evening. We're so sorry to disturb you." Lance plastered on his most charming and debonaire smile. "We're renting the cabin adjacent to you and having issues with our water. We couldn't find anyone at the front desk and noticed your lights on. We thought we would check to see if it's a global issue with all of the cabins or just our bad luck."

She opened the door farther, confident that we weren't going to attack her. "You too? I'm so frustrated with Hoff. Maintenance has gone downhill around here. I told Erik that we're not going to continue paying our monthly HOA fees until things are fixed."

"So it's not just us?" Lance asked, offering her a conspiratorial smile. "I suppose that's a relief."

"It took Hoff hours to fix our water. I'm sorry you're having issues too. My advice is to speak with Jess at the front desk. She had to stay on top of Hoff to get him to finish the work. It's been a problem for a while. I keep bringing the topic up at our monthly owners' meetings. Hoff used to be much more attentive, but in the past year or so, he's been awful. I raised the question of whether we should keep him on. You know, he has free housing in addition to his salary. That's a good deal, if you ask me. His job as the head of maintenance is to fix things when they break, but he likes to take his own sweet time."

"But he did finally fix it?" Lance peered behind her like he expected to see water gushing from the faucets. "Is your water working now?"

"Yes, but it took five hours. I have no idea what that man does. He moves at the speed of the banana slugs you find in the forest around here. He kept leaving to get different parts. I told my husband he was gone long enough to drive to Ashland and back, but what's more likely is that he was loitering in the grounds smoking." She wrinkled her nose like she could smell his cigarettes. "I've complained to Jess and Erik about that, too. There's no smoking at the resort, but Hoff seems to think the rules don't apply to him. I've caught him dozens of times smoking in the lobby, the restaurant, and all around the grounds. Do you know that he tosses his cigarette butts on the ground? He's ruining our local ecosystem, and he's going to end up starting a forest fire and burning the entire resort down. I don't understand why management keeps him around. He should have been fired years ago. But then again, Jess is not much better. She's always running around the resort, sneaking off with people she shouldn't be."

My senses perked up. Who was Jess sneaking off with?

"At least your water is working again," Lance offered before I could follow up about Jess.

"For how long, though? With his shoddy work effort, I wouldn't be surprised if it goes out again tonight." She pressed her hand to one of her curlers like she was worried it was going to fall out.

"Let's hope that's not the case," Lance said, shaking his head. "Sorry to bother you. We'll take another look for Jess and hope your water stays on." He crossed his fingers.

"Good luck finding her. She slinks around those cabins over there all hours of the day and night." She pointed a shaky finger away from the main path.

That was exactly what Steph had said about her. "You mentioned her sneaking around? With who?"

"That's the gossip, isn't it? Rumor has it there's a hot and heavy affair going on, but I don't pass on gossip." She wrapped her robe around her tighter.

I hoped she would say more, but she changed the subject, bringing an end to the conversation.

"Have a good stay. Are you honeymooners?"

"How did you know?" Lance planted a sloppy kiss on my cheek.

"Feel free to stop by anytime. We live here year-round, so I know everything about the resort, and I always have a teakettle on." She waved good-bye and shut the door.

"Honeymooners, really?" I wrinkled my brow. "There's going to be a huge scandal when she sees me holding hands with Carlos tomorrow."

"It will *really* give her something to talk about, especially when she sees me and Arlo. The gossip will be fabulous." He threw his head back and laughed wickedly.

"I'm kidding, of course. She's the sweetest, but before they send a search party out for us, what did we learn?"

"That Hoff did end up fixing her water, but that it took him five hours, and he disappeared for long stretches in the process." Her report matched what I already had been mulling over. Hoff had disappeared for too long. He easily had enough time to kill Erik, especially since it would have been nearly impossible to fix the water without his tools.

"Which confirms that he could be our killer," Lance added. "If she's telling the truth—and for the love of all things good, why wouldn't she be?—then he had ample time to sneak down the trail, push Erik, and return without anyone noticing."

"I should have asked her when he finally got her water working again," I said, scolding myself for not thinking about that sooner.

"Why?" Lance kicked a pinecone off the path.

"What if it was not long ago? His toolbox must factor in. She mentioned him leaving to get parts, but his toolbox was in the kitchen for most of the afternoon. Without his tools, it's no wonder it took him so long, and I keep coming back to the idea that he accidentally left the toolbox behind."

"Yes, tell me more." Lance led the way back with his phone as our guide. In the short time we'd been chatting, the sun had fully vanished.

"Here's a theory. Erik's murder was premeditated. Hoff used the repairs as his excuse and now his alibi, but he forgot one critical detail—his tools. In his haste to get over to cabin eight to establish his whereabouts, he left behind his toolbox."

"Thereby negating his alibi."

"Exactly."

"We're so clever." Lance patted himself on the back. "Look at us on the case, chasing down killers and out-smarting the police."

"I wouldn't go that far."

"I would, darling." Lance sounded incensed. "We're a dynamic crime-solving duo. You simply can't argue with that fact."

I could, but my efforts would be futile.

"The other possibility we should consider is that Jess and Erik were having an affair. If people gossiped about her sneaking around, maybe it was her and Erik. What if he broke it off?"

"And she pushed him off a cliff in retaliation? I like it." Lance snapped his fingers twice. "A lover scorned is dangerous territory."

"Yeah, but we have no proof at the moment."

"What next?" Lance paused as we approached the lodge.

"Dessert." I massaged my stomach. "I was promised dessert, and I've had my eye on Steph's banana boat cup-cakes all day."

"Fine, but this doesn't end here. Our work isn't fin-ished until Erik's killer is behind bars, understood? We alone can solve the case. It's our duty as citizens of the planet."

Lance's over-the-top theatrics weren't new to me. "The Professor and Detective Mars might have a difference of opinion on that."

"Nonsense. I'm sure they're grateful for our assistance." Lance held the door open for me.

We didn't get far, though, because Jess was slumped next to the lobby doorway with her head buried in her hands. Her shoulders heaved as she sobbed audibly.

"Jess, are you okay?" I asked with concern.

Had something else happened?

She wiped her nose on her sleeve and looked up at us with bloodshot eyes. "I'm fine."

"You don't look fine." Lance removed his pocket square and handed it to her. "Use this."

She stared at the creamy silk and rubbed it between her fingers. "This is, like, a legit old-school, uh, what are they called?"

"I believe the term you're looking for is pocket square or handkerchief," Lance said.

"I can't use this." She gave it back to him. "It's too nice."

"No, I insist." Lance pressed it into her hand.

She hesitated before using it to swab her eyes. Then she sniffed like a car engine trying to warm up. "Sorry. I'm a total mess. I know I'm supposed to be professional, but everything is falling apart. Everything. It's on me, and I don't know what to do. I'm in way over my head. Erik was a nightmare, but at least he knew how to get things done."

"I'm sure it's overwhelming," I said, crouching to be closer to her. Was she also distraught because she'd killed her secret lover? "Sterling and Steph said the same thing about the kitchen. Maybe the three of you can put your heads together and make a plan."

She wiped her eyes again and then balled up the silky square in her hands like a security blanket. "Yeah, I feel bad for them. They just started, and now everything's imploding."

"Have you considered calling an owners' meeting?" I

suggested. "I'm sure the cabin owners will have ideas and will be able to offer you help."

"But who's in charge in the meantime?" Jess asked. "Me? I run the front desk. I don't know how to do payroll, taxes, accounting, manage staff, or any of the other things that Erik did. He did everything himself. He wouldn't even let me come into his office. It's always locked. I don't even have the password for his computer."

It sounded like Whaleshead had a serious gap in organizational planning. We had backups upon backups at Torte, flowcharts in terms of who was in charge, and an entire document our team could use to operate without Mom or me.

"I'm sure the police will be able to help with that," I said. "They have technology experts, but Erik must have left that information somewhere. Have you looked in his office yet?"

She wadded the square tighter. "No, like I told you, he doesn't let me in. I don't have a key."

"Yes, but, dearest, he's dead." Lance stated the obvious.

"You think I should just go in there without permission?" Jess asked, crinkling the material and then smoothing it out on her thigh. "Like, break into his office?"

"Have you spoken with the police yet?" I asked. The Professor or Detective Mars would have likely already gained access to Erik's office.

"About what?" She blinked rapidly and sniffled like a small child.

"About this situation," I replied. Her demeanor had shifted. I got the sense she wasn't telling us the truth, or at least the full truth.

"You mean about going into his office?"

Lance sighed and mumbled something unintelligible.

"Uh, yeah, I let them in earlier, but I wasn't sure that I should go in because Erik made it clear that his office was completely off-limits to everyone on staff, including me."

My instincts were right. She contradicted herself. I glanced around the empty lobby. Mary Beth's artwork had been secured on the walls. Jess's desk was neatly organized, and a fire burned low in the fireplace. Erik's office door was shut. There were only two ways in and out of the lobby—through the front doors or through the restaurant.

"How did they get in?" I asked, wondering if Jess might slip up again.

She dropped the pocket square. "Huh?"

"You said you let them into Erik's office, but you don't have a key, right?"

"No. No. I don't have a key. They had the key. I meant that I showed them where his office is—well, was."

She picked up the pocket square and tried to hand it back to Lance.

"Keep it. I insist." Lance pursed his lips and held his hands out to stop her.

"Okay, thanks." She wiped her nose and stood up. "I appreciate you both listening. I'll talk to Sterling and Steph. Maybe we can organize a meeting with the owners tomorrow."

"Good idea," I said. "We'll be around and are happy to help in whatever way we can."

We left her and headed into the dining room for dessert. Our conversation had ended with catching her in a lie. Was that because she was overwhelmed and emotional, or could she be hiding something else?

# Chapter Sixteen

The last of the dinner plates were being cleared when Lance and I returned to the dining room.

"Quick, darling, this way." He yanked me toward the kitchen. "We need to establish our own alibi, and I do indeed have a little something for our chefs." He flashed a dazzling smile and burst through the kitchen door.

"Geez." Steph threw her hands back and dropped a flat-edge spatula on the island.

"Sorry. We had to sneak in to tell you, brilliant show, you two. Brilliant show." Lance applauded, giving them his version of a standing ovation.

Sterling plated conchas on silver platters. "Thanks, man. I'm glad you enjoyed it."

"Enjoyed it?" Lance scoffed, flicking his wrist like the sea lions on the beach flicked their tails. "It was an utter masterpiece. You've outdone yourselves. I can't wait for tomorrow's brunch encore." He reached into his jacket pocket and procured two small envelopes sealed with a navy wax crest.

He'd given Jess his handkerchief from the same pocket.

Was he some kind of a magician or a modern Mary Poppins?

I waited for him to pull a rabbit out next.

Instead he walked over to Sterling and pressed the envelope into his hands.

"What's this?" Sterling asked.

"Consider it a little opening gift." Lance handed Steph her envelope. "But don't open it yet. Save it for later. We won't keep you, but we will eagerly await dessert." With that, Lance turned on his heels and gestured for me to follow him.

I wondered what was in the envelopes as we returned to the table.

"How was your errand?" Mom asked, giving me a knowing look. "You were gone for a while."

"Interesting?" I suggested.

Lance kicked me under the table to silence me.

I hadn't intended to say more, but I dropped the subject anyway.

Dessert was even more delicious than I anticipated. The banana boat cupcake was moist and tender with a hint of cinnamon and a gooey chocolate and marshmallow center. "I'm going to dream about these," I said, helping myself to a second.

"The animal cracker is so good, too," Mom said, swiping a taste of buttercream with her finger. "We'll have to ask Steph if we can pay tribute to her at Torte by recreating these."

"I love that idea."

"Maybe we should have a Sterling and Steph special when we return," Carlos suggested. "We can tell people if they want more, they have to make a trip to the coast."

Ramiro tried one of each cupcake. "I'm voting s'mores. My friends want to build a bonfire on the beach tomorrow. I could bring these, and we could make s'mores with s'mores cupcakes."

"You should film it," Arlo suggested. "That sounds like it would be a huge hit with the team. Maybe we can steal your idea for our campout next week."

Arlo coached the Southern Oregon University women's softball team.

"Do it." Ramiro gave him a fist bump. "As long as you save some for me."

Our waiter came by with a fresh pot of decaf coffee, tea, and pencils so we could fill out the feedback survey.

"Why did they limit themselves to five stars?" Mom asked, putting on her reading glasses. "This was a ten out of ten for me."

"It's going to be hard to give them any constructive feedback," I agreed. "There wasn't a miss."

"Perfection." Lance doodled hearts on his paper.

We lingered for a while, enjoying each other's company, along with hot coffee and cinnamon tea. My eyes began feeling heavy. I fought to keep them open and stay upright as the conversation drifted to end-of-summer travel plans.

"Julieta, are you ready to go?" Carlos asked, picking up on the fact I was starting to fade—fast.

"Yeah, I'm beat. The day has finally caught up with me," I admitted.

"And you'll be in the kitchen at five a.m. tomorrow morning," Carlos said with a fake scowl.

"Me?" I touched my shoulders in protest. "Never."

Everyone cracked up.

"Shall we reconvene for brunch at a more reasonable

hour?" Lance asked, folding his napkin on the table in a perfect square. "Preferably after the sun has come up."

"Excellent idea," Mom said. "I'm on vacation and wouldn't mind sleeping in."

We agreed to meet at ten and called it a night. Carlos, Ramiro, and I made the short walk to our cabin. They stayed up drinking tea and resuming their board game battle.

I slept like a baby—or like I was growing two babies. Carlos was still snoring lightly when I woke to a dim, purple sky. I tiptoed out of bed and tugged on a pair of jeans that were getting snug in the waist, a hoodie, and my tennis shoes.

I left him and Ramiro a note on the Whaleshead letterhead in the cabin to let them know I was assisting Steph and Sterling with breakfast prep and I would see them for brunch later.

The cool, misty air was refreshing as I stepped outside. According to the weather report, there was a chance of rain later, but the sky was clear and speckled with stars. The entire resort sat in a sleepy slumber. I loved this time of the morning when the day still held the mystery of good things to come.

I took the short path to the lodge. The lights were on inside the building, but no one was out and about at this hour. I tugged the door open and stepped into the rustic lobby. The woody scent from last night's fire lingered in the room. Jess, or another worker, had pushed the shelving units in front of the surf and gift shop to close it for the night. Her desk was tidy and organized. I noticed stacks of paperwork on the corner.

That couldn't be Lucy's paperwork?

I took a quick look, but it was simply reservations and vendor contracts.

I was about to head for the kitchen when I noticed that Erik's office door was open.

I couldn't resist the temptation to take a peek. Blame it on Lance.

*It's just a quick look, darling,* I could imagine him saying.

My rational brain tried to convince me to reconsider, but my feet moved forward, and the next thing I knew I was pushing the door open.

I flipped on the lights. There was nothing that immediately seemed out of order. Erik's office was clean and organized, yet soulless. There wasn't a single photo, artwork, or any personal touches. Nothing that indicated Erik had used the space. It was like stepping inside an office showroom. A map of the resort hung on one wall, and posters from previous events were tacked to the other wall.

His desk contained a computer and some basic office supplies. The bookshelves were filled with local guides and brochures and a handful of nonfiction business and marketing books.

A small filing cabinet caught my eye. Could this be where Erik stored financial records and employee files?

I peered around the door and checked to make sure I was alone.

I don't know why I bothered. I doubted that Jess or any of the other staff would be up for hours. The only other people awake were likely Steph and Sterling, and neither of them would fault me for snooping.

I inched toward the filing cabinet, being extra cautious

just in case I was wrong, and tried the top drawer. It was locked. So were the rest of the drawers.

*That's a dead end, Jules.*

*And it's a bad idea for you to be here.*

*You're potentially tampering with evidence.*

Then I spotted Erik's notebook resting on his desk.

*It wouldn't hurt just to flip through.*

I picked it up carefully and browsed the pages. His handwriting was meticulous and in all caps. The first few pages were notes about repairs and upcoming events.

Then his writing shifted into what appeared to be a code. There was a drawing of a fish with Travis's business card taped to one of the pages. Dozens of tally marks were listed in neat rows.

I pulled out my phone and snapped a picture, not wanting to take the time to try and decipher the meaning now.

Then I flipped through his remaining notes and gasped when I turned to the final page with writing on it.

Jess's name was circled on the top.

Erik had drawn a map of the resort. Cabins were numbered, and different spots were marked with red X's.

The bench where he'd fallen was circled in dark red ink.

Above his drawing of the infamous bench, he'd written: *JESS, MEETING SPOT?*

Did that mean he and Jess were supposed to meet at the bench?

Why?

When?

Questions assaulted my mind.

Could this be the proof we needed that they were having an affair?

I took another picture and closed the notebook.

Had the Professor and Detective Mars already looked through Erik's notes? According to Jess, they entered his office last night. But why wouldn't they have taken the notebook into evidence?

Or could there be another explanation?

Why was his office open now?

I sighed, turned off the lights, shut Erik's office door, and made a mental note to speak with the Professor about it later.

*It's time to be an adult and stop snooping,* I chided myself as I snuck past Jess's desk and bumped straight into her.

She was dressed in all black and wearing disposable blue plastic gloves.

"Oh my God, what are you doing here?" She jumped and threw her hands over her chest in a protective stance.

"I'm helping in the kitchen." I pointed in the direction of the dining room. "Sterling and Steph asked me to come in early."

She gulped and darted her eyes from left to right. "Are you here alone? Are the police with you?"

"No, it's just me. Why? What's going on?"

"Nothing. A minor emergency. One of the cabins has a clogged toilet, and Hoff's not answering his phone. I have to grab the master keys." She pointed to her desk. "You scared me. I didn't expect anyone to be up this early."

"Sorry. Baker's hours."

"Right, okay, I better get the key." She hurried to her desk, rummaged through the top drawer, grabbed the keys, and took off.

I watched her skirt along the dimly lit pathway until she was out of sight.

Had I caught her about to do something else?

Part of me wanted to stop her and ask her more, but I needed to be strategic and think this through.

Like Hoff, where were her tools? She wasn't carrying a plunger, and those gloves weren't made for heavy cleaning. They were the kind you find at a doctor's office. If she was actually fixing a toilet, I would think she would opt for different gloves like the kind we had at Torte—thick and yellow that went up to your elbows.

What was Jess really doing?

Had I interrupted her about to do something else—like destroying evidence?

# Chapter Seventeen

I sighed and took a minute to compose myself. I didn't want to stress Steph and Sterling out.

The kitchen was already in full swing. Music blared from the overhead speakers. The overhead fluorescent lights reflected on the stainless-steel counters.

I inhaled the scent of freshly brewed coffee and cinnamon bread.

Steph was deep in bread dough while Sterling cracked eggs into a large mixing bowl.

"Good morning," I said, washing my hands and tying on an apron.

"There's coffee. I made a pot of decaf for you, Jules. I know it's not the same as fully leaded, but Andy sent us a huge box of roasts. We were planning to test them over the next few days to see if there are any standouts for guests and then talk to Erik about switching to make Andy our preferred coffee vendor. He said he would do a custom SeaBreeze blend, but now that Erik's dead . . . I don't know—" Sterling tossed eggshells into a compost bin and nodded to the coffeepot. "It's all up in the air."

"Yeah. I know, it's so hard to make longer-term decisions until you know more."

"I'm sure we're going to figure it out. It's just weird to be in limbo."

"The one thing I can say with certainty is you're a gem for this," I said, blowing him a kiss. "Honestly, my morning coffee is as much about the ritual as anything else. I don't even miss the caffeine, at least not as much as I thought I might. It's the sensory experience of pouring the rich brew into a hot mug, stirring in a splash of heavy cream, and cradling the drink in my hands."

"Carlos had better watch out. You have a serious love affair with coffee." Steph sprinkled flour on the counter. She massaged the dough into a large ball and then used her palms to begin kneading it.

I poured myself a cup of coffee and studied the whiteboard near the sink, which had the menu and prep schedule for breakfast. "What can I tackle for you?"

"Sterling's making the brunch lasagna, and I'm making butterscotch sticky buns." Steph's arms flexed as she worked the dough. "Do you want to start on the rhubarb crumble?"

"Sure." Their menu was adventurous and also smart. In addition to the breakfast lasagna, which included layers of hash browns, sausage, and a creamy egg bake, and the butterscotch buns, they were featuring a pizza frittata, a blueberry and lemon breakfast cake, and individual soufflés. "You're serving everything buffet style?" I confirmed.

"That's the idea," Sterling said, whisking the eggs with heavy cream. "We'll set everything up in the dining room under heat lamps. We figured for opening weekend, it would be better to streamline our efforts and focus on pre-paring larger quantities of a limited selection of dishes. With the buffet, guests can serve themselves, so we don't need extra waitstaff. It should also reduce wait times, since we won't need to turn over tables, but everything is a gamble this weekend."

"Trial and error is the only way you learn," I reassured him. "I think it's a very smart plan, and people love a buf-fet brunch."

I wanted to bring up my strange interaction with Jess, but not until I had a good handle on what they needed help with.

Steph used a marble rolling pin to form the dough into a large rectangle. I gathered the ingredients for the crumble. Then I creamed butter, sugar, and vanilla together until they were light and fluffy. I beat in eggs and alternated adding milk and dry ingredients—baking powder, salt, and flour.

I greased baking dishes and spread the batter evenly over the bottoms. Next I washed and chopped fresh rhubarb into cubes. I mixed that with sugar, cornstarch, orange juice, and orange zest. Once the rhubarb was coated, I layered it over the batter.

The final step was to mix oats, flour, brown sugar, and cinnamon together. I cut chilled butter and used a pastry cutter to combine it with the oat mixture, working it until it resembled coarse sand. I sprinkled the crumbly topping over the rhubarb and set the cakes in the oven to bake for forty-five minutes. We would serve the slices at room tem-perature with a dollop of whipped cream.

"Okay, what next?" I asked Steph, brushing flour from my hands.

"You're making us look bad, Jules. How do you work that fast?"

"Years of muscle memory." I cracked my fingers. "And the faster I bake, the faster I get to eat. That's the—uh, gift—of pregnancy."

"How do you feel about soufflés?" Steph asked, biting her lip.

"They're my worst nightmare. The worst. I avoid them like the plague." I stuck out my tongue and made my eyes bulge out. "Mom always says, 'Soufflés wait for no one.'"

"That's what I'm worried about." Steph frowned, gnawing on a purple fingernail. "They're out of my comfort zone. I've only made a few and it's been years."

"Totally. I understand. I'm teasing. We've got this. Soufflés get a bad rap, but they're actually much easier than you might think. I made them all the time on the *Amour of the Seas*, but you're right; they're not really a staple at Torte. My best piece of advice is to focus on precision. Let's walk through it." I tapped into everything I had learned in culinary school about the delicate French desserts, shifting into teaching mode. "They require precise measurement of the ingredients. You can't eyeball a soufflé. You have to measure exactly. Another key is achieving the right consistency with the egg whites. They need to be stiff, but you can't overbeat them, and once you start folding them into the base mixture, you have to proceed with caution and do it very gently so you don't deflate the air bubbles that give the soufflé lift. On the other hand, you need to make sure you mix it thoroughly so you avoid large pockets of egg white in the final bake."

"Never mind, see, this is what I remember about making them," Steph interrupted me, waving me off with both hands. Her nails were painted the SeaBreeze pistachio. I'd never seen her wear colors other than black and purple. "Forget it. I can't have a baking fail on my first weekend."

"I'm not even done yet."

"Uh, yeah. Kind of my point." She made a slicing motion across her neck. "I'm out."

"We're doing this, my friend. Listen, they can be a touch finicky, but the payoff is so worth it. They'll be showstoppers, I promise."

"But what about the ovens?" Steph motioned to the large industrial oven. "I know you can't open the oven door while they're baking because they'll collapse. How are we going to keep the door shut with everything else that has to go in?"

"That's true, but we'll be super smart about timing. It's not a problem. If we're doing them in individual ramekins, they only need to bake for fifteen or twenty minutes. We can do them last."

Steph chomped on her bottom lip, dragging her teeth through her eggplant lip gloss. "I don't know. Maybe we should scrap them for individual bread puddings or something easier."

"It's your menu and your restaurant, so I won't force the issue, but I think they'll be great for your confidence." I locked my eyes on her to show I was serious. "They are so elegant in terms of presentation, and you'll get to show off your culinary skills. Plus, the effort and timing involved in baking soufflés make them perfect for a special occasion like this. Most people can follow a basic recipe for a bread pudding, but I doubt that many of your guests have ever attempted a soufflé. They're the highlight of a gourmet meal."

"She's going hard on the soufflé," Sterling said with a laugh. "I'm convinced."

"You don't have to bake them, though." Steph frowned.

"Come on, let's live on the edge and go for it," I said, rubbing my hands together. "One savory and two sweet, according to your notes. Chocolate, berry, and a classic cheese, right?"

"Okay, but can I watch you first?" She sounded unsure.

"Of course. We'll have mini soufflé school."

Steph finished the sweet rolls, and then we cleaned a workspace.

"Did either of you see Jess this morning?" I asked, separating egg whites into the industrial mixer.

"No, was she supposed to come in this early?" Steph looked at the clock. It wasn't yet seven.

"I'm not sure when the front desk opens, but I bumped into her on my way in." I told them about our strange interaction and how she was wearing gloves and seemed very eager to get away from me. "Here's what makes it even odder—Erik's office was open. She told me yesterday that it's always locked and that she wasn't ever allowed inside."

"Let me guess, you went in, didn't you, Jules?" Sterling held his wooden spoon and flicked it like he was scolding me.

I grimaced. "I'm not proud of myself, but yes, I did take a quick look around."

"And?"

"I found his notebook. I'm surprised the police didn't take it last night. It's almost like someone else put it there."

I turned the mixer on low. The egg whites need to be whipped low and slow to form stiff peaks.

"Are you saying you think that Jess put it there?" Sterling asked, chopping onions without so much as shedding a single tear. One of the tricks I'd taught him early on in his days at Torte was to refrigerate onions. Chilling them before chopping reduces the amount of volatile compounds released in the air, which is what leads to eye irritation and tearing.

"I'm not sure," I admitted. "The timing feels too coincidental. Is she really fixing a toilet? Or was she on her way to grab the notebook when I bumped into her, hence the gloves?"

"Why wouldn't she just have taken it to begin with?" Sterling asked.

That question had been bugging me, too.

"I'm stuck on that." I watched the egg whites carefully, waiting for them to start to develop a glossy sheen.

"Unless she was planning to rip out the pages pertaining to her," Steph suggested, taking notes on each step in the process on her phone while we worked.

"Interesting. I hadn't considered that. Maybe she left to grab gloves because she didn't want to leave her fingerprints on the notebook." I turned the mixer higher as the egg whites became glossy.

"She could have known the police found it last night." Steph leaned closer to get a better look at the mixer.

"Why wouldn't she have taken it, then?" Sterling asked, scooping the onions and peppers into a bowl and pressing seasoned hash browns into the bottom of a large baking dish.

"Yeah, I don't understand why the police would have

left it." I couldn't wait to speak with the Professor. In Ashland, he always stopped by Torte before we opened for a cup of coffee and a pastry. I hoped he would do the same today.

"Bait?" Steph dipped her pinkie into the mixture and held her finger upside down to see if the egg whites would run off.

"Bait," I repeated, considering the idea. "Hmm. They knew there was incriminating evidence in the notes, so they intentionally left the journal in plain sight to see if Jess would try to destroy it." I wasn't sure if that was exactly the Professor's style, but then again, he wasn't in charge of the investigation. He was simply assisting Detective Mars. Perhaps she'd suggested the setup.

"That would explain why Jess is up so early." Sterling scooped cooked sausage over the hash browns. "I haven't seen her before eight or eight thirty the entire time we've been here."

"She usually rolls in closer to nine," Steph said. "She said something to me the other day about needing her beauty sleep and how she couldn't imagine how brutal it must be to work the morning shift in the kitchen."

"I hope you told her our early hours keep us young and spry."

"Is that how you're trying to spin it?" Sterling teased, pretending to stifle a yawn.

"I don't need to spin it because it's true." I patted my cheeks. "And our skin stays so supple and dewy from all of the steam and heat."

Sterling shook his head and laughed. "I love the positivity."

"Have you heard anything about her sneaking around? Could she and Erik have been having an affair?"

Steph dragged her teeth along her bottom lip. "No, but that would make sense. She's always vanishing from the reception desk. Although I got the sense they didn't like each other very much."

"Enemies to lovers?" Sterling suggested.

"I guess." Steph didn't sound like she was on board with the idea. "Props to you for knowing your tropes."

"Come on." Sterling leaned back like he was offended. "I've seen plenty of Jane Austen in my day."

I laughed.

I finished teaching Steph my method for fail-proof soufflés. We carefully folded the egg whites into the roux base of butter, flour, milk, egg yolks, Gruyère cheese, and Parmesan. We filled ramekins with the mixture and smoothed the tops with a flat spatula to make them rise evenly. My secret trick was to run a knife around the rim to create a channel between the edge of the ramekin and the batter, which forced the soufflé to rise up instead of expanding out. I had Steph take the lead on the chocolate and berry soufflés and dropped the topic of Erik's murder.

There were too many questions that needed answers. As soon as we finished breakfast prep and the buffet was ready for guests, I intended to find the Professor and see if he might be able to fill me in on anything new. I wasn't sure what Jess's motive might be for killing Erik, but her behavior was highly suspicious, and it was nearly impossible to dismiss the fact that her name was circled in his notebook, marking the exact spot where he'd been killed.

I had a lot more to learn about Jess and the rest of the staff and guests at Whaleshead. I just hoped we'd be able to figure out who had taken such a terrible and drastic step before it was time to return home to Ashland.

# Chapter Eighteen

As anticipated, the soufflés were a huge hit. They puffed like fluffy erupting volcanos and added a wow factor to brunch. Guests raved about the spread and begged Steph and Sterling to make the soufflés and his savory breakfast casseroles permanent additions to the menu. I was glad to see that people made quick work of my rhubarb crumble. Brunch was elegant yet understated in the best possible way. There were no lattes or highly crafted coffees. Instead, there were pots of French roast, decaf, hot water for tea, and an assortment of fresh-squeezed juices. It was like stepping back in time. I remembered similar brunches in my childhood here at Whaleshead. Dad would puzzle over the crossword and a strong cup of black coffee while Mom would sketch cake designs in her notebook, and I would go back to the buffet for second and third helpings of crepes with lemon butter and marionberry jam and pigs in blankets.

Carlos and I often talked about how the simplicity of a meal often elevates it, not adding dozens of extra garnishes or making a dish unnecessarily complicated.

Carlos and Mom helped with setup, but once brunch

was in full swing, we joined Lance and Arlo at a table in front of the window. Morning light spilled in, warming my cheeks and making the entire restaurant look like it was lit up with a disco ball. Puffy white clouds and red-tailed hawks floated through the aquamarine sky. So much for rain or an impending storm. The weather couldn't have been better. The beach was calling me. I couldn't wait to dig my toes into the balmy sand and dip them into the ocean.

"My compliments to the chef," Lance said, lifting his cranberry juice in a toast. "We never should have let these two out of our grasp. They're absolutely killing it." He gasped. "Sorry, sorry. I realized it's way too soon. That was a Freudian slip, but since the topic of murder is on the table, is there any news?"

"You? A Freudian slip?" Arlo shot him a skeptical glance.

"Mais oui, mon ami." Lance shifted into French, a habit he employed when he was caught in a lie. He ignored Arlo and turned his attention to Mom. "How is Doug doing? Were they up all night trying to catch the killer?"

Mom knew Lance as well as I did. She smiled non-committally. "It was a long night, followed by an early morning. He said that he would try and drop in for a bite, but I haven't heard from him yet."

"Cell service is abysmal here," Lance said, reaching into his pocket for his phone and checking the connection. "One measly bar. How am I supposed to communicate with the team in Ashland with such a spotty connection?"

"You might try speaking with Jess," I suggested. "She has a landline. Actually, I might join you. I'd like to give Marty a call and make sure everything is running smoothly at Torte."

"Excellent idea." He tucked his phone in his pocket and shifted in his seat like he was about to get up.

I was sure that if we left again, everyone would assume we were coming up with another ploy to snoop, but I genuinely wanted to check in with the bakeshop. I wasn't anticipating that anything would go wrong, but I wanted a report from Marty about how the new staff were doing with their training.

Before we could sneak out, the Professor strolled up to the table. "Good morning, all. I've been doing my best to avoid the siren song of the spectacular aromas emanating from the dining room, and I've finally caved. I simply cannot resist for another minute." He bent closer to kiss Mom's head.

"You should sit, Doug." Carlos motioned to the empty chair next to Mom. "Let me get you a plate."

"Oh, there's no need. Don't go to any trouble."

"No, no, I insist." Serving was in Carlos's blood. There was no point in arguing, he was already on his feet and halfway to the buffet tables.

"Coffee?" Mom asked, offering him the carafe.

"Yes, thank you." He filled his cup. "It's always a shame to think the Bard never had the chance to let this nectar touch his lips. He would have been familiar with ale and wine, of course, but coffee had yet to make its mark on England during his time. I wonder what stories he might have penned fueled by the mighty bean."

Lance chuckled. "I'm positive he would have been of the mindset to never trust anyone who doesn't drink coffee."

The Professor raised the cup to his lips, closed his eyes, and breathed in the scent. "Ah, agreed."

Carlos returned shortly with a plate piled high with every item on the buffet. "I brought one of each, but don't be shy, there's plenty more."

"I won't be able to move for the remainder of the day if I devour all of this." The Professor rubbed his belly. "But then again, it might be worth it."

We gave him time to enjoy his meal in peace without bombarding him with questions about Erik's murder. Carlos refilled our coffees, and Ramiro ambled in with sleepy eyes. He shielded his face with his hoodie.

"You look tired. Why are you up?" Carlos asked.

Ramiro removed his hoodie and brushed a strand of hair from his eyes. He slumped in the chair next to the Professor. "I don't want to waste the day, but I binged the final six episodes of a show last night. It was so good, I couldn't stop."

Everyone laughed.

"Ah, the curse of youth." The Professor patted his shoulder. "In my day, we didn't even have the ability to record shows. You watched whatever was live, and that was it. In fact, if you can believe it, programming ended shortly after midnight, and then the TV screen went to nothing more than gray static."

"Hence, the draw of the theater," Lance added with a dramatic flick of his wrist. "Full immersion in the atmosphere and performances."

"I feel you on the binge. I've done the same thing. It used to be different when we were kids because you had to wait a week for the next episode of a show to come out,"

I said to Ramiro. "I've gotten sucked in to shows, too, and it's hard not to keep watching because there is no end."

"Unless you binge the entire series like me." Ramiro ran his hands through his hair like he was trying to wake up his brain cells. "I'm meeting my friends in thirty minutes to go to the beach. I need coffee."

"And food," Carlos said, sounding like a concerned parent. "Maybe this afternoon you need a siesta."

"For sure." Ramiro stirred cream into his coffee and brushed sleepy dust from his eyes.

"I'm meeting Detective Mars soon," the Professor said, topping off his drink. "Before I go, I thought I might check to see if you've heard anything that could be valuable in our investigation."

Lance raised his hand like he was in class.

"Yes, Lance, the floor is yours." The Professor tipped his head and held out his palm.

"If you insist. Twist my arm." Lance rotated his arm in small circles and winked. "I do have a bit of news. I happened to bump into the owner of cabin eight last night."

I had to force myself not to give him a little kick in the shins. *Happened to bump into* was a stretch, but I was glad he left me out of it.

"She mentioned that Hoff was in and out of her cabin all afternoon and that it took him an inordinate amount of time to fix her water."

The Professor made a note.

Lance nudged me. "Juliet, tell him what you saw."

My mind raced to our chat with the owner last night. Had I seen anything?

"Which part?" I asked Lance.

"About our chat with Jess," he said, motioning for me to keep going.

"Right. We found Jess crying in the lobby last night. She was upset about Erik and said she didn't have access to any of the employee records, payroll, or even his office. It seemed odd." I hesitated. I needed to tell him about what I'd found in Erik's office earlier, but I didn't want everyone to know how much I'd been snooping.

"She was a mess," Lance interrupted. "Juliet and I have theorized she could be a lover scorned. There's talk around the resort of secret affairs and late-night trysts. She's lying about something. I'm convinced of that much."

"But you don't have any specifics to expand on?" the Professor asked, hiding a smile.

"Not yet. However, that's never stopped me before, so there's no reason to think it should stop me now." Lance turned his face to the sky, soaking in the heat from the windows.

Arlo buried his face in his hands. "Oh, no. You've woken the beast."

The Professor closed his notebook. "Juliet, would you happen to have an hour or so to accompany me to speak with the fishmonger? I could use your culinary insights."

Fish was more of Carlos's department, but I wasn't going to argue about the opportunity for some time alone with the Professor. Not to mention, I was curious why he needed to speak with Travis. The fish drawings and tally marks in Erik's notebook popped into my mind.

What if Travis discovered Erik had been documenting his every move? What if Erik and Travis were wrapped up in something together? A partnership gone wrong, perhaps?

Could the Professor have evidence linking the local fisherman to the crime? Had they found a link with Travis's towel? Were we closing in on the killer?

# Chapter Nineteen

"I sensed you might have more to share, and I genuinely want your thoughts and insights on Travis," the Professor said as he navigated the steep driveway. He kept his eyes focused on the road, but I knew I had his full attention.

"You're always so astute," I said, feeling a sense of appreciation and gratitude move through me. "How did you know?"

"Years of practice, my dear." His tone was kind. "That, and you're one of my favorite people on the planet. I can tell when something is bothering you."

Tears welled in my eyes. Knowing he was in touch with my emotions made me even more grateful for our connection. After Dad died, I never imagined having someone like the Professor in my life who could fill that role.

"There's a lot bothering me," I admitted, keeping my eyes glued to the windshield to try and keep the morning sickness at bay. "But before we get into it, I need to tell you something. I'm feeling guilty about what I did this morning."

"Would it help to have a nonjudgmental listening ear?"

His voice was soft and languid, like he had all the time in the world to hear whatever I wanted to say.

"Always." I clutched my hands in my lap as we descended through the forested hillside and turned onto Highway 101. The ocean paralleled us on the right. I opened my window a crack and stared at the rhythmic waves crashing onto the shore. I was in the most serene and stunning place in the world. I couldn't lose sight of that. Sunlight sparkled on the water, casting a bejeweled spell on the whitecaps and making the sand appear luminescent. Yes, I wanted to get to the bottom of Erik's murder and make sure the rest of the weekend went as smoothly as possible for Sterling and Steph, but I also needed to remind myself of the commitment I had made to self-care and carving out time just for me. No matter what else happened, I was making time this afternoon to read on the beach.

"She's quite majestic, the sea, isn't she?" He sounded wistful. "Being near the ocean always reminds me of one of my favorite passages from *The Winter's Tale*: 'When you do dance, I wish you a wave o' th' sea, that you might ever do nothing but that; move still, still so, and own no other function; each your doing, so singular in each particular, crowns what you are doing in the present deeds, that all your acts are queens.'"

"That's lovely."

"It makes me consider what Shakespeare thought about the sea, much as I wonder what he would have thought of coffee. It's a shame we haven't invented time travel yet, isn't it? If only we could travel back and witness his creative genius live, yet alas, here we are in the present, and I'm rambling while you have something to tell me."

I couldn't help but wonder if his so-called rambling was intentional—a way to take the pressure off and give me a minute to collect my thoughts. I appreciated the sweet gesture, but ripping the Band-Aid off and coming clean with him was the only way forward.

"I found something in Erik's office this morning, but I know I shouldn't have been there," I blurted out. "I feel bad for even going in. I realize it's not an excuse, but I was overcome in the moment because Jess mentioned his office is always locked, and she doesn't even have a key."

The Professor clicked off the radio. "That's what she told us as well. Although we had no trouble procuring a key."

"Well, it wasn't locked this morning. The door was propped open when I arrived early to help Sterling and Steph."

"Propped open. Is that so?"

"Yeah. It took me by surprise, and I guess I didn't really think about it, and I went inside." I felt silly admitting this to him. I was smarter than this. "I'm sorry, I know that was not my brightest move."

He shrugged noncommittally. "We're allowed mistakes. It's what we do with our mistakes, isn't it? For example, letting me know you entered the office is appreciated. Did you find anything of interest?"

I was relieved he was letting me off the hook. I wasn't so sure I was ready to give myself the same grace, but I told him about the notebook and, specifically, the pages about Jess and Travis. "Did you leave it there? It seemed weird it wasn't taken in as evidence."

"Detective Mars recovered the notebook and took digital photographs of each entry. She decided it might be interesting to leave it in place and see if any of our suspects took the bait. However, she didn't mention unlocking his office."

"I ran into Jess shortly after," I said, going on to explain about our exchange and her claim that she was up early fixing a toilet.

"Ah, so she's moonlighting as a plumber. Interesting." He steered past a group of bikers in brightly colored kits. "Do you think she and Erik planned to meet at the spot where he was killed? It seems like too much of a coincidence, unless they were lovers. I'm not sure about that angle, though. Steph knows her the best, and her take is that Jess and Erik didn't get along well. But if they weren't sneaking off together, what's her motive—that he was a terrible boss?

"Sadly, people have killed with lesser motives." He checked the GPS as we got closer to town. "I don't believe in coincidences in circumstances like these. Although I agree that at this stage, it's a flimsy motive at best."

"Could they have been having an affair?" I asked, thinking out loud. "Or what if Erik was trying to use his position of power?"

"Every possibility is currently on the table." Signs pointed to the commercial docks. He turned off onto a small single-lane road. "If you have an opportunity to speak with her further, it would be most helpful to see if she might open up more with you."

"I'll do my best."

"Excellent." He tapped the map on his phone. "Does this look like the right turn to you?"

I zoomed in on the map and confirmed his directions. "Why are we visiting Travis, by the way? Did you already get the forensic report back on the towel I found at the crime scene?"

He laughed. "Ah, I wish. Alas, the world of criminal investigation does not move at that speed."

"Do you think he could have followed Erik down the trail after he dropped off the fish delivery? I know for a fact he had a towel just like that with him then. He was angry about payment. Maybe he tracked Erik down, demanded he get paid, and things took a turn."

"It's a possibility." The Professor nodded as the smell of freshly caught fish grew stronger. I hoped that my stomach would cooperate.

"Like many of our other suspects, including Jess, details about Travis's whereabouts from other witnesses don't match his account. I have some further questions for him, and I'd appreciate your insight into his business practices, which I find odd and, shall we say, inconsistent."

"No problem." I was happy to be of any assistance, especially after admitting I'd trespassed in Eric's office earlier. I was also curious about the tally marks in Erik's notebook. It seemed plausible that he and Travis had concocted a deal of sorts. Could Erik have been skimming from the resort? Maybe overbilling Whaleshead and splitting the difference between him and Travis? Travis could have pushed for a bigger share, and when Erik refused, he decided to kill him?

I sighed. The road changed to weathered wooden slats. We bumped along like it was a carnival ride.

"I'm hopeful our conversation will be illuminating on a number of levels." The Professor pulled into an empty gravel space in front of the docks. Fishing vessels of varying sizes, from commercial ships to family-owned boats, were moored tightly together, rocking on the waves. The wooden docks were weathered from salt and storms. Adjacent to the docks were seafood processing facilities and open-air fish markets where the catch of the day was being cleaned and prepared.

The smell of diesel from the boat engines and tuna and halibut assaulted my senses as I got out of the car. Seagulls circled above us, attempting to snatch up a discarded fish or bait. They could gladly have my share, I thought as my stomach gurgled.

*Keep it together, Jules.*

I swallowed hard, not wanting my brunch to resurface. Why hadn't I thought to tuck an extra package of mints into my pockets before we left?

I concentrated on the activity around us to distract myself. Fisher workers clad in heavy rubber boots mended nets and unloaded their catches. There was a flurry of activity in every direction. Handwritten signs directed us to fish stalls where we could purchase today's offerings. Prices were sketched informally in chalk.

"I believe we're this way." The Professor pointed to the docks to our left.

We passed boats bearing the scars of many voyages with peeling paint and barnacle-encrusted hulls.

Travis's boat was draped with nets, drying in the sun. It was painted a slate gray with yellow trim. CATCH OF THE DAY was painted on the side of the fishing vessel, which looked like it had weathered many storms.

He was on his knees in his waders, scrubbing the deck.

"Greetings," the Professor called, announcing our presence.

Travis looked up from his work and tossed the scrub

brush into a bucket of bleach. He appeared resigned as he stood and wiped his hands on his shirt. "Do you need something?"

"I have a few follow-up questions." The Professor sounded casual. I knew this meeting was anything but. "You've met Juliet, correct?"

"Briefly." Travis gave me a nod of acknowledgment and folded his arms across his chest. "What do you need? I have a lot of work to do."

"Understood. I'll make this as brief as possible." The Professor smiled and leafed through his Moleskine notebook. "You mentioned being out at sea yesterday between the hours of three and five, correct?"

"Yep." He stood and dried his hands on a towel—a towel that looked exactly like the one I'd found on the bench.

"Yet, from a commercial standpoint, dawn and dusk are highly favored by your colleagues. According to them, the fish are more active and prone to feeding frenzies during the lower light levels, making them much more likely to bite. From my inquiries, it also sounds as if fish seek deeper waters during the heat of the day. Cooler morning and evening temperatures bring them closer to the surface and shore. Do you agree?"

"Yep." He folded his arms across his chest, signaling he wasn't going to give the Professor anything easily. He was impossible to read with his closed, protective body language and one-word answers.

"Is there a reason you chose to go out in the middle of the day, in nonideal conditions?" the Professor pressed.

"I've been doing this for a long time. I know the behavior patterns of fish. I know these waters better than anyone."

"You mentioned you weren't successful with your catch, though."

"Yep. That's why they call it *fishing*, not *catching*."

"Clever." The Professor made a note and then reached for his phone. He scrolled through his photos until he found what he was looking for. "Is this your boat?"

Travis barely glanced at the screen. "Yeah."

"And this is your spot on the dock?" He showed him another set of photos. "*Catch of the Day* is always docked here."

"Yep."

"According to your statement, you were on the water from three to five. Do you maintain that is correct?" the Professor repeated his early question.

"What is this about?" Travis snapped the straps of his waders against his chest. "I told you and the other detective this yesterday, and you're asking me all of the same questions."

"Standard procedure in a murder investigation."

"Murder? Who said anything about murder?" Travis scowled and glanced around us like he was expecting to see a dead body nearby. "I thought Erik fell?"

"We've determined that he was pushed," the Professor said.

I watched as Travis processed this information. He wrinkled his tanned brow, trying to make sense of the Professor's statement. "When was he killed?"

I wasn't sure if I believed his reaction or not. I suppose if he hadn't been back to the resort since the incident, he might not have heard, but then again, he might be putting on an act.

"Between three and five," the Professor answered slowly.

"Okay, so what's the deal, then? I already told you a million times that I was out on the water then." He shot his thumb behind him toward the bay. "How would I have killed him?"

"That's a very good question." The Professor put his notebook away. "What sort of arrangement did you and Erik have regarding delivery of and payment for your product?"

"What?" Travis nearly slipped on the deck as he took a step backward. "I don't know what you mean."

"You supplied SeaBreeze Bistro with their fish and sea-food, correct?"

"Yeah, what's that got to do with anything?" Travis sounded defensive.

"Did you deliver daily, biweekly? Did Erik pay you directly?"

"Yeah, everything was standard, on the up-and-up. I haven't delivered as much lately because the place has been closed. Now that they have the kids in charge, who knows, maybe they'll finally be the ones to revive the place, but I don't have high hopes. Erik was notoriously late on payments. I told him that he couldn't have any more credit. I have bills to pay, too, you know."

"I'm sure you do."

For a minute, I thought the Professor was finished with his questions, because he started to turn toward the car, but he stopped and held his index finger as if he'd just had a new thought. "Before we let you back to your work, you didn't mention how often you deliver."

"I don't know. It depends on what I get and what Whaleshead needs. I don't keep records. My clients know me. That's how things work around here. I usually just put a sticky note on the delivery box, and I get paid."

"Let's narrow it down to the past few weeks. How often have you delivered?"

"Probably twice. Maybe three times. What does this have to do with Erik?"

"I'm not at liberty to share those details." The Professor gave him a half bow. "Thank you very much for your time. Good luck with the fishing. Do be sure to stay in town or let Detective Mars know if you have any plans to leave."

"Yeah, okay, fine." Travis returned to scrubbing the deck.

I followed the Professor back to the car. "Was that a successful conversation?" I asked, unsure if he had learned what he was hoping to find out.

"Indeed." He didn't start the car but rather scrolled through his phone and then handed it to me. "Take a look at the video surveillance from yesterday afternoon. It's sped up to the window of time when Erik was murdered."

I watched the footage of the boats speeding in and out of the harbor. They looked like miniature toys floating in a bathtub.

"Pay attention to the dock, specifically Travis's boat." He pointed to the spot on the video.

I studied the dock where the moored boats danced in rhythm with the tides and the waves, rocking back and forth like they were being lulled to sleep. "Wait, Travis's boat never leaves."

"No, it does not, and yet, according to his earlier statement and what you just heard, he claims to have been out fishing the entire time. It's unclear why he lied."

"He must not realize there's video footage," I said, trying to make sense of it. "Otherwise, he's not very smart."

"I don't get that impression. In fact, I would say he's quite crafty." The Professor took his phone back and plugged in directions to Whaleshead. "Does anything strike you as odd about his accounting practices?"

"Yeah, everything. He doesn't keep records and gives clients sticky notes. I understand that this is a small community, but even so, that's a terrible way to track sales. I can't imagine any restaurant, even a mom-and-pop shop, being okay with that level—or lack thereof—of accounting."

"An astute observation, Juliet." The Professor backed the car out of the space. "As it turns out, I believe there's much more than sales receipts missing when it comes to Travis and his business practices."

# Chapter Twenty

I watched the docks get smaller and smaller in the rear-view mirror, processing what I'd observed and the Professor's hints. "Do you think that Travis and Erik had a side gig going?"

The Professor navigated the bumpy wooden bridge and turned onto the highway. "I suspect that's exactly the nature of their professional relationship. We've uncovered a variety of inconsistencies in Erik's record-keeping. Detective Mars believes Travis was selling to Whaleshead under the table and at below-the-market rates."

"Why?" That didn't line up with my theory he and Erik had been overcharging the resort.

"Our best guess at the moment is that he and Travis struck a clandestine deal. Their arrangement allows the SeaBreeze Bistro to boast the freshest fish in town at very competitive prices, and on Travis's end, he would have guaranteed sales without having to worry about market fluctuations or dealing with anyone in the middle."

"That makes sense. Until something went wrong." The farther we drove from the water, the less fishy the smell. I breathed easier and deeper.

"Until something went wrong," the Professor agreed. "The signs certainly point in Travis's direction—the moored boat, the towel you found at the scene, witness statements of them arguing, and staff reports about their ongoing issues with payments."

"Could Erik have been selling the overstock fish at a higher rate to exclusive private clients or other restaurants in Brookings?" I asked. That would explain why he had been so uptight about locking his office and keeping the financial records hidden.

"Detective Mars shared yesterday that there have been murmurs around town about Travis for the last few months. Other restaurants have complained about shortages of the best catch, but oddly, the SeaBreeze hasn't been affected."

"Even though it hasn't been open. Why would they still be receiving deliveries?" I drank in another gulp of pine-scented air as we zoomed along the highway. The tree line paralleled us to my right and the ocean to my left. It was always such a juxtaposition to see the mountains loom over the sea. They towered over the coastline like sturdy, unmovable giants.

"Exactly my question." The Professor picked up speed as we started to crest a hill and move away from the ocean. "I've been impressed with Detective Mars and her team. She had her staff interview a number of people in the industry, and in addition to rumors about shortages, there has been chatter about Travis's recently improved financial status."

"Okay, so if he and Erik had a deal going on, then Erik could have gotten greedy or the other way around. Maybe Erik threatened to call it off. Maybe he realized that people in town and the industry were catching on, and they needed to end their partnership, but Travis was too far in. He refused. Things came to a head, and he killed him." The words came out in a jumbled mess, like I was trying to make a vase out of a lumpy, wet ball of clay but couldn't get the pottery wheel to spin.

"It's certainly a consideration." The Professor pointed out a patch of tall, spiky purple lupine. The native wildflower was a favorite. In addition to his extensive Shakespearean knowledge, he was also a bird and wildflower buff. "It could be that Travis is delivering more than fish. We're looking into that angle. Perhaps the fish is a front for drugs or other illegal endeavors."

That made a lot of sense. "What will you do next?" I asked, wondering what I should do next.

"Detective Mars is reviewing both of their personal financial accounts and having her staff check for any other discrepancies. Next she'll do the same for Whaleshead and the restaurant. I'll continue to interview suspects and follow a few leads."

"Thanks for bringing me along. I'm not sure how much help I offered."

"Plenty, my dear. Plenty." He gave me a knowing smile that I couldn't quite decipher as he took the turn to Whaleshead, and we wound our way up the curvy road to the lodge.

We arrived back at the resort. There was more activity than earlier. The deck was packed with people enjoying lunch with a view. Families lugged backpacks and picnic baskets on the trails en route to the beach.

"If you happen to cross paths with Jess and she's willing to talk, I would appreciate any other insight," the Professor said, helping me out of the car. "But don't go to any extra trouble."

"No, I'd be happy to chat with her. I have some questions of my own, and since we already had an awkward meetup this morning, it will be natural for me to apologize and check in with her."

"Excellent, but be careful. Remember, there is a killer on the loose. I don't want you taking any unnecessary chances."

"I'll be safe, I promise." I gave him a kiss on the cheek. "You do the same."

We parted ways in the lobby, agreeing to connect for a beach bonfire later.

Not surprisingly, the reception desk was empty, and Jess was nowhere in sight. However, a group of tourists was trying to find someone to rent them surfboards while another group waited to check in with a pile of bags and suitcases.

Where did Jess go? And how did she still have a job when she was never at her desk?

I went to the kitchen and found Steph and Sterling packing lunch baskets. Premade sandwiches, cold pasta salads, fruit, and cookies were organized in neat rows. They had a system down. Steph checked off orders, handing Sterling each item, which he proceeded to tuck into picnic baskets labeled with guests' names and cabin numbers.

"Hey, great timing." Sterling held up a wicker basket with red and white gingham lining. "We just finished packing the best basket of the day. This one is for you."

"For me?" I pressed my hands to my chest. "I didn't order a basket, although now I'm wishing I had, because everything looks delicious."

"You're in luck. Carlos ordered it." Sterling pointed to

his name on the tag. "You're supposed to meet him and Ramiro on the beach. We were told to send you there with a basket once you got back from your excursion with the Professor."

I came closer. "Can I peek?"

"Not until you get to the beach," Sterling teased with a mischievous smile.

"Hey, I don't know if this is your domain, but there are some guests interested in renting surfboards, and Jess isn't at the front desk."

Steph pounded her palm onto her forehead. "She's such a flake."

"Can I do anything?"

"No, I'll go help them." Steph untied her apron.

I took the basket and went to the cabin to grab a few things before heading to the beach. As I took the pathway, the noon sun burned through the marine layer, filling me with a feeling of déjà vu and a slight dread.

Was it really only yesterday that Erik had tumbled to his death?

I passed the garden boxes humming with pollinators and followed the path as it curved into the trees. I was even more careful to watch my footing and stay far away from the edge. Pine needles baked into the dirt, giving the air a woodsy aroma. The scent reminded me of childhood descending on this very path through the lush, fragrant forest to the sandy shores below.

I spotted a motion to my left and stopped to get a better look as I came around the first bend.

It was nothing more than a skittish squirrel scrambling up the base of a tree.

*Jumpy much, Jules?*

The path was empty. I could hear the sounds of people at the beach and the soft rush of waves, but otherwise, it was me and the birds.

Usually, nature is my great escape, my happy place.

Today, the empty trails felt foreboding.

Despite it being unseasonably bright and warm, I couldn't shake the feeling that someone was watching me.

*It's just nerves.*

*Don't blow things out of proportion.*

I tried to be kinder to myself as I skirted around a pinecone in the center of the path and the spot where Erik had been killed came into view.

*Of course you're nervous, it's normal—a man died here yesterday.*

My little pep talk made my heart rate slow a bit.

That was until the infamous bench came into view, and I realized there was someone sitting on it, staring out into the sea.

"Jess?" I skidded to a halt and stared at her. She was sitting with her back to me, staring at the jagged rocks and coastline below like she was in a trance. Her body was as rigid as a statue.

"Jess, Jess, are you okay?" Blood rushed to my head. She wasn't responding. Was something wrong?

I stepped closer.

Why was her body so rigid?

Was it too rigid?

"Jess, it's Jules," I said cautiously.

*What if this is a trap?*

*What if she realized that I know about Erik's notebook?*

*Could this be how she killed him?*

*Is she about to do the same to me?*

I tried to silence the relentless questions bombarding my brain.

I moved close enough to tap her shoulder.

She startled and whipped her head around. "Oh my God! What are you doing?"

"Sorry. I called your name, but you didn't respond."

"I didn't?" She pounded her forehead with her fingertips. "I guess I'm kind of in a daze. I can't believe he's dead. I can't believe this is where he died. I wonder if he knew he wasn't going to survive the fall. Did it hurt? Did he die instantly? Do you think he's in a better place?"

Was she asking rhetorically?

Or could I be witnessing her trying to process her guilt?

Maybe they had been an item.

"I don't know," I answered truthfully. After my dad died, I didn't find platitudes helpful. People would say things like "He is in a better place" or "Time heals all wounds." Their words may have been well intended, but they weren't effective. I found it much easier to sit with my pain and grief. There was no escaping it, so it was better to let it in.

Jess rolled her shoulders like she was warming up for a yoga class. "It looks like you're on your way to the beach."

"Yeah, but if you have a minute, I'd love to chat."

She didn't look great. Her hair was frazzled and stringy like she'd gone for a swim in the ocean and toweled it off. Her cheeks looked hollowed in. Instead of her professional attire, she was dressed in a tie-dyed pair of baggy sweats and matching sweatshirt.

"Sure." She scooted over to make room on the bench for me, wrapping her hands in the pockets of her sweatshirt.

"I've been out here for an hour contemplating my bad life choices, so I might as well have company."

*Her bad life choices?*

*As in killing Erik?*

I sat next to her, using the picnic basket as a shield between us. I didn't think she would try anything in broad daylight, but I wasn't going to risk it. Erik had been killed in the middle of the afternoon. If she had done it, I wondered how she could have pushed him. She wasn't particularly tall. Her feet barely grazed the ground. How could she have overpowered him?

Maybe the element of surprise?

Or maybe an argument got out of control.

If they had tussled near the edge of the trail, Erik could also have lost his footing and slipped.

"What life choices?" I asked, trying to silence my active mind.

"Everything. I'm in way over my head." She swung her feet like a little kid.

She had said those exact words yesterday.

"You mentioned that before. I know Erik managed everything at the resort, but is it more than that?"

"How did you know? Is it obvious?" Her bottom lip quivered uncontrollably. She laced her fingers together and wiped her nose with the back of her sleeve. "I knew it was going to come out. I told him. I said that we had to be more careful. That people were going to talk, but he wouldn't listen. He said he was so in love with me that he didn't care if the entire world knew, but obviously, that wasn't true. I'm an idiot. I believed him, even though it's a lie."

Jess and Erik *had* been a couple!

That explained her mysterious disappearances and the rumors about an affair.

"You and Erik were in love?" I asked.

She recoiled, sticking her tongue out and shaking her head like she was about to gag. "Erik? What? No."

"I'm confused. Was Erik in love with you, and you didn't reciprocate his feelings?" My internal protector mode switched on. Had Erik used his position as her supervisor to try to coerce her? If that was the case, I wanted to get the Professor involved in our conversation immediately because that completely changed the narrative.

"No. I'm not talking about Erik. I'm talking about Cody." She yanked her hands free from her sweatshirt and massaged her head with her index and middle fingers.

"Cody? Who's Cody?"

"One of the cabin owners. You wouldn't know him." She made circles in the dirt with her foot.

"I'm still not tracking."

She kicked the dirt and bark chips around, rubbing away the circle like she was trying to wipe out a memory. Then she let out a heavy sigh. "Everyone is going to hear about it soon enough, so I guess there's no point in trying to keep it a secret anymore."

I waited for her to say more. Over the years, I've learned that holding silence and space for someone is the best way to encourage conversation.

"Cody and I met last year right after I took the job. He spent the summer here working on a fishing boat part time—on and off when he was here at the resort. He and his wife were separated. She stayed home in Portland and filed for divorce. We got pretty close. Their marriage hadn't worked for either of them. They got married right out of high school and then grew up and grew apart." She rolled her neck from side to side as she sighed. "Then, out of the blue, she showed up shortly after the holidays and begged him to give their marriage another chance. He's not interested, but it's complicated because, technically, she owns the cabin. We've been meeting in secret. This is our spot. We'll meet here after the sun starts to go down and have a cocktail and watch the ocean together, but Erik caught us and threatened to tell everyone. Now it looks bad for me, really bad." She pressed her heel into the dirt, kicking another rock hard enough to send it sailing over the ledge. "I'm sure the police are going to arrest me."

# Chapter Twenty-one

"Why does it look bad for you?" I asked, already having a sense of Jess's answer, but I wanted to hear it from her.

She reached into her sweats and pulled out a crumpled sheet of paper. She smoothed it on her thighs and passed it to me. "Because of this. This was in Erik's notebook on his desk. He'd been following me. He knew each of my meeting spots with Cody. He was tracking them. I don't know what he was going to do with the information, but I know it wasn't good."

"Was he blackmailing you?" I couldn't believe she was being so forthcoming. Did this mean that I was right? Had the gloves been because she went back to Erik's office after I left her and ripped out the pages?

"No, not officially. He threatened to tell Cody's wife about us."

That sounded like blackmail to me.

"And did you argue? Was there an accident? If there was, it's important to come clean about everything that happened. The Professor—Doug—is my stepfather. He's very wise and kind. If you tell him the truth, he'll be fair and advocate for you."

She crinkled her brow and scrunched her nose. "What are you talking about?"

"If you accidentally pushed Erik off the cliff, the police can help. They may be able to reduce the charges if you explain what happened and tell them it was an accident."

"Wait—wait," she stuttered. "Wait, no." She held her hands up to stop me. "I didn't kill Erik. I wasn't anywhere near here when he was killed."

"You weren't at the front desk, though." I pushed the issue to see if she would tell me more. "You've been missing from your station a lot this weekend.

"Yeah, because I've been with Cody. I haven't wanted to say anything to the detectives because it's complicated with his wife. I swear their marriage was over before we hooked up. Not on paper, but they've been separated. I don't feel good about sneaking around. This wasn't what I imagined for my relationship, but we didn't want to give her anything she could use against him in the divorce proceedings. And he still cares about his soon-to-be ex-wife. He's not in love with her anymore, but he's a good guy. That's why we were so careful and made sure to meet here at times he knew she wouldn't see us."

"Why did you rip the page out of Erik's notebook?" I wanted to believe her. She sounded sincere, but until there was definitive proof, I didn't want to take what she was saying at face value.

"I wasn't thinking. I got the call early this morning about the broken toilet. I'm so frustrated with Hoff. It's his job. He's supposed to be on call. That's why his housing is comped in addition to his salary. It's one of the perks of working here. Whaleshead might not be fancy, but not having to pay rent is a lifesaver. Anyway, Hoff didn't answer, and I couldn't leave the homeowner waiting. I went to the lobby to find supplies, but Erik's office door was unlocked. I don't know why; it was like the universe was giving me a gift. I flipped through the notebook and found the pages about me after I saw you. I ripped them out and instantly regretted it. I was going to toss them over the cliff here, but then I realized that would be idiotic—if the police search the area, they'd find the pages which would only further implicate me."

New questions began to form, like where Hoff was this morning and who else knew about Jess's affair.

"Is that why you were wearing gloves?" I asked, shifting on the bench to try and get comfortable."

"Huh, gloves?"

"The blue gloves," I said. "You were wearing them this morning when I bumped into you. Were you planning to destroy the evidence in Erik's notebook?

"No, no. It wasn't like that at all. I really had to fix the toilet." She pressed the paper on her legs in an attempt to smooth it out. "Trust me, I would have been doing anything else. Fixing toilets isn't supposed to be in my job description, but I love this place and I couldn't leave the cabin owners hanging."

I dropped it for the time being. "Was Erik the only one who knew about you and Cody?"

She folded the paper and stuffed it in her back pocket. "No, Mary Beth figured it out. She said she spotted us, but I don't know how because her cabin and studio are on the opposite side of the resort. She's been decent about not saying anything. I'm not sure I trust her, though. She's an odd woman."

"Odd, how?"

"I don't know. She has a mean streak. You should see some of her art—it's super dark. You can almost see her rage on the canvas. Have you been in her studio?"

"Not yet."

"You should go see it if you have a chance. She's talented and slightly twisted. You know, you said I've been missing, but she's the one who is constantly flaking out. She was supposed to be helping set up her display at the lodge and restaurant twice and never showed. We had to scramble to get everything ready before opening night because she kept flaking."

I made a mental note to add a trip to Mary Beth's gallery to my list. "What about Hoff? There seemed to be a lot of tension between him and Erik. Do you think he could have done it?"

"Yeah." She thought about it for a minute. "I've been thinking there's a good chance that he and Lucy did it together. They've been hanging out a bunch and having hushed conversations. She was trying to get people to sign off on the resort sale last night. It was like she was suddenly in a rush to make it happen. I don't know what else they could be working on together."

"Do you know any more about her plans for development? It sounded like Erik wasn't a roadblock."

"That's not true. He was definitely a roadblock. She had the most to gain with him dead. That's why I think Hoff did it. He did her dirty work for her in exchange for being guaranteed a position and housing at the new resort. She told me she was going to town for a council meeting, but I saw her and Hoff on my way back from meeting Cody. They're working together, I would bet my life on it."

"Let's not bet any lives." I knew it was a figure of speech, but one death was too many for me. "There's already been enough loss."

"You know what I mean." She rubbed her fingers together like she was trying to soothe herself.

"Have you told the police all of this?"

"Not all of it," she admitted with another sigh. "I knew they would ask where I'd been when I saw Hoff and Lucy, and then I'd have to tell them about Cody. Do you think they already know?"

"I think it's highly likely that in their extensive search of Erik's office and the property, they've already documented everything in the notebook." I didn't want to tell her directly what I knew, but it wasn't such a stretch to imagine that the police were well ahead of her.

"Oh no, it's going to look like I killed him. He has this bench circled with my name," she wailed.

"That's why I encourage you to call Detective Mars or the Professor and share everything you've shared with me immediately. The longer you put it off, the worse it's going to look for you. They'll also be able to confirm your alibi with Cody, which will only help you."

"Yeah, you're right." She rounded her shoulders like she was about to cry. "I'm just worried that they're going to ask me why I didn't tell them this sooner."

"I'm sure they will," I said truthfully. I didn't want to give her false hope that Detective Mars or the Professor would let her off the hook for not sharing this critical information sooner. "The only thing you can do is be honest, and don't leave anything out this time."

She rubbed the top of her sweats as if trying to create friction or build up the confidence to follow through. "I guess this forces the issue between Cody and me. No more hiding. It's a relief, if I'm being honest. I'm tired of it. I'm sure you must think I'm a terrible person."

It wasn't my job to judge her. I thought back to my conversation with the Professor and took my lead from him. "I think the beautiful thing about choices is we can always make new ones."

"Thanks for listening. I feel better."

"Good. Are you going to speak with the police now? I can give you the Professor's number."

"I have it. They both gave me their contact information. I'm going to call them now before I lose the courage." She brushed her hands together.

"Smart." I reached for the picnic basket. "Hey, one more thing before I go. Did you notice anything odd about Erik and Travis's interactions?"

"You mean Travis, the fisherman from Catch of the Day?"

"Yeah. Erik handled payments and deliveries, right?"

"Everything. Erik didn't trust any of us. Every financial transaction went through him, but come to think of it, I did overhear them arguing a couple of days ago—it was about payments. Erik is always late paying vendors. Half the time, I'm surprised that the lights stay on at the resort."

"Was Travis angry that Erik hadn't paid him for delivery?"

"No, that's the weird thing. Travis didn't bring any fish with him that day. They barricaded themselves in Erik's office. I wasn't intentionally eavesdropping, but it was impossible not to hear. Travis kept saying something about his cut and how it needed to be bigger. I didn't think about it at the time, but now that I'm remembering, it was weird."

"You should make sure to pass that on to the detectives, too." I stood and hooked the picnic basket over my arm. "If you need a listening ear, I'm around anytime."

"Thanks, I appreciate it."

I left her and continued down the path to the beach. I was eager for sand between my toes and sun on my cheeks. However, my conversation with Jess raised a number of new possibilities. Could she be right about Hoff and Lucy working together? What was the truth when it came to Lucy's redevelopment plans? Was Erik the last thing standing between Lucy's grand vision for a new and improved Whaleshead? What did Hoff stand to gain with Erik's death—job security, a more prestigious role?

Jess's comment about Mary Beth's dark side made me very curious to see the rest of her artwork. Could one of her paintings be the clue?

And then there was Travis.

It was hard to ignore the tangible evidence against him, like the fact that he claimed to be on the water fishing at the time of Erik's death, yet his boat was moored at the dock. Was Erik's death merely about financial gain?

The problem was I kept adding reasons that everyone could have killed him. What I needed to do was start eliminating suspects.

# Chapter Twenty-two

I found Carlos, Mom, and Ramiro on the beach. They were hard to miss with their large yellow-and-blue-striped sun umbrellas, blankets, beach chairs, and inflatable balls. Waves rushed ashore, devouring the sand. The tide was out, giving beachgoers ample room to wander among the tide pools, searching for purple sea urchins, starfish, and anemones. Kids screeched as they traipsed ankle-deep through the frigid waters, splashing in the waves.

"Did you move in for a week?" I teased, giving a wide berth to a group of preteens constructing a towered sand-castle nearby. "How did you cart everything down?"

"Down was no problem," Mom said, peering at me from beneath her polka-dot sun visor. "It's up that's going to make our muscles fire, but not to worry, Carlos drove the car, so you don't have to make the trek back up."

"That's sweet." I caught his eye.

He blew me a kiss. "Anything for you, mi querida." He looked completely at home on the beach in his light blue swim trunks. The humidity brought out the natural curl in his hair, and his skin glistened under the sun.

"Did someone say lunch?" Ramiro asked, running over

to greet me. His cheeks were flushed with color, and his skin was coated in sand, like he was prepping for a scrubbing massage.

"Yes, and I was told that under no circumstances could I peek until we were all together, so have at it." I handed him the basket.

He plopped onto the center of the beach blankets and opened the basket. "We've been playing volleyball for two hours. My legs are burning. I promise I won't eat the entire basket, but you might have to hold me back." Ramiro lifted each item from the basket. They were wrapped in parchment paper with notes and little doodles handwritten in Sharpie. I recognized Steph's delicate scroll. It was a lovely touch. "Ham and cheese sandwiches on buttered baguettes, French onion flatbread, quiche Lorraine muffins, Camembert cheese, plums and grapes, and madeleines."

"I sense a theme," Mom said, putting her book down. "Très French."

"Lance will be thrilled." I surveyed the beach. Couples strolled hand in hand through the foamy surf, teens boogie-boarded, and kids dragged heavy buckets through the sand. "Are they meeting us for lunch?"

"Oh, yes, he and Arlo should be here any minute." Mom glanced behind her to the rocky monoliths jutting out of waves. "They went for a walk and promised not to miss lunch."

"How could they with this?" Carlos pulled out a low beach chair and helped me sit. "Can I pour you a sparkling lemonade?"

"Yes, please." I leaned my head back and soaked up the sun.

"How was your outing with Doug?" Mom asked, helping Ramiro unwrap the food and set out plates.

"Good. Have you seen him since we got back?"

"No." Mom plated sandwiches and passed around napkins and bamboo silverware. "He texted to let me know he'll be wrapped up most of the day in further investigation. He mentioned reviewing footage of the council meeting and boat dock, so I assume that's at least two key suspects that he's narrowing in on."

"Unfortunately, I think they have even more suspects right now." I was about to fill them in when Lance and Arlo approached our temporary enclave.

"Hello, hello, my lovelies," Lance called, wiggling his fingers in a greeting. "If you're talking murder, you're in deep, deep trouble, Juliet. Were you about to dish without me?"

"He never takes a break, does he?" I asked Arlo.

Arlo shrugged. "He hates it when I say this, but he's like a sleeping cat when it's just the two of us. This is all for your benefit—so performative. He'd have pages upon pages of notes for an actor bringing this kind of energy to the stage."

Lance gasped. "Lies, blatant lies." He gave Arlo a terse smile before breaking out in a wide grin. "Come on, hit us with the goods, darling."

Mom passed around plates.

Ramiro scarfed down his lunch in three bites, then grabbed two more sandwiches and hurried off to join his friends in their extended game of beach volleyball.

I helped myself to a sandwich, a slice of onion flatbread, a muffin, and fruit to start. I skipped the soft cheese. There would be plenty of time to enjoy Camembert after the twins were born. "Before we were so rudely interrupted, I was telling them our list of suspects is growing instead of shrinking," I said, hardening my gaze at Lance.

"Apologies." He made the sorry sign on his chest. "I simply cannot miss a single detail. This case requires the utmost concentration. Do tell, you must have one suspect who is on the top of your list."

I told them about Travis and his lie about fishing in the Pacific while in reality his boat had been tethered to the dock. "The Professor has irrefutable video evidence—his boat, *Catch of the Day*, was moored all afternoon. I don't get why he would lie so blatantly. He must know the police will find out. It also makes me wonder about the towel I found on the bench. He could have followed Erik right after we saw him in the kitchen," I said, turning to Carlos. "That would explain why the towel was there."

"Sí, if they fought, he could have accidentally dropped the towel and forgotten about it in his hurry to get away before anyone spotted him," Carlos suggested.

"Right." I nodded in agreement. "There's also Jess. She and I had a lengthy conversation right before I came to the beach. I found her on the bench, contemplating her bad life choices—her words, not mine. At first, I thought she was confessing that she and Erik had a fling, but it turns out she's been in a secret relationship with a cabin owner."

"The question is, do we believe her?" Lance popped a grape in his mouth and crushed it between his teeth. "She could be spinning a sob story to try and win you over."

I wasn't sure I would classify sneaking around with a married man as a sob story, but he could be right about her. She had sounded genuinely upset, but for all I knew, she could be a great actor.

"Jess mentioned that Hoff and Lucy have been working closely together," I continued. "If they have a mutual goal to demolish Whaleshead as we know it and build a shiny new resort, that gives them a clear motive."

"Hoff as the henchman," Lance said. "I can see that. She could have bought him off."

"They were both near the scene of the crime right after the murder. Hoff's alibi is flimsy at best, and we're waiting to hear what the Professor learns about Lucy's motive and whereabouts when Erik was pushed."

"That could seal the case against them." Mom offered me a chocolate-dipped madeleine. The scallop-shaped French butter cakes were a culinary treat. I was glad that Steph was stretching herself. First soufflés, now madeleines. They were giving the SeaBreeze menu a major "glow-up," as Bethany would say.

"Pass those my way, please." Lance ran his tongue along his lips. "I read an article in *Bon Appetit* many years ago that has attached itself permanently to my brain cells. It went something like, 'The cookie that launched a thousand memories—a literary masterpiece.'"

"I'll eat to that." Arlo bit into the soft, pillowy cake-like cookie.

"The other person we can't dismiss is Mary Beth," I said, helping myself to a coconut madeleine. "Jess said that Mary Beth confronted her about her affair and mentioned our artist-in-residence has a dark side that apparently comes out in her paintings."

"The tortured creative soul. It can be a curse if not channeled properly," Lance said in all seriousness.

"Jess suggested we visit Mary Beth's gallery. It was almost like she was hinting there's a clue in one of the paintings, although that seems far-fetched." I was impressed when I bit into the scalloped, tender cookie. The butter-forward sponge was the ultimate cake-cookie hybrid. I thought I just might daydream about these for days or weeks to come. I had a bad feeling they were going to be my new pregnancy obsession.

"Yesterday, we would have said that Erik not only falling to his death but being pushed was far-fetched," Mom added wisely.

"So true, Helen." Lance tipped his head in a rare show of brevity. "I say after a leisurely lunch and an afternoon siesta, we visit said gallery."

"I vote beach nap," I said, stretching out farther on the blanket.

"Me too." Mom reached into her tote and pulled out a paperback and an e-reader. "I brought a book and my Kindle just in case."

I used a towel to prop up my head and let my eyes drift shut. The calming sound of the waves breaking on the shore mingled with the nearby laughter of Ramiro and his friends playing volleyball. I found myself sinking deeper into the warm sand. Blurry visions of Mary Beth splattering blood-red paint on a giant canvas and Hoff and Lucy counting stacks of money flickered in and out of my head. Visions of chocolate-dipped madeleines floating above the waves like the kiteboarders made me semi-aware that I was dreaming or daydreaming, but I was too content to want to wake up.

The next thing I knew, Carlos was gently shaking my shoulder.

"Sorry to disturb you, Julieta, but I agreed to assist Sterling with dinner preparations."

I yawned and stretched, gazing out toward the ocean. The sun was lower on the horizon. My fingers tingled. I shook them awake as I sat up and inhaled deeply, rubbing sleep and sand from my eyes. "How long was I out?"

Lance and Arlo had already left. Mom was propped in a low beach chair reading her book, and Ramiro and his friends had swapped volleyball for a game of Frisbee.

"Almost two hours." Carlo smiled.

"No way." I blinked, adjusting to the sunlight.

"Sí, you were snoozing." He rested his head in his hands and closed his eyes briefly. "I might have even heard a snore or two."

"I don't snore." I pursed my lips and jutted out my chin.

"When you're pregnant with twins, you snore. It's adorable." Carlos ducked to avoid being hit by the towel I launched in his direction. "Do you want to stay? I can give you a ride, or I can leave the car for you. Either way is fine with me."

"I'll come back. I'd like to take a shower and rinse off the sand." That was true, and I also wanted to check out Mary Beth's gallery. He helped me to my feet. We gathered our things, said good-bye to Mom and Ramiro, and headed back to Whaleshead.

I was happy to have a ride. The trek up the hill might have done me in after everything that had happened in the stretch of two days. I still couldn't believe it was only yesterday that Erik had been killed. It didn't seem possible. On one hand it felt like we'd been at the beach for days, and on the other it felt like we'd just arrived.

Carlos dropped me off at our cabin. "Julieta, I want you

to rest. Read. Relax. Put your toes in the hot tub and enjoy the afternoon. I'll assist Sterling with dinner. You're banned from the kitchen or any work for the rest of the day, sí?"

"If you insist." I gave him a broad smile.

"You don't fool me, Julieta—I know you and Lance will be traipsing around, but be careful and take it easy, please. Don't overdo it."

"I promise, I won't. I'm looking forward to reading on the deck with a nice cup of tea."

"I like the sound of that." He left me with a kiss.

I appreciated that he didn't try to convince me to leave the case alone. He knew me better than that. I would take his warning to heart. I had zero plans to put myself in any kind of danger, but I still wanted to check out the gallery. First, I needed a hot shower and new clothes.

The shower felt refreshing. I let the warm water wash over me and scrubbed my sandy skin with orange and lemon soap, creating my own personal spa. Once I'd changed and tied my hair into a ponytail, I grabbed my book and a cup of tea and followed Carlos's instructions.

The deck had a view of the long driveway and turnaround in front of the lodge, but if I moved the chair to the very end, I could just make out a hint of the sea. I positioned an Adirondack chair so it had a peekaboo view of the ocean through the trees and escaped into my book.

The story was a modern mashup of Shakespeare's *Merchant of Venice* and Jane Austen's *Emma*. I got sucked in immediately, abandoning my ruminations about Erik's murder. My tea went cold as I devoured the story.

I needed to take more time for myself. In Ashland, I always had dozens of projects in the works, people to manage, and fires to put out. I'd been intentional about carving out family time—this past year. That was one of the many gifts of having Ramiro live with us. He forced me to reprioritize. I was grateful for every minute I got to spend with him and Carlos. Making space for myself was my next hurdle, especially since once the twins arrived, I had a feeling there wasn't going to be a minute to spare.

My reading break was cut short an hour later when Travis's truck rumbled up the driveway and stopped in front of the lodge. Had he changed his mind about delivering to the resort? This was my chance to talk to him alone. I wanted to follow up on our earlier conversation and ask him about his boat.

I left my book and hurried to stop him before he unloaded crates of fresh fish. He was still in his waders and boots. I wondered if he'd come straight from the boat. Also, this was the time he claimed to be on the water yesterday. Why wasn't he on his boat now if this was his peak fishing window? His story had too many holes.

"Do you need a hand?" I approached his truck from the side, so as not to startle him.

"Oh, hey, it's you." He stacked crates of salmon and halibut on ice on the ground. "Nah, I got it."

"Do you deliver daily? As a restaurant owner, I know there's nothing like being able to serve the very freshest fish and produce." I snuck a glance into the back of the truck. There were dozens of plastic-lidded tubs filled with fish on ice. Nothing seemed out of the ordinary, but seeing his packed truck made me even more curious if he could be using his fishing vessel and delivery truck for other purposes—like to smuggle drugs, perhaps?

Maybe he and Erik were involved in something darker.

I knew there was a serious and deepening drug crisis in the region. Could he and Erik have been involved in criminal activity? Drug smuggling that went wrong? Weapons? My mind raced to dozens of possibilities—all of which would mean he could be very dangerous.

"We live on the coast. Every restaurant in town has fish on the menu." Travis looked at me like he was stating the obvious.

He was, but I had to open the conversation somehow. I didn't want to say anything that might upset or trigger him. I didn't know what I was dealing with in terms of his personality, so I had to play it cool.

"I'm surprised you're not fishing now." I nodded toward the ocean. "I thought you mentioned this was potentially a good time to be out on the water."

"It is." He grabbed another tub and set it on the ground.

He was a man of few words. Extracting a complete sentence from him was as difficult as trying to extract a cake from an ungreased pan.

"But you're here now." I stated the obvious again and prepared myself for a curt retort.

"My boat's broken. It's wrecked. Pretty hard to fish without a boat." He wiped his hands on his waders.

"Wrecked?" I said with genuine surprise. He hadn't mentioned anything about that during our conversation with the Professor earlier. I knew his boat was moored, but wrecked was another story.

"Yeah, the fuel line is busted. It's been docked for almost a week. Such a bummer. I depend on my boat for everything—my livelihood, my living. It's sucks, and it's not a cheap fix. The repairs are going to set me back a ton of cash."

My skin tingled, and the tiny hairs on my arms shot up. Had I just caught him in a blatant lie?

I knew I should probably let it go and tell the Professor so that he and Detective Mars could question Travis further.

But was I really in danger, out in the open in front of the lodge? Could he smack me with one of the crates or take off and make an escape?

Doubtful.

There were dozens of people outside on the deck.

Travis wouldn't risk hurting me in broad daylight in front of an audience.

I had to go for it and ask.

"How were you fishing yesterday if your boat is broken?" I held my breath, waiting for his reply. Maybe I should have left the questioning to the Professor. I never anticipated this twist. Why would he admit something so damning?

"I've been using my buddy's boat." His eyes slanted, and his mouth hung open slightly as if he were coming to a realization himself. "Wait a minute. Wait, wait, wait. Is that what those detective's questions were about this morning?"

"You'll have to ask him," I replied. "Why didn't you mention that your boat was broken, though?"

"I didn't know I needed to. I told him the truth—I was out fishing. Does he think I killed Erik?"

"You failed to mention your boat was broken and moored. Why wouldn't you have told him that you borrowed a friend's boat? If other witnesses noted that your boat was on the dock, that doesn't match the statement you gave the police, does it?"

"No. It's not like that. I answered his questions. Everyone knows my boat is busted. It's not a secret. I've been borrowing my buddy's boat. It's what we do—we help each other out. This is a small community. We make our living on the sea."

"It seems like a critical detail you left out."

"Because it didn't matter. I thought he was asking everyone questions. Why would I be a suspect?"

I considered my choices. Was Travis telling the truth about his boat? It should be relatively easy for the Professor to confirm his story with his friend. Or was he scrambling to cover up for his slip because he had killed Erik?

# Chapter Twenty-three

Travis stared at me, the horror of his situation sinking in. "Oh, crap. They really think I killed Erik? Why? I didn't say anything about my boat being busted because everybody knew. I swear. The docks are like a family. We all help each other out. Everyone knows everyone else's business. I wasn't hiding anything, because it wasn't a secret. You can ask anyone. We can go right now."

I half expected him to get in the truck and beg me to come with him.

"Look, like I said, you'll have to speak directly with the detectives. I can tell you that I've heard rumors floating around the resort about a deal between you and Erik, so it looks pretty bad that you lied about your boat."

"But I didn't lie." Red splotches spread up Travis's neck to his cheeks as his jaw tensed. He sucked in air through his nose and rocked back on his boots. "Are you serious? This is nuts."

"I'm only repeating what I've heard. I have no idea what's true."

"This isn't fair. I'm not a killer. I didn't touch the guy."

Travis pounded his fist on his truck bed. "Leave it to Erik to mess with me even after he's dead."

"Leave it to Erik how?" I wondered how long it would be before someone walked by. I was so close to getting the truth out of him that I didn't want to be interrupted now. The lobby was mere feet away. Odds were good someone would show up to check in or return a surfboard. I had to get as much out of him as possible now.

"Okay, yeah, fine—we got in a fight, but I swear I didn't kill him." He banged on the tailgate with both fists. "Erik fought with everyone. No one liked the guy. I'll admit that. I didn't like him either, but I swear I didn't kill him. I was fishing with my buddy yesterday. I did your friends a favor by dropping off the delivery. I didn't have to do that. Erik owed me. The only reason I delivered was because I felt bad for those two. It's tough breaks working for Erik, especially young chefs like them. But I went straight out on the water after I left here. You can check with my friend. He'll tell you. You can call him right now."

I wasn't sure why he thought I could do anything about his situation or his alibi.

"What kind of arrangement did you have with Erik?"

"He had connections with exclusive clients, wealthy guests who have cabins at Whaleshead for investment purposes only. He approached me because he wanted to be able to offer some of his high-profile clients special bonuses."

"Like fish?" That didn't add up. Was my theory about smuggling drugs or weapons correct? I took a step backward, just in case. I didn't think Travis was dangerous, but I wasn't taking any chances.

Travis's cheeks burned with heat. "Not just any kind of fish, fish that isn't exactly legal."

Now I was really intrigued.

"You probably know this since you work in the restaurant industry. There are tight regulations on what we can fish and when we can fish. Erik was aware of those laws and encouraged me to bend them. Pacific razor clams, Dungeness crab, king salmon, and steelhead trout all have strict rules. You can't sell wild steelhead or harvest clams or crabs out of season, but there's a very strong underground market for smuggled delicacies, and Erik wanted to capitalize on that."

Smuggled delicacies?

Never would I have predicted this was what Travis would share.

I was familiar with regulations, and what Travis and Erik had schemed up was most certainly not legal. Still, I was relieved we were talking about smuggling fish, and not something much more dangerous like narcotics.

"We'd sometimes have bidding wars if I was able to bring in a rare catch out of season or break my quota. No one got hurt, and I pocketed some extra cash." He shrugged. "It's not like I'm a millionaire. The fishing industry is tough and getting tougher by the day. I'm always on the grind, trying to make ends meet, pay my rent, afford groceries and gas."

I felt for him. Earning a living wage was becoming more challenging every day. "Did anyone else know about your arrangement?"

"Nope. Just me and Erik." His eyes drifted to the lodge. "He paid me under the table in cash, so there were no records or anything."

"Were you still working with him when he died?" The music on the deck grew louder. I glanced in that direction, wondering if Steph and Sterling had turned the speakers up. Nearly every table was taken. People chatted happily and toasted with fluted glasses of bubbly drinks. That was a good sign for the restaurant.

"Yeah. I was supposed to deliver a special order today. Now it's going to another friend, a restaurant in town who won't ask any questions."

"Did Erik want to end your partnership?"

"No. Why would he? We were both making money."

"But you were fighting about payment shortly before he died."

"Yeah, that was his idea. He thought we could sell it better and distance ourselves from each other by acting like we had beef. He paid me in cash right after that."

"And you didn't have any intention of ending your deal?"

"No way. Now I have to see if I can find someone new. I've got a system down and know how to avoid Fish and Wildlife regulators. I'm not giving this up. I'm going to see what my friend has to say about striking a deal. I just have to be careful who I tell. I don't want anyone to give me up. That was the great thing about Erik—I knew he had my back." He lifted another crate from the truck. "Look, I've got to go. I have more deliveries. I know you're connected with the police. Will you tell your detective friend about my boat? I'd appreciate it if you'd keep what I told you on the down-low. Word around here spreads like wildfire. If people see me with the police, they'll talk. It's bad for business. Gossip around here is the worst, and I've already had a couple of run-ins back in the day with the police."

"You need to speak with Detective Mars or the Professor as soon as possible." I wished they were here now. This was potentially game-changing information for their investigation. "I'm betting you're one of their top suspects. If you want to clear your name, they have to know about your boat. I won't say anything about your arrangement with Erik, but the police are looking into everyone's financial records. It will be much better for you if you come clean with them about everything. I'm sure they'll be willing to speak with you somewhere in private."

"But they might shut me down and revoke my commercial license."

"If I were you, that's a risk I would take. The alternative is doing jail time for a murder you didn't commit."

He sounded dejected, hanging his head and punching his fist into his palm. "Yeah, I guess so. Freaking Erik. I never should have partnered with the guy."

"Murder is a serious charge," I said, wishing I had any kind of authority in this situation. I needed to contact the Professor—stat. "You know your towel was found at the scene of the crime, too."

"My towel?"

I motioned to the back of his truck to his Catch of the Day towel. "A towel just like that was found on the bench where he died."

"So what? I gave Erik a bunch of those. Another buddy of mine gave me a good deal on two hundred towels to use as marketing. I've got stacks of them on the boat. Erik probably had it with him—I don't know why. But I never left the lodge. Like I told you, I dropped off the fish and took off."

He sounded truthful, but it wasn't up to me to decide. "Regardless, you should get in touch with the police."

"Yeah, I get it." He rubbed his forehead and temples. "Let me drop off this order, and then I'll get in touch with them."

I watched him heave the crates over his shoulder. As soon as he was inside, I called the Professor. He didn't answer, so I left him a detailed message explaining everything Travis had revealed to me. Hopefully, he'd get the message before Travis had a chance to reach out to his friend to provide him with an alibi.

I tended to believe him, but it was the Professor and Detective Mars's job to follow up on his claims and potentially rule him out as a suspect.

Travis's explanation sounded plausible. I didn't get the impression he was the type of person who would make up an elaborate story involving contraband fish on the fly, but I didn't trust him either. It could be that part of his story was true, but he'd rewritten the ending. If Erik had decided to end their partnership or if Travis had gotten greedy and decided to cut Erik out as the middleman, that would have given him a solid motive for murder.

I was about to return to my book, but my phone buzzed with a text from Lance.

"Mocktails and a little murder chat? Meet me on the SeaBreeze deck in twenty?"

I could go for a mocktail, and I was curious to hear if Lance had learned anything new, so I shot him back a "Yes" and went into the lobby. It was empty as usual. Since I had a few minutes before meeting Lance, I took a closer look at Mary Beth's art.

None of the displayed pieces struck me as dark or full of rage as Jess had suggested. There was a variety of watercolors depicting scenes from the resort, the beach, and the surrounding trails. Her work was fluid and smooth. I could almost hear the sound of the waves in her broad strokes. There were paintings of the resort from the vantage point of the deck and the hiking trails. Many of her pieces were of the same swath of the beach but with small points of differentiation—cloud cover and rain hitting the waves on a gloomy winter day, a fishing boat cutting through the glass-like waters, a lighthouse at the cliff's edge, sea lions frolicking in the waves.

Small notes and pricing were posted next to each painting. Some were titled, and some were simply numbered. Each painting was original, and Mary Beth's rates ranged from the high hundreds for her smaller pieces to five figures for her larger canvases.

There was one painting in particular that drew me in—it was the same canvas I'd noticed when Mary Beth was hanging her artwork. Maybe it called to me because, like Erik's notebook, it featured the very bench where he was killed. Out of every potential location around Whaleshead, why had Mary Beth picked this specific spot?

Sure, the view was incredible, but there were plenty of other lookout spots along the trail.

Could she be leaving clues in her painting? Hiding things in plain sight?

I read the description. The painting had already sold.

Her notes read *Sunset at Whaleshead. Killer views of the killer whales.*

I looked closer and noticed she had painted a pod of orcas bobbing on the waves. The majestic creatures were dwindling in number. Not long ago, I read an article about how Oregon was considering adding them to the endangered species list.

Mary Beth was lucky to have captured them in the wild. I wondered when she had painted the scene.

There was no date on the note.

Her phrasing, "killer views," gave me goose bumps, but the clever title matched the painting. Chances were good that I was reading way too much into it.

"Well, aren't you a vision?" Lance slunk toward me with long, exaggerated, catlike strides.

"I'm wearing capris and a T-shirt." I ran my hands over my outfit.

"You're wearing them well, darling. That's the key." He struck a pose, stretching one arm to his knee and resting the other on his chin. "Much like yours truly. What do you think of the 'fit, as the kids like to say?"

"The kids?"

"Don't leave a debonair hanging." He'd changed into white tailored slacks and a pale pink paisley long-sleeve shirt. His matching boat shoes with a tiny ship pattern finished the look to perfection. A white sweater was tied around his neck like he was auditioning for the part of a preppy character from an '80s movie. "I've changed into my evening attire. What do you think?"

"Lance, there's never been a single instance when you haven't been the best-dressed person in the room, let alone in the entire resort, theater, or town."

"Oh, stop. You're making me blush." He fanned his cheeks. "But do feel free to go on. I look devilishly handsome in pink if do say so myself."

"Arlo's a lucky man."

"He is, isn't he? I try to remind him of this most days. We wouldn't want him losing sight of that, would we?"

"As if there was a chance," I scoffed. "Arlo is absolutely smitten with you."

"Same. Same." He dropped the act and cleared his throat. "There's actually something I've been wanting to talk to you about." He retied his sweater and wandered toward the fireplace.

I followed him, glad for once that Jess was nowhere to be seen and we had the lobby to ourselves. He sat on the hearth and patted the spot next to him. His eyes were soft and filled with an inner sparkle.

I waited for him to speak. He paused, laying his hand on his heart and swallowing like he was reining in his emotions.

I cherished the rare opportunities when Lance broke character and revealed the rawer pieces of himself. I could tell this was one of those times.

"I've been starting to think about our long-term plans," he said, forming a steeple with his hands. "I can't believe I'm going to say this out loud, but, Jules, it might be time to for me to pop the question soon."

"Are you serious?" I clapped my hand over my mouth, unable to contain my delight. "A Lance and Arlo wedding, oh my goodness, I don't have any words to express how happy this makes me."

"Slow down. Don't get ahead of yourself yet. I said it might be time, emphasis on *might*. I am ridiculously happy, which terrifies me. Life feels too good. I keep waiting for the bottom to drop out or something to go horrifically wrong."

"That's the anxiety talking," I said, recognizing my own patterns. "I know it's hard to silence the negative voices in your head, but you deserve happiness. The bottom isn't going to drop out. Getting engaged and married is only going to deepen your connection. I've watched you and Arlo, and what you have is special. It's real. That's not going to change or go away. I can tell you from experience it's only going to get better. I can't guarantee that you won't go through hard times, but you'll go through them together."

His eyes misted. He gave my hand a light squeeze. "Thanks. It's scary to love him this much. It's a first for me."

"I get it, and I agree, but taking the leap is always worth it."

"Says the woman who jaunted off to elope in Marseilles." He nudged my waist.

"I highly recommend it, but selfishly, I want a Lance wedding." I couldn't even fathom how fantastic his nuptials would be. "We get to bake the cake regardless, right?"

"An elopement might be just for us, but don't worry your pretty head. I'll never turn down the opportunity to throw a bash, and Torte must make the cake and cater the entire event. I wouldn't have it any other way."

Was Lance actually going to propose?

"How are you planning to pop the question?" My toes bounced on the floor in eager anticipation. Between Lance's romantic heart and theatrical flair, I couldn't begin to imagine what he might have in store for a proposal.

He tapped his fingers together. "I don't know, darling. Is that a bad sign?"

"What do you mean?" I leaned closer, trying to get a better read on what was bothering him.

"There's so much pressure. It has to be perfect. Nothing less. I'm at a complete loss. A romantic dinner at our favorite restaurant is too pedestrian, and yet he would hate a grandiose gesture like having the entire cast of *Much Ado About Nothing* serenade him. Something with his players and the softball team could be sweet, but that might be stepping over a line. Too invasive? Not romantic enough?"

"Oh, Lance, you're way overthinking this. The proposal doesn't have to be perfect. It just has to be heartfelt. Trust me, that's all Arlo will want."

"Yes, we'll see." He brushed his hands together and stood up, offering me his hand. "I believe this goes without saying, but please keep this to yourself. I have to decide on the right place and time to take a knee."

"My lips are sealed." I pretended to zip them shut with my finger and thumb. "My only advice is not to worry too much about the ideal proposal. You and Arlo are such a great couple. I know that he adores you, and no matter how you ask, the answer is going to be yes."

"Obviously." He rolled his eyes and ran his hands over his chest. "Who would turn down this?"

I chuckled as we linked arms and went outside. I couldn't believe my best friend was ready to make a life-long commitment to the man he loved. I wouldn't tell a soul, but I couldn't wait for him to do it so we could start planning the wedding of the century.

# Chapter Twenty-four

"Go sit," Lance said, pointing me to the sole empty table on the deck. "I'll get us drinks. What's your poison?"

"Anything sounds good, surprise me." I couldn't believe the turnout for SeeBreeze's inaugural happy hour.

Steph and Sterling offered a limited happy hour menu with cocktails, mocktails, and light snacks. By the looks of the crowded deck, it was not only popular but likely to become a permanent event. Every table was occupied with guests sharing bowls of spiced popcorn and antipasto. Music wafted on the outdoor speakers, and the flower boxes beamed with color.

I noticed Lucy seated by herself at a two-person table in the far corner. She sipped on a pineapple spritzer. Her face was buried in her phone, and she looked concerned, like she'd just received bad news.

"Is everything okay?" I asked, approaching her table.

She clicked off her phone and turned it upside down. "Am I that obvious?"

"No, I don't think anyone is paying attention. Everyone is happy to be outside in the sun, soaking up the vitamin D." I glanced around us at guests wrapped up in their own conversations. "You had a worried look on your face, so I thought I would check in. I'm sure you're on edge, like the rest of us, with Erik's murder."

Her phone buzzed twice. She silenced it and pressed the bridge of her nose with her finger and thumb. "I am worried because the police in this town are utterly incompetent."

"Really, why?" Detective Mars had struck me as professional, and the Professor had only said good things about her.

"I was just on the phone with the detective, and she's insisting that I'm not on the video surveillance of our council meeting." She stared at her phone screen and then flipped it over.

That meant that, like Travis's, Lucy's alibi was collapsing too.

"I was absolutely there. I told her to review the footage again. There were at least a hundred residents in attendance. People are angry about new zoning near the beach, and for reasons unbeknownst to me, many residents are resistant to our plans for development. I've been playing the political game and trying to explain the many benefits the town will receive by building a modern luxury resort. We're going to attract tourists from new markets, not just southern Oregon and northern California. This will be a boon for the local economy. Every restaurant and shop in town will be packed by this time next year. Mark my words. They'll be kissing my feet and thanking me."

I wasn't sure about the part about kissing her feet.

"Did you speak at the council meeting?" I asked, hoping for further clarification. How would one hundred people have missed seeing her there?

"Well, technically no, but that's why the police are

useless. I was the last person scheduled to speak. They stopped filming because there was a minor walkout and protest." She glossed over her words by reaching for her drink and taking a long sip. "It's ridiculous. Talk about shooting yourselves in the foot. Why protest the best thing to happen around here in decades?"

"A protest?"

"It was announced that I would be the next speaker. I was stuck outside the main room, listening from the hall because the crowd was so large. I don't think they anticipated the turnout. Before I could even push my way to the front to give them my pitch and hard numbers on the economic impact, everyone walked out. It was a mass exodus. I'm sure they were hoping to hurt my feelings. They didn't. I have thick skin." She pressed her finger into her arm as if to prove her point.

"Everyone left?" That sounded like an exaggeration.

"They staged a protest—signs, bullhorns, chants, the works. The council members must have stopped recording. They had to have been forewarned, but they did nothing. No one called the police. You need proper permits to protest in the streets. No one stayed to listen to my presentation. It's unacceptable. I've never experienced this degree of unprofessionalism on all levels. If the police had done their job, they would have seen me with their own eyes. Instead, they're accusing me of murder. I'm impatiently waiting for my lawyer to return my call." She checked her phone again.

"Did anyone see you? Surely someone in attendance must be able to vouch that you were there. Surely the local press would have covered the meeting." I was struggling to believe Lucy's story.

"Hardly. Dozens of people saw me, but no one has come forward. The press refused to interview me. I tried to give them a statement. This is a modern day witch hunt." She reached for the numbered whale on the table and held it for a waiter who dropped off a basket of sweet potato fries and spicy aioli sauce for dipping. "I'm waiting to be run out of town with pitchforks next."

I understood local residents weren't happy about the possibility of their iconic and beloved resort being torn down and a mega-resort being constructed in its place, and I found it difficult to believe people would stay silent, knowing the stakes.

"Greetings," Lance said, handing me a cocktail glass adorned with a lemon slice and a paper umbrella. "A cherry lime shrub for the lady." He set his martini on the table and extended his hand to Lucy. "I don't believe we've had the pleasure."

I made introductions. "Lucy was just sharing that the entire town appears to be against renovations at the resort. She was at the council meeting, but no one will vouch for her—not even the press."

"Dreadful." He didn't miss a beat. "Mob mentality is the bane of my existence. One tiny boo from a disgruntled theatergoer, and the entire audience can turn on the cast like that." He snapped his fingers.

"It's ridiculous," Lucy repeated, dipping a fry into the sauce. "They don't know what's good for them. This development is going to flood the local economy with money. It's the best thing to happen to the southern Oregon coast in years, and they're treating me like a common criminal."

I didn't appreciate her attitude or use of "they," as if the local residents were uninformed and incapable. I would have felt the same way if a large corporation threatened to tear down the OSF campus and build a giant theater complex in its place. There was no doubt I'd be on the streets protesting, too.

"What do the police say?" Lance used his teeth to peel the olive from his cocktail pick.

"Nothing. I was explaining to your friend how terrible their treatment has been." She motioned to me, dabbing another fry into the aioli.

"I'm sure someone will verify that you were there," I said. "What about the council members?"

"Worthless." She stared at the sky and shook her head. "They're fighting amongst themselves. The good news is the majority of the council members are completely on board with the development. They recognize that they'll have a much smoother path to reelection once the economy is flooded with new tourist dollars. None of this is deterring me. I just need to get done with this silly police business and organize the meeting for the final vote. I'm confident that by this time next week, we'll have a signed contract, and we'll be ready to begin demolition before the weather turns."

"Lofty goals." Lance swirled his drink.

"We intend to be ready to reopen by early next spring at the very latest." She peered around us. "This is the busiest I've ever seen it. I stand corrected, those two young chefs might be on to something. An empty resort is a resort that does not bring in any money, and my business partners are fans of making money over spending it."

"What will happen to the current staff?" I was asking on behalf of Sterling and Steph. It was good to hear she was pleased with turnout for happy hour.

"We'll attempt to keep everyone on who wants to stay on, but there will also be some redefining of positions and roles. We'll be hiring contractors, but we'll need staff on-site to coordinate workflow as well as develop new menus and new guest activities and so forth."

"Will the restaurant stay open during renovations?" I wanted to know if I should offer Sterling and Steph their old jobs back before we left.

"Yes. Everything will be done in stages." She tasted another fry, like she was a restaurant critic. "This is one of the better fries I've had—crispy with nice seasoning. I need to schedule time to meet with your friends. We're starting on the west side of the resort. We'll demo cabins and what's being used as an art gallery first. Then we'll work our way through the rest of the property. The lodge and restaurant renovations are planned for stage three. We're adding a pool and tennis courts, and the gallery will become an exclusive members' lounge."

"It sounds like it's going to be unrecognizable," Lance said, running his finger around the rim of his martini glass.

"I hope so." Lucy turned to look behind us. "It's an eyesore now, if you ask me. At least your friends cleaned it up, but this is so circa 1980. We need to get this place into this century. Yet another reason I'm unclear why there's so much resistance."

"Lots of people grew up here, myself included," I said, a touch of nostalgia creeping in. "Whaleshead has never been fancy, but that's one of the reasons it's beloved. Families come year after year. It has a real sense of place and community."

"You sound like Erik." She rolled her eyes. "He was oddly sentimental. I don't understand it."

"He didn't want to sell," Lance prompted.

"That's an understatement," she scoffed. "He did everything in his power to undermine my efforts. If he had been smart, he would have worked with me instead of against me, but he didn't know what was for his own good."

Her tone changed.

It was impossible to ignore the hate laced between her words.

"It's terrible to say, but I'm not heartbroken that he's gone. It's going to make the transition so much smoother."

"I thought you didn't need his approval for the sale to go through." I caught Lance's eye. He nodded to show me that he had picked up on her change in demeanor as well.

"I didn't. I'm just glad I don't have to work with him moving forward."

Her phone rang.

"This is my lawyer. If you'll excuse me." She stood and grabbed her phone.

"She's not even mildly broken up about Erik's death," Lance said.

"Or trying to hide it."

"I say we keep a close eye on that one." Lance closed one eye and tapped his finger on his temple. "Methinks she's trouble."

# Chapter Twenty-five

We opted to do a late meal with everyone—but Mom and the Professor were taking a stroll on the beach, so Lance and I lingered over happy hour drinks and snacks, reviewing each of our potential suspects and what we'd learned about them.

"The more I think about it, the more I'm convinced that Lucy did it," I said, popping a handful of nuts into my mouth.

"When it comes to motive, she takes the cake, to borrow a pastry phrase." Lance grinned slyly. "But, in all seriousness, I agree. I'm surprised she's not the one who met an untimely end. It sounds as if the entire town is out to get her."

"And the resort staff." I crunched the nuts, which had been toasted in a trio of spices, brown sugar, and coconut. They were equally sweet and salty, my favorite combination. "I wonder if Mary Beth knows about Lucy's plans to renovate her art space and turn it into an executive lounge."

"There's one way to find out." Lance tipped his glass and finished his drink. Then he stood and bowed as if we were at a Regency ball. "I, for one, am slightly buzzed and can't think of anything I'd rather do until the dinner hour than spend time with you perusing some beachy art. If Arlo and I do tie the knot, we'll need to expand our art collection. What a better place to start than here? I'm envisioning Bigfoot statues carved out of driftwood."

"You're not far off. I saw a number of those in town, but I believe that paint is Mary Beth's medium."

"The question we must answer is whether her medium is also murder."

We followed the main path, past the infamous bench, and then turned off onto a smaller trail leading to Mary Beth's cabin and workshop. This was the first time I'd ventured to the east side of the resort. I didn't have any recollection of coming this way when I was younger. There probably wouldn't have been a need. I would have been singularly intent on getting down to the beach. Come to think of it, I wondered how long Mary Beth had been living and working at the resort.

"What do you think?" Lance asked, motioning behind us as the narrow pathway curved deeper into the forest. "We're not walking particularly fast, and it took us mere minutes to vanish from the main trail. Mary Beth could have practically ambled away from the murder scene without breaking a sweat."

"I was thinking the same thing. She must be familiar with every trail in the resort." Clumps of moss dripped from the trees. This side of the resort was permanently shaded by dense trees.

"That's also true for Jess and Hoff and likely Lucy. If she's a good businesswoman, redeveloping the property would mean touring every square inch of it." He stepped carefully to avoid getting his shoes dirty.

"Unfortunately, you're right. I was hoping we might rule suspects out, but I bet even Travis knows most of these trails."

"There's no need to wrinkle your brow. Let's see what we can extract from Mary Beth."

Her studio was tucked into the forest. It reminded me of the witch's house in "Hansel and Gretel." The shingled roof was coated in a thick layer of moss. Ferns grew up between the slats in the sagging porch, and the arched stained-glass windows were cracked and fading.

"No wonder Lucy wants to bulldoze this. It looks like it's about to crumble into a billion tiny pieces." Lance made a face. "Is it safe to enter? The roof might sink in on us. How has this building not been condemned?"

"It needs a monumental amount of TLC," I said, stepping carefully over broken boards with nails jutting up through the porch slats.

Lance rapped on the door.

We heard shuffling inside, but Mary Beth didn't answer.

"Should I try again, or do we just go in?" He tapped a small handwritten sign next to the door with the gallery viewing hours. "According to this, she's open."

"Maybe knock one more time," I suggested.

He pounded louder on the door.

"Come in. I'm painting," Mary Beth called.

Lance opened the door and waited for me to go inside first. The studio wasn't at all what I was expecting. The cedar plank floor was splotched with paint like Mary Beth had experimented with splatter techniques. Huge canvases in varying states of completion hung from the walls. Mixed in were smaller works. There were stacks and stacks of paintings propped on the floor and on end tables. A large antique cabinet housed brushes, a kaleido-scope of paints, palette knives, and spatulas. It reminded me a bit of the tools we used at Torte to paint cakes.

Mary Beth had her back to us. She wore a paint-covered smock and oversized glasses. "I'll be right with you. Feel free to look around. Everything is for sale, and everything is negotiable."

Lance and I viewed her paintings while she dabbed paint onto her current project. Most of the pieces were like the ones on display in the lobby—landscapes of the natural world—with a few portraits mixed in. But like Jess had mentioned, there were a handful of canvases with a very different energy. Lance paused in front of one of them and elbowed me. "I'd call this sinister," he said under his breath.

Angry, harsh black, gray, and maroon brushstrokes collided with force across the canvas. Red dots dripped from the sides, like a cut that had been slashed open and wouldn't stop bleeding. The piece was finished with barbed wire Mary Beth had strung across the front like a barricade.

"Oh, it's you," Mary Beth said in a singsong voice, pulling her attention away from her work. She dipped her brush in a jar of water and walked toward us. "I see *Gloom's Caress* has caught your eye. What do you think of the painting? Does it elicit any specific emotional response?"

"Terror?" Lance whispered to me.

"What's that?" Mary Beth asked, leaning closer and cupping her hand over her ear.

"It brings out a sense of melancholy for me," Lance replied in complete seriousness.

"Interesting." Mary Beth nodded her head in approval. "When I created this piece, I wanted to challenge the viewer to connect with their discomfort. It's important to see the allure of darkness and how we try to avoid it. I find companionship in the shadows. This piece was born during a period of deep introspection, where the quiet state of my despair became the canvas for my emotions."

"I can see that," I said, nodding. "What does the barbed wire represent?"

"Being caged in. Not having control. The blood scars that come with breaking free and following our own destiny." Mary Beth reached to prick the tip of her finger on one of the barbs. "It's a metaphor for how pain and struggle are the price we pay for our independence."

"Wow. I wouldn't have picked up on that much on my own." I took a closer look at the painting, seeing it in a new light. Mary Beth's perspective on her piece was exactly why talking to artists and asking them questions was important. Art, whether it be on a canvas or cake, was subjective, but having an understanding of what the artist was trying to convey gave me a better understanding. However, I couldn't separate her perspective from Erik's murder. Could the painting be a metaphor for her breaking away from him and from the shackles of the resort?

"The contrasting shades and textures are meant to highlight the complexity of the darkness of human emotions. I want this to be an invitation for you to explore your own darkness and the depths you might go to find the tiny spark of light in the dark."

"Bravo. Well said." Lance clapped, using his fingers against his palm.

"Thank you. I'm very proud of this piece in particular."
Mary Beth circled in the other direction. "As you'll see,
there are plenty of other options if this one doesn't speak
to you."

"You're quite prolific." Lance's gaze drifted around the
room. "And this is a live/work space, yes?"

Mary Beth pointed behind double glass doors near
her easel. "Yes, my living space is in the back. It's not
anything special—a bedroom, bathroom, and small
kitchen."

"Have you been at Whaleshead a long time?" I asked,
glad Lance was shifting the conversation in a new
direction.

"Going on thirty years now."

"So you must have been here when I was a kid. We visited
the resort every summer. Has this always been a studio?" I
tried to recall any memories of the physical space, but nothing came to mind. Like Mom had mentioned, we probably
never ventured to this side of the resort.

"Not exactly. It was originally a mediation center. One
of the caretakers lived here then." She flicked a paint
chip from her thumb. "When I took a job at the front
desk, the role Jess is in now, I was offered the cabin, and
over the years, I've made it my own."

"You and Erik must go way back," I said.

"He was only hired four years ago." She avoided the
subject and moved on to show us another painting. "If
you're in the market for something more calming, this style
is a fan favorite. A classic, quintessential beach landscape."

"It's lovely." I wanted to keep her on topic. "Did Erik
implement a lot of changes when he took over?"

"If you mean butting heads with everyone he came in contact with, then yes." She didn't say more.

I couldn't tell if I was making her uncomfortable or if she was mostly concerned with selling us a piece of art.

Probably both.

"It sounds like Erik made work miserable for everyone." Lance strolled to the next painting. "He didn't have many friends, did he?"

"Erik didn't care about Whaleshead," Mary Beth snapped, her tone turning pitchy. Had we hit a nerve? "He was in this for himself. For the money. He cared about profit and profit alone. He was ready to abandon the people—the people who made this place. I've said it before, and I'll say it again, I'm not heartbroken he's dead."

I decided it was best not to belabor that point. She'd been very clear about her feelings for Erik. "I didn't realize there was a ton of money to be made at a small, local, family-friendly resort," I said.

"Erik had his ways." She adjusted a painting of a seagull perched on a rock. "He had all kinds of deals going."

Did she know about his arrangement with Travis?

I decided to try another tactic. "What will happen to your space when Lucy takes over?"

"Lucy's not taking over." She recoiled. "Where did you hear that? It sounds like you're listening to rumors, because I have it on good authority that the sale has *not* gone through."

"Sorry, wrong choice of words. I meant when the sale goes through and the resort is renovated."

"The sale isn't going through."

"Really?" Lance pulled his attention away from a group

of three paintings—each had a slice of the monolith that the beach was known for. Each painting contained a section of the highly recognizable rock, and when hung together, they created one image.

"No. There's not a single person aside from Lucy in favor of the sale."

"Are you sure?" I asked, trying to catch Lance's eye. "Lucy made it sound like it was basically a done deal."

Mary Beth laughed, but there was no humor in her tone. "She's sorely mistaken. There is zero chance the sale will go through now that Erik's dead." She stopped herself like she'd said too much.

"Erik? I thought he was against the sale."

She moved to her supply cabinet and picked up a thin-tipped brush. "There's too much to settle now with him gone. Lucy will lose interest and move on before the legal team reviews all of the paperwork."

I could only imagine the amount of legal paperwork associated with the sale and subsequent property development.

"Are either of you interested in purchasing a piece? If not, I have to get back to this." She dabbed the brush in mint green paint.

"I'll have to bring my boyfriend back," Lance said. "I can't make a choice without him."

I wasn't ready to go. I had more questions for her, but Mary Beth's stance and firm lips made it clear she was done with us.

"Thanks for letting us take a look. You're very talented."

"You can see yourselves out." She turned her back to us and studied the canvas.

I wished I could think of anything else to ask her that

wouldn't be obvious, but my mind drew a blank. Lance ushered me to the door.

Once we were outside and had made it back to the bench, he asked, "What say you, Juliet? Have we found our killer?"

# Chapter Twenty-six

"Did she just slip up?" I asked, glancing behind us to the cabin. "She said now that Erik's gone, there's no chance the sale will go through. What if we have it wrong? What if Erik was working with Lucy to encourage homeowners to support the buyout? It makes so much more sense. I think Mary Beth is telling the truth about Erik being in it for the money. We've proven as much, what with his setup with Travis, payments under the table, bookkeeping, and potentially preparing to blackmail Jess. If Erik was trying to push the sale through, that gives Mary Beth a strong motive to want him dead. She will lose her housing and art studio if the sale is successful."

"She painted it for us, didn't she? It was right in front of us. The rage in the painting tells the whole story." Lance ran his fingers along his chin in contemplation. "There's just one thing that doesn't make sense—why would Lucy remain tight-lipped if she and Erik were in cahoots?"

"Good question. Could they have a similar arrangement as his deal with Travis? What if Lucy was offering him a bonus or extra cash under the table? Maybe Mary Beth found out about it and knew that her only way to 'break free' like her painting was to kill him."

"I like it. I like it a lot." Lance nodded, stepping around a slug. "There's only one problem—how do we prove it?"

"We need to speak with Lucy again." I followed the path, noting the weathered wood signs pointing us to the main trail.

A branch snapped behind us.

Lance grabbed my arm and swiveled around.

"Are those footsteps? Is she following us?" I whispered.

He pressed his finger to his lips and kept his eyes glued behind us.

My breath quickened.

*Mary Beth wouldn't do anything rash, would she? Then again, if she killed Erik . . .*

I didn't want to finish the thought.

"We're okay," Lance said, pulling his gaze away. "I don't see anything."

He kept his hand on my back, pushing me gently forward.

I appreciated the sweet, protective gesture.

"It's her, isn't it?" I asked, mindful of my footing while still trying to keep pace. I wanted to get out of the tree cover and back on the main trail as quickly as possible.

"Following us?" Lance twisted around again. "I don't hear anything. It was probably a squirrel. We're both understandably jumpy, but I've got you, Juliet. I won't let anything happen to you."

His chivalry made me want to turn around and smooch his cheek. "No, I mean Mary Beth. She's the killer," I said, power-walking faster as the sound of the waves grew louder and the sky lightened. We were close.

The bench came into view. I breathed with relief.

"You sound convinced," Lance said, stopping at the bench and taking out his phone. "Should we call Doug?"

I wasn't sure what our best option was. I didn't want to go back to the gallery, but I wasn't sure we had enough, other than my hunch and her terrifying paintings, to force the Professor away from whatever he was currently working on. "If we can get Mary Beth to tell us the truth about whatever she and Erik had cooked up, then we can alert the Professor."

"You won't be alerting anyone." Mary Beth's voice pierced through the woods.

Lance and I froze and turned toward the sound.

She appeared below, bursting out of the woods with a shovel in one arm.

Was that a side trail or even some kind of animal trail?

Where had she come from?

Had she heard our entire conversation?

"Why did you have to come snooping around?" She trudged to the base of the bench, dragging the shovel behind her.

It created a ridge through the middle of the trail.

What was her plan?

Or did she have one?

From the wild look in her eyes, I doubted she'd given any thought to following after us.

She positioned herself between the bench and the cliff-side. "You should have left it alone." She yanked the shovel over her shoulder.

What was she going to do with a shovel?

She was at least twenty years older than us. Even

pregnant, I knew I could easily outrun her. Not to mention, there were two of us.

"Look, no one else needs to get hurt." I raised my hands to show her I was unarmed.

She propped the shovel higher in her arm and held it tight with both hands like a sword or a knight preparing for a jousting duel.

"Dearest, you don't actually think you're going to take us out with a shovel?" Lance's tone was almost condescending.

I didn't want to make her angrier.

"No, here's what's going to happen." She jerked forward in a threatening stance. "You're going to get moving now. Get. Disappear. Vanish. If you so much as say a word to the police, I will launch off the side of this cliff, just like I sent Erik tumbling to his death. But it will be on your shoulders. Not mine." She stabbed at us and inched backward near the edge of the trail.

I sucked in a quick breath.

She was threatening to jump?

"Mary Beth, please don't." I could hear the shakiness in my voice, but I didn't care. I couldn't handle another death. "You don't need to do this. Like I said, no one needs to get hurt, including you."

"Then get away from me," she yelled, keeping the shovel between us. "I'm not kidding, I will jump."

"No one is jumping," Lance said in an even, commanding tone. "Juliet and I will do as you say. We're going to slowly walk up the trail and let you take whatever time you need to pack up your things and get a head start. You have my word that we will not contact the authorities until we've given you ample time. It's going to take the police a while to arrive, and Juliet is pregnant, so we'll have to set an easy pace getting up to the lodge."

I couldn't believe he was going to let her get away, but the alternative was much worse.

I wanted to pull out my phone and call the Professor, but I didn't want to risk having Mary Beth make true on her threat to jump.

"See? We're taking our first step," Lance said, grabbing my hand and moving backward, making sure to use his body to shield me. "You can keep your eye on us as long as you want."

It was thoughtful of him to use his body as protection, but it was clear the only person in danger was Mary Beth. She wasn't stable, and she was inches away from the edge of the cliff. I didn't trust that she wouldn't jump even without being provoked.

"Go. Get. Move." Mary Beth used the shovel to try to prod us onward.

Every time she made the slightest movement, I held my breath.

"This is bad," I whispered to Lance. "I'm scared she's going to do something drastic. Should we stay?"

"No, trust me," he said through a toothy smile. Then he raised his voice for Mary Beth's benefit. "We're taking our time, slowly, because we don't want Jules to lose her footing," Lance said, tightening his grasp on my arm as we continued walking backward up the hill.

Mary Beth glanced over the ledge like she was considering how far the fall would be. Her flowy scarves fluttered in the wind. One misstep or jerky movement, and there was nothing to stop her.

I felt helpless.

*What else could we do?*

"We're making progress. You can go ahead and move away from the edge," Lance articulated our every move like he was announcing a soccer match.

"I'm worried she's not stable," I said to Lance, keeping my voice low.

"She's not. There's no doubt about that." He steadied me. "That's why we're going to let her do whatever she feels is necessary."

"Why are you moving so slow?" Mary Beth yelled, her body still precariously close to the edge.

"We're going," Lance responded carefully.

I was impressed with how calm and collected he was in an emergency situation. Gone were any traces of his over-the-top persona.

"How far do we go before we call for help?" My head started to spin. I wasn't sure if it was from walking backward, nerves, or stress.

"We're coming to the bend." Lance remained locked in on Mary Beth. His body was rigid and his posture perfect, like he had a long stick attached to his spine. "We should be to the garden boxes in a minute or two. I hope once we're out of sight, that will be enough proof for her."

I hated not knowing if Mary Beth was safe. Not that I condoned violence. It was terrible she killed Erik, but I didn't want anyone else to die. She obviously needed help. Her mental health was in a terrible state.

"Are you sure we shouldn't try to reason with her?" I hesitated.

"She's beyond civilized conversation, darling. Our best bet is to get far enough way for her to move and feel safe. Then we'll call for help."

My breath was heavy as we climbed backward. My lungs burned, and my legs quaked. Not from overexertion, though. I wasn't even winded. It was definitely nerves.

Fortunately, Lance was right. As the trail meandered around a clump of trees, I lost sight of Mary Beth.

"I'm calling the Professor," I said, reaching for my phone without hesitation.

"Just keep your voice low. Sound travels," Lance cautioned.

The Professor answered on the first ring. "Juliet, to what do I owe the pleasure?"

"It's Mary Beth. She confessed, and she's at the bench threatening to jump," I blurted out in a rushed whisper.

"I'm sorry, I didn't catch that. Can you repeat what you said?" the Professor asked. Static crackling on the line.

*Oh, no, not bad service now.*

*Please don't let the call drop.*

I raised my voice ever so slightly and repeated my plea for help. "It's Mary Beth. She's at the bench. She admitted to pushing Erik. She's going to jump."

He heard me this time. "Stay where you are. I'm close. We're on our way."

"What did he say?" Lance asked, leading me past the garden boxes.

"They're coming. He said they're close. I just hope they're really close." I exhaled with relief I wasn't sure was real. Mary Beth might jump if she felt threatened by the police, but at least the Professor and Detective Mars were trained for situations like this.

Lance paced between the garden beds.

Waiting was agony.

I hated not being able to see what was happening.

Had she heeded Lance's advice and made an escape?

Or were we about to experience déjà vu?

I didn't have to contemplate either question for long. Within what felt like seconds, the Professor and Detective Mars sprinted past us. He hadn't exaggerated about being close. They must have been at the lodge.

"Do you want to go inside?" Lance asked, already inching forward.

"Yes, but no." I chomped on the inside of my cheek. "We're in it this far. I want to make sure she's okay."

Lance didn't say anything. He simply held out his hand.

We retraced our footsteps in silence.

We didn't need to speak. I knew we were both thinking the same thing.

As the bench came into view, there was no sign of the Professor or Detective Mars.

Mary Beth had vanished.

I hoped that meant that she had headed for her cabin. I didn't want to consider any other possibility.

"They wouldn't leave if she jumped, right?" I asked Lance.

"Wait here." He skidded to a stop. "I'll look."

I gulped. I felt terrible for Lance, but I couldn't do it again. Not while the image of Erik was still burned into my head.

The dizziness came in waves as I watched him inch toward the bench, and then carefully peer over it. "All clear," he called, shooting me a thumbs-up.

*Thank goodness.*

"They've got this," Lance said with a level of assuredness I didn't share. He glanced down the trail. "They're probably tracking her down as we speak."

Time moved like honey pouring from a jar.

Lance put his arm around me to keep me warm. "It's going to be okay. We have the best of the best in charge."

He was right about that. I trusted the Professor implicitly. If anyone could defuse the situation and bring Mary Beth to justice, it was him.

I wasn't sure how much time had passed before the Professor's voice broke through the quiet. He jogged out of the path. "We've got her. She's safe and in custody. Detective Mars and I will be bringing her to the lodge soon."

I sighed in genuine relief this time.

Mary Beth was safe. Erik's killer had been apprehended. And no one else had been hurt. Thank goodness for small miracles.

# Chapter Twenty-seven

The deck hummed with chatter and questions—murmurs about why the police had just been seen sprinting down the trail and rumors about another person falling off the cliff. Lance and I ignored the electrified atmosphere and went to the kitchen to find everyone.

Sterling, Steph, and Carlos were transitioning to dinner service.

"What's going on out there?" Sterling asked, wiping his hands on the towel tucked into his apron. "I delivered the last round of happy hour snacks, and people are saying there's been another accident. Have either of you heard anything?"

"I can assure you that not only has there not been another accident, but Erik's killer has also been apprehended, thanks to yours truly." Lance patted his chest and bowed with a flourish.

"What?" Carlos looked at me. "Is this true?"

"Partially," I said, swatting Lance. "The Professor and Detective Mars have arrested Mary Beth."

"Mary Beth killed Erik?" Steph gasped. "Why?"

"We'll have to wait for the Professor to share the

details. I'm sure he'll be able to tell us more. When Lance and I went to her gallery and saw her artwork—it gave us an entirely new perspective on Mary Beth's health and well-being. Jess was correct in labeling it dark."

"Gruesome comes to mind," Lance interjected.

"She killed him because of her art?" Sterling sounded confused as he snipped green onions onto a spring salad.

"No, but her art reflected her internal turmoil," I said. Being in the kitchen made me feel more grounded. The aromas of their daily specials—chicken picante and halibut seared in a lemon and dill butter sauce. "We believe she became desperate when she discovered Erik was actually in favor of selling the resort and secretly working with Lucy to encourage cabin owners to push the sale through."

Lance helped himself to a breadstick. "She's had a good thing going here. I don't blame her for her desperation. Don't get me wrong, I'm not condoning murder. I simply understand how she became triggered. She was losing her entire lifestyle and livelihood. She couldn't give that up. She was smart enough to realize her gig was up as soon as Lucy took over."

"Exactly," I agreed. "Lucy's vision for a new and improved Whaleshead does not include a run-down art gallery tucked deep in the woods, and I would guess Lucy intends to take away Mary Beth's grandfathered perks—like free housing. It's not the same as you two, Hoff, or Jess. You all work in exchange for room and board, but Mary Beth's profiting on the sale of her paintings in addition to getting comped housing. In my exchanges with Lucy, she made it clear that big changes were afoot. I can't imagine her allowing Mary Beth to keep her setup."

"I'm surprised she didn't target Lucy," Sterling said, reaching for a bunch of fresh parsley to add to the salad.

"Who knows? She might have intended to do just that." I surveyed their prep. Like yesterday, everything was in order and ready for plating. I wouldn't mind a distraction, and there was no better way to get out of my head than baking. "Do you need help?"

Carlos cleared his throat and pointed to the dining room. "Lance, please escort my lovely wife to her table. She's banned from the kitchen tonight. I have a plate of chicken picante with your name on it, and a bottle of raspberry rosé sparkling juice waiting in the fridge for you."

"Fine." I didn't have the energy to protest. "Tomorrow morning? One last breakfast prep?" I asked Sterling and Steph.

"Sure, we'd love your help." Steph glanced at Carlos. "As long as we don't get in trouble with this guy."

"I'm the one who will be in trouble for banning her tonight." Carlos grinned.

"That's right. You better watch out later." I pretended to scowl at him before turning to Sterling and Steph. "Good luck with service, and if I don't see you again, I'll be here dark and early."

"Are we on for the bonfire tomorrow night?" Lance asked, grabbing another breadstick.

"Yes," Sterling replied. "We don't serve dinner on Monday nights, just picnic boxes to go, so we're already planning on it—a classic cookout on the beach for Ramiro with hot dogs and s'mores."

"Wonderful. Then I bid you adieu." Lance folded his hands and bowed.

We joined Mom, Arlo, and Ramiro for dinner. The

first course was an arugula and kale salad with pickled onions, hard-boiled eggs, marinated olives, house-made garlic croutons, and a lemon vinaigrette. It paired beautifully with my chicken picante and Mom's halibut.

The Professor and Detective Mars were too busy with Mary Beth's arrest to join us, but Jess and Hoff stopped by our table as dessert was being served with a stack of paperwork.

"None of you are cabin owners, are you?" Jess asked. "We're handing out ballots to vote on the sale of Whaleshead. I'm sure you've heard by now they've arrested Mary Beth."

"As a matter of fact, we have. Juliet and I were integral in bringing her to justice," Lance said, stabbing his strawberry rhubarb pie with his fork.

"Oh, good." Jess sounded unsure what to say next.

"Not really, the police are taking care of the situation," I said, shooting Lance a look.

"I can't say I'm shocked she did it." Hoff pointed to the seascape painting hanging nearby with his thumb. "The woman was unhinged."

"Yeah, she was," Jess agreed. "She threatened to tell Erik about me and Cody. She spotted us a couple of times on the trail and kept warning me she was going to get me fired. There was no reason for that. It didn't impact her at all. I think she just wanted everyone to be miserable."

"Or she was going to blackmail you eventually," Hoff suggested.

"True. I wouldn't put it past her." Jess held out the ballots. "Anyway, none of you are voting members, right?"

"I've been curious about ownership," Lance said, reaching for a ballot. "Would I speak with you about potential available properties?"

"I think so." Jess shrugged and looked at Hoff. "We're passing around ballots in hopes that we can put Lucy and the sale of the resort behind us. Contrary to what Lucy says, most cabin owners don't want to sell."

"It would be good for both of you if the sale doesn't go through." I had a few lingering questions for both of them, and this was my chance to clear them up.

"I guess. We want to keep our jobs, if that's what you're hinting at." Jess readjusted the stack of ballots. "Hoff, back me up here. People don't want to sell."

"They don't." He shook his head. "They want things to change and improve, but they don't want a mega-resort."

"Can I ask you something about improvements?" I swirled honey into my tea.

"Go ahead." He folded his arms across his chest.

"How did you fix the water issue in cabin eight?"

"It's my job. I fix everything that breaks around here. I'm hoping under new management I'll finally have funds to be able to make the repairs that are needed. Erik never had enough cash for the basics. I had to run to town three times for parts and supplies on my own dime." He paused and looked at Jess. "I'm turning in reimbursement receipts for that, by the way."

I squeezed lemon into the hot tea, careful not to let it squirt into my eyes. "Oh, you were back and forth to Brookings?"

"Yep. Why?"

"You left your toolbox in the kitchen. We couldn't figure out how you were working without your tools."

"I needed specialized tools for the water pipes. I told Erik at least a dozen times that we need to stock the tool-shed with basic supplies, but he refused. Assuming the owners don't vote to sell, I'm going to demand to be part of the interview process for a new manager. Whoever we hire needs to have a basic understanding of maintenance and what goes into keeping a resort of this size functioning."

So that explained where Hoff had been during Erik's death and why he'd left his tools in the kitchen.

Mom scooped a bite of her raspberry panna cotta. "Will Lucy be involved in the vote?"

Jess shook her head. "She can't be. I mean, she's already spoken her piece and done her best to try to sway votes. I heard she was trying to get owners to sign a petition at dinner the other night, but these are the official ballots." She patted the stack. "Owners have until tomorrow at four p.m. to cast their vote. I'm also sending digital ballots to people off-site. By this time tomorrow, we'll know our fate."

"Will you both stay?" I asked.

They nodded in unison. Jess answered first. "I'd love to. Cody, my boyfriend, is in hotel management, so ideally it would be great if he could take over Erik's role. He's managed a chain of hotels in Portland, so he has the experience, expertise, and obviously knows the ins and outs of Whaleshead."

"I'd be good with that." Hoff jutted out his chin as he considered the idea. "Frankly, anyone will be better than Erik. Though I'm sorry he died, truly."

Jess bowed her head and sighed. "Me too. I feel terrible. It's going to be weird picking up the pieces and figuring out how we move on, but the cabin owners are so wonderful, and the resort is a gem. We just need to stick together. Whaleshead is already something special, and I know we can make it even better." She glanced at Mom and me and then motioned to the crowded dining room. "Sterling and Steph are amazing. We owe Erik for that. I feel like they're setting the tone for what Whaleshead could be. They see its potential, and I'm excited to work together. I can't even imagine what this place might look like a year from now."

Her enthusiasm gave me renewed hope for Sterling and Steph.

"Good luck with the vote." Lance crossed his fingers. "And do let me know about potential properties. I wouldn't mind touring a few before we leave."

They moved on to continue passing out ballots. I was glad to hear they were both committed to Whaleshead. It was a good sign. Now we just needed the vote to come out in their favor.

# Chapter Twenty-eight

The next morning, I woke to the patter of rain on the roof. The storm that never materialized yesterday must have rolled in overnight. I scooted out of bed and pulled on a pair of jeans and a sweatshirt. Everything was misty and cool outside. Pine needles and bark squished under my feet on the short walk to the lodge. It felt fitting to have the clouds and light rain wash away the events of the last few days like an ultimate cleanse.

As I walked through the lobby, I wondered what would become of Mary Beth's art and whether Jess would stay on. Would she and Cody manage the resort? Would the owners vote against selling? Or had Lucy done enough to sway people to sell and demolish Whaleshead as we knew and loved it?

Hoff and Jess sounded committed and eager to make some serious changes and improvements, but was it too late?

My thoughts drifted to Steph and Sterling. They had proven they were capable of running SeaBreeze. But would they want to? After everything that had happened, I was curious to hear where their heads were at.

"Morning, Jules." Steph greeted me with a half wave, looking up from her pie dough. "Did you get drenched on the walk in?"

I brushed tiny drops from my sweatshirt. "Barely. It's just misting. Is it bad to admit that it felt good?"

"I said the same thing to Steph." Sterling cracked eggs into a large stainless-steel bowl. "I bet it will be clear when the sun comes up. It felt refreshing."

"Agreed." I poured myself a coffee and looked over their brunch menu. Today's buffet featured a French toast casserole, spinach quiche, sweet potato hash, spiced zucchini bread, orange cardamom granola with house-made yogurt, and peach cobbler muffins. "Wow, this all sounds delish. What can I help with?"

"Would you make the peach cobbler muffins?" Steph asked, flouring a cutting board to roll out the piecrust. "This is for the quiche. Sterling's making the sweet potato hash, and I'll start the zucchini bread next. The yogurt is resting in the fridge, but we still need to make the granola and the French toast casserole, which should come together easily at the last minute."

"I'm on it." I took a long sip of my coffee and studied her recipe. The muffin base involved creaming butter and sugar together and adding vanilla, eggs, and buttermilk. Once a smooth batter had formed, I would sift in flour, salt, and baking powder. Finally, I would stir in chunks of fresh peaches. "How are you both feeling about everything?" I asked after tying on an apron and gathering the ingredients.

"You mean about Whaleshead?" Steph asked.

"Yeah. Have you heard anything more about the next

steps? We heard last night that the members are voting today. I'm guessing it's too soon to know anything else yet?"

Sterling cracked eggs one-handed, like an expert, using the flat surface of the countertop. It was a pro-chef trick I'd taught him his first week at Torte. Using the side of a bowl to crack eggs makes it more likely to break yolks or end up with eggshells in the bowl or pan. "Not much yet. According to Jess and the head of the owners' association, we still have jobs if the sale fails, so I guess we'll take that as a win for now."

"You two have done such a phenomenal job, especially given the extraordinary circumstances." I added butter to the industrial mixer and turned it to low.

"Yeah, but you're biased, Jules." Steph rolled her eyes while rolling out the piecrust.

"You and Lance both," Sterling agreed. He glanced at Steph. "Speaking of Lance, is it okay if I tell her?"

"No, go ahead." She shook her head.

"Tell me what?" My interest was piqued.

"You know those envelopes Lance gave us?" Sterling asked, cracking another egg into the bowl. "Well, they contained fifteen thousand dollars—each."

"Really?" I wasn't entirely surprised. Lance was incredibly generous with his wealth, although ironically, it was the one thing he was also extremely private about. Most people had no idea about the extent of Lance's personal philanthropy. "That was thoughtful of him."

"Fifteen thousand, Jules. Fifteen K," Steph said in disbelief. "We can't accept that. It's way too much money. He wrote us sweet notes about it being 'a little seed money,' and how proud he is of us and of what we've already accomplished with the restaurant. Honestly, it made me almost tear up, but I don't feel right keeping his money."

Sterling scooped eggshells into the compost bin. "Me too. It's super generous, but it's too much."

"Listen, if Lance gave you money as a gift, it's because he really wants to help you get started. He wouldn't have done that if he didn't want to, and I guarantee you there's no chance he'll let you give him the money back."

"Yeah, but thirty K, Jules." Steph stopped rolling the pie dough and rubbed her fingers together. "Thirty K."

"Don't worry, Lance is good for it."

"What do you mean?" Sterling picked up a whisk and began whipping the eggs.

"All I will say is that I'm sure that amount is a 'little seed money' to him."

"You're sure?" Steph didn't sound convinced.

I turned the mixer up as I added sugar and creamed it with the butter. "I'm positive."

"You think we should keep the money?" Sterling asked, seasoning the eggs with salt, pepper, and chopped fresh herbs.

"I think Lance would be devastated if you didn't. He cares deeply about you both, and this is a way for him to show you that and also to give back. He would never say this to anyone, but I know it makes him feel good to share his wealth with people he cares about. I would think of it as an investment in your future."

"That's exactly what he said in the note." Steph pressed the crust into a pie plate and crimped the edges.

I slowly incorporated eggs, vanilla, and buttermilk into

my batter. Then I added the dry ingredients, keeping the speed low so as not to send flour flying everywhere.

"We're going to owe him, big-time," Sterling said.

"That's not how gifts work." I watched as my batter began to thicken. "I'm sure he'd appreciate a thank-you note, but the best thing you can do in thanks is to accept his generosity and use it to launch this new phase of your careers—wherever they take you."

"Thanks for your input, Jules, it's helpful." Sterling added heavy cream, spinach, and cheese to the quiche mixture.

Steph handed him the first piecrust while I stirred juicy peach chunks into my muffins and scooped them into silicone trays. I used an ice-cream scoop to ensure the muffins would be uniform. Then I cut cold butter into small squares and used a fork to incorporate cinnamon, sugar, and flour for my crumble topping. I sprinkled the topping on each muffin and slid the trays into the oven to bake.

It was just like Lance to do something so sweet for Steph and Sterling without wanting any recognition. Whether they decided to stay at Whaleshead and try to make a go of SeaBreeze or opted for something different, his gift would give them a nice start.

With the muffins baking, I turned my attention to the granola. For that, I combined oats, honey, a trio of warming spices, cardamom, coconut oil, coconut flakes, and the zest and juice of fresh oranges. I tossed the ingredients together with my hands and then spread them out on parchment-lined baking sheets. It would cook for twenty minutes, which gave us plenty of time to allow it to cool before serving it with Steph's house-made yogurt.

"Are you leaning toward staying for a while, assuming

the sale doesn't go through?" I asked as I took the first tray to the oven.

"You mean at Whaleshead?" Sterling poured the egg mixture into a piecrust and leveled it with a flat spatula. "Yeah, I think so, right, Steph?"

She set another crust in front of him. "Why not? We're young. It's low risk as long as the new management continues to comp our housing and agrees to keep us on."

"I'm sure they will. Everyone has raved about the food all weekend long. Happy hour was packed. The food, service, and ambiance have been perfect, even with a murder investigation going on in the background." I didn't have a shred of doubt that Sterling and Steph had solidified their job status with what they'd accomplished in the opening weekend.

Opening weekends were notoriously difficult. Customers had high expectations for trying a new restaurant, and first impressions were critical. If word-of-mouth was negative right out of the gate, it was an uphill battle to try and climb back from that. Operational challenges tended to come to light, even after doing dry runs and soft openings. I'd experienced my fair share of unforeseen issues in the kitchen getting exposed during an opening weekend—delays, mistakes in orders, inconsistencies in the food.

Sterling and Steph had sailed through the relaunch of SeaBreeze without any of these.

"I hope you're right, and I hope people vote against selling," Steph said, fluting the edges of the last piecrust. "I guess the smart move is to sock away Lance's gift, see if we can make things work here, and then come up with plan B if we bomb."

"You're not going to bomb," I said reassuringly. "I'm always a phone call or a text away. The same goes for Mom, Carlos, and everyone on the team. We're all cheering you on."

Steph smiled.

"And, as I've said at least a million times, you always have a job at Torte."

"We know. We know. You're starting to sound like a broken record." Sterling pretended to shush me. His bright eyes crinkled with gratitude. "Thank you for that, though. It's good to know we have Torte in our corner."

"Team Torte forever." I gave them both hugs, and we shifted into final brunch prep mode. Spending the weekend with them softened the sting of losing them. It was clear they were more than ready for this next step. Pulling off a successful opening weekend in the midst of a murder investigation showed me they were fully prepared to make their mark on SeaBreeze Bistro. I would be cheering them on from afar and eager to see where this adventure led them.

# Chapter Twenty-nine

Once the sun set, we returned to the beach, where Carlos and Sterling constructed a massive bonfire. The earlier mist and rain had passed on, leaving black, crystal-clear skies in their wake. Moonlight beamed on the waves, casting an incandescent glow. The coastline was dotted with other fires farther down the beach. The smell of woodsmoke and the crackle of the flames made the scene even more magical.

Mom and Steph spread out blankets, electric lanterns, and enough food to feed a small army. Ramiro, Lance, Arlo, and the Professor all joined our oceanside dinner. We gathered around the bonfire in a circle, huddled in blankets and jackets, as nighttime breezed in over the Pacific.

"Tell us everything; don't spare a single detail," Lance said to the Professor, passing around bottles of wine and a thermos of hot chocolate. "We were on the edge of our seats last night, waiting for news."

Sterling grilled hot dogs to order over the open flames while Steph filled plates with potato salad, corn on the cob, and house-made potato chips.

"Apologies, but duty called. I'm afraid the downside of

policework is the hours and hours of paperwork that accompany every arrest." The Professor reached for a pickle spear. "I believe you already know the highlights. Mary Beth didn't get far yesterday evening after you so wisely alerted us as to where to find her. Detective Mars apprehended her on her way to her cabin. She didn't put up a fight. She confessed and told us everything, which should make building a case against her much easier."

"Was it because of Lucy and the plans to tear down Whaleshead?" I asked, pouring myself a cup of the steaming hot chocolate.

"Yes. As fate would have it, we had already found financial links in Erik's office. Lucy was indeed buying him off. She gave him multiple bonuses for trying to sway property owners her way. In reviewing her work history, we learned that she's extremely motivated for the sale because she'd had a number of failed ventures, and her bosses have put extreme pressure on her. Her job is on the line." He tucked his hands into his windbreaker.

"Why didn't she tell you that, especially when there wasn't proof that she was at the council meeting?" Steph handed me mini marshmallows to add to my hot chocolate.

"The money was a bribe. It didn't go through legal channels. She needed this sale desperately to save her floundering career. Detective Mars questioned her again yesterday afternoon after she had a chance to speak with her employers and review Lucy's bank accounts and tax records. That's why we were close by. She told us the full story once we produced financial receipts of her payments to Erik. She didn't want anyone—namely her bosses—to know she'd funneled him bribe money. We would have closed the case even sooner had she cooperated from the beginning.

She was at the council meeting, by the way. One of the members came forward and made an official statement and there was an article about it in the local paper."

"Mary Beth killed Erik because she learned about the bribes and realized that Erik was fine with tearing down her cabin," Lance confirmed, pouring a generous glass of wine for Arlo. "When Jules and I saw her painting, we both had a similar reaction that she had worked out some rage on the canvas, which is understandable. However, once she launched into her tirade, it became clear that her rage went deeper than her art."

"Exactly. It's a shame." The Professor ran his finger and thumb along his chin. "We spoke with Jess a short while ago, and it's official—the ownership has voted not to sell the resort."

"No way." Sterling lifted the hot stick above his head in a cheer. "She told us she felt confident the owners weren't going to vote to sell, but we've been waiting to hear."

Steph smiled wider than I'd ever seen. "That's huge."

"Despite Lucy's and Erik's best efforts, the resounding sentiment is to keep Whaleshead the rustic treasure that it is." The Professor clapped Sterling on the back. "It appears your successful venture with SeaBreeze helped tip the scales in favor of a 'no' vote."

Everyone cheered.

That was a bit of much-needed good news.

Sterling and Steph would keep their jobs, and the resort of so many of my childhood memories would live on for the next generation of Capshaw kids.

"Well, if we're sharing good news, then there's no better time than the present for this." Lance set his wineglass in the sand and stood up. "Everyone, excuse me. If I could borrow a minute of your time. There's something I need to share, and it simply cannot wait."

I sat taller and wrapped a blanket around my shoulders.

Lance cleared his throat and signaled Ramiro with a nod.

What had he and Ramiro cooked up together?

Was this about Steph and Sterling and the money he'd gifted them?

Or about Ramiro returning to Spain?

Ramiro queued a song on his phone and paired it with the portable speakers propped next to his chair. He moved the speaker closer to the center of our little circle so everyone could hear. Adele's sultry voice filled the sparkly night air.

Lance stood in front of the fire, the flames casting a soft glow on his skin.

As soon as I realized the song Ramiro was playing was "Make You Feel My Love," I had a good idea of what was about to happen. I reached over and squeezed Carlos's hand.

He turned to me with a look of confusion. "What is it, mi querida?"

"Just watch," I whispered.

Lance wrung his hands together in a rare show of nerves and paused as if working up the courage to speak.

Arlo most have noticed his partner was at a loss for words, because he scooted his chair closer and studied Lance with concern. I thought he was about to get up and rescue him, but Lance pressed his lips together and inhaled slowly. "Ah, what a delight to be surrounded by the people I love tonight." He chuckled, placing his palm on his throat. "That wasn't even an intended rhyme. Sometimes I simply can't help myself."

Mom leaned into the Professor's embrace. She caught my eye and grinned.

I wondered if she had an idea of what was going on, too.

"Rhyming aside, I hope you all know how much I love and adore you." Lance fiddled with his sleeve and let his eyes linger on Arlo. "One of you I love particularly dearly."

Arlo blew him a kiss.

"Which is why, as we're gathered here together beneath a canopy of stars with the lulling rush of the ocean nearby and a fire lapping up the flames, I must profess my flame burns bright for the man seated in front of me."

If Adele and Lance's nerves hadn't cued Arlo in to what was happening, there was no mistaking it now.

He started to move, but Lance motioned for him to stay. "No, sit. Please. I have to see your face to do this properly."

Arlo's smile beamed brighter than the moon above. He patted his heart and nodded for Lance to continue.

"I've spent the better part of my lifetime staging love. Grandiose productions, star-crossed lovers, romantic heroines, dashing leading men, passionate kisses, and tender embraces. Yet never, never in my visions of blocking out a love scene so real that it sweeps audiences off their feet did I even imagine that the love of my life would feel so utterly, wonderfully mundane."

"Hey," Arlo interrupted him, clearly not anticipating this was where Lance's profession of love would go.

I couldn't blame him. No one wanted their love affair to be labeled "mundane."

"Hear me out," Lance said, grinning slyly. "I said wonderfully mundane, emphasis on *wonderfully*."

Arlo acquiesced, crossing one leg over the other and waiting for Lance to continue.

"What I've learned is that chasing love on the big stage is nothing compared to finding the real thing. I don't need over-the-top gestures and out-of-this-world performances when the man of my dreams sits right in front of me." Lance's voice caught.

I felt the happy sting of tears. Carlos scooted closer and tucked his knees under my blanket. "This is so romantic, Julieta."

"I know." I brushed a tear from my eye.

Everyone waited with bated breath for Lance to continue.

"What I've failed to realize until finding you, dear Arlo, is that love is Saturday strolls through Lithia Park, soup night, crossword puzzles and French press coffee, softball—who would have ever thought that yours truly would know so much about softball?"

We all laughed.

Lance was just getting started. "Sure, you can always bring a guy an overflowing bouquet of flowers, and I'll never turn down a bottle of bubbly and a date night in matching tuxes, but I'll take you exactly like this. I want all your future bonfires. I want taco Tuesdays and sweaty Saturdays when you force me to—oh, for the love of God—run. What is it with you and exercise, anyway?"

Arlo shrugged. "It could be the health benefits."

"Health benefits, *schmealth* benefits." Lance waved him off. "Fine. I want your endless need to exercise and force me to drink green smoothies. I want your warm arms

wrapped around me on a cold winter's night, and I want
to wake up every day knowing that we belong to each
other."

Now the tears really started to flow. Not just with me.
Mom was weepy, too, as were the Professor, Carlos, and
even Steph. I was fairly sure we were all going to be a
blubbering mess by the time Lance finally got down on a
knee.

"I want to be there for you. I want to hear about your
favorite soccer team and memorize the players' numbers.
I want to take you dancing in Paris and glamping in the
Florida Keys. I want every moment. I want every breath
we have left."

His chin quivered as he reached into his pocket and
dropped down to his knee. "Arlo, what I'm asking so inel-
oquently is, will you spend the rest of your life with me?"
He pulled out a purple Ring Pop and held it like a token.

Arlo threw his head back and laughed at the sight of the
candy ring. He got out of his chair and down on one knee,
too. "Lance, you better marry me."

They collapsed into each other's arms and kissed.

We cheered and applauded. I was sure our happiness
drifted down the beach into the scattering of fires flicker-
ing in the distance. There were hugs and tears and more
hugs and more tears. Lance had actually done it and in the
sweetest most humble way possible.

He had done it. He had really done it.

My best friend was engaged.

There were rounds of toasts, speeches, and cheers. I
couldn't contain my happiness. My cheeks hurt from smil-
ing so much.

As the flames began to flicker, I pulled Lance aside. "I

can't believe you proposed. You were so intent on coming up with the perfect plan and the ring and all of it earlier. What changed?"

"You, darling. You." He kissed both of my cheeks. "You."

"What? I don't understand, but I do have to say I love the Ring Pop."

"I had little to work with, but the candy store in Brookings came through in a pinch." He wrapped me in a tight hug. "Your words stuck a chord. Why wait on love? I don't need the perfect setting, moment, or even a ring to declare to the world this is the man who I love and want to spend the rest of my life with. You've taught me more than I think you'll ever know, Juliet Montague Capshaw, and for that, I'm forever grateful."

"Right back at you, Lance Rousseau." I held him tight, not wanting this moment to end.

"Chin up, darling," Lance said, finally releasing me. "We have much to do upon our return to Ashland—a wedding to plan, a new staff for you, perhaps a coffee adventure or two. The Fair Verona Players are selling out shows. There's news afoot with OSF that I'm not yet at liberty to share. And we must plan a watch party for Richard Lord's television debut on *Make a Millionaire Match*."

I'd nearly forgotten about Richard Lord's impending stardom on the new dating show. Lance was right. There was so much to look forward to. He moved on as Arlo called him over to take a selfie.

I glanced at our little impromptu engagement party, feeling entirely overcome with emotion and gratitude. Tears poured from my eyes as I looked at everyone I loved, backlit by the flame and the dark ocean. Lance was getting married, I was having twins, Sterling and Steph had successfully launched a new restaurant, Ramiro was soon off for his next adventure, and Mom and the Professor were ready to kick back and enjoy their golden years.

Mary Beth had sunk into the darkness, but I was choosing the light. There were so many reasons to celebrate every form of love, and that was exactly what I intended to do.

# Recipes

### Chocolate Cherry Sponge Cake

**Ingredients:**
**For the sponge cake:**
6 large egg whites
½ teaspoon vinegar
1 cup sugar
1¼ cups flour
½ cup cocoa powder
2 teaspoons instant coffee
1 tablespoon cornstarch
1 teaspoon baking powder
1 teaspoon salt
6 large egg yolks
¼ cup warm water
1 teaspoon vanilla extract
½ cup vegetable oil

**For the cherry compote:**
2 cups Bing cherries, pitted and halved
¼ cup sugar

1 tablespoon lemon juice
1 tablespoon cornstarch mixed with 1 tablespoon water

**For the chocolate whipped cream:**
1½ cups heavy cream
¼ cup cocoa powder
¼ cup powdered sugar

**For the topping:**
Dark chocolate shavings
Whole cherries with stems

**Directions:**
Preheat the oven to 350°F. Grease two 9-inch round cake pans and set aside. In an electric mixer or by hand, beat egg whites and vinegar until soft peaks form. Gradually add the sugar, continuing to beat until the mixture is glossy and stiff peaks form. In a separate bowl, sift together the flour, cocoa powder, instant coffee, cornstarch, baking powder, and salt. Whisk the egg yolks in another bowl with the warm water, vanilla extract, and oil until smooth. Slowly add the egg yolk mixture to the dry ingredients, mixing until well combined. Carefully fold the beaten egg whites into the batter.

Divide the batter evenly between the prepared cake pans. Bake for 25–30 minutes or until a toothpick inserted into the center comes out clean. While the cakes are cooling, make the compote by combining the cherries, sugar, and lemon juice in a saucepan. Cook over medium heat until the cherries release their juices and soften, about 10 minutes. Stir in the cornstarch mixture and cook until thickened. Remove from heat and let cool.

In an electric mixer, whip the heavy cream until soft peaks form. Add the cocoa powder and powdered sugar, and continue to whip until the mixture is fluffy. Once the cakes and compote have cooled completely, assemble the cakes by placing one layer of the chocolate sponge on a serving plate. Spread a generous layer of half of the cherry compote over the cake, followed by half of the chocolate whipped cream. Top with the second layer of sponge cake and repeat the process. Finish by topping the cake with dark chocolate shavings and stemmed cherries.

## Sterling's Sunday Sauce

### Ingredients:
2 tablespoons olive oil
1 large onion, finely chopped
4 cloves garlic, minced
2 pounds fresh tomatoes, chopped
¼ cup fresh basil leaves, chopped
Juice and zest of 1 small lemon
¼ cup heavy cream
Salt and pepper

### Directions:
In a large skillet, heat the olive oil over medium heat. Add the onion and sauté until translucent, about 5 minutes.

Add the garlic and cook for another 1–2 minutes, stirring frequently to prevent burning. Add the chopped tomatoes to the skillet. Stir well and cook over medium heat until the tomatoes break down and form a sauce, about 15–20 minutes. Stir in the chopped basil leaves and fresh lemon juice and zest. Lower the heat and stir in the heavy cream. Season with salt and pepper to taste. Let the sauce simmer for a few more minutes and serve over your favorite pasta with meatballs and Parmesan.

### Rhubarb Crumble Cake

**Ingredients:**
½ cup unsalted butter, softened
1¼ cups sugar
1 teaspoon vanilla extract
2 large eggs
2 cups flour
2 teaspoons baking powder
½ teaspoon salt
½ cup milk
2 cups fresh rhubarb, washed and chopped into cubes
1 tablespoon cornstarch
¼ cup orange juice
1 tablespoon orange zest
½ cup rolled oats
½ cup brown sugar
1 teaspoon cinnamon
½ cup unsalted butter, chilled and cubed
Whipped cream for serving

**Directions:**
Preheat the oven to 350°F. Grease a 9-inch square baking dish and set aside. In a large mixing bowl, cream together the softened butter, 1 cup of the sugar, and vanilla extract. Beat in the eggs one at a time. In a small bowl, combine 1½ cups of the flour with the baking powder and salt. Alternate adding the milk and the dry ingredients to the butter mixture. Mix until just combined.

Mix the chopped rhubarb with the remaining ¼ cup sugar, cornstarch, orange juice, and orange zest in a separate bowl until the rhubarb is well coated. Spread the cake batter evenly over the bottom of the greased baking dish. Layer the coated rhubarb over the batter.

In a new bowl, combine the oats, remaining ½ cup flour, brown sugar, and cinnamon. Using a pastry cutter or fork, cut the chilled butter into the mixture until it resembles sand. Sprinkle the crumbly topping evenly over the rhubarb layer. Bake for 45 minutes or until the cake is golden brown and a toothpick inserted into the center comes out clean. Allow the cake to cool to room temperature. Serve slices with a dollop of whipped cream.

### Breakfast Lasagna

**Ingredients:**
2 tablespoons olive oil
4 cups frozen hash browns, thawed
Salt and pepper, to taste

1 pound breakfast sausage
1 small onion, finely chopped
1 bell pepper, finely chopped
1 teaspoon garlic powder
1 teaspoon paprika
10 large eggs
1 cup heavy cream
1 cup shredded cheddar cheese
½ cup shredded mozzarella cheese

**Directions:**
Preheat the oven to 375°F. Grease a 9x13–inch baking dish
and set aside. In a large skillet, heat the olive oil over medium heat. Add the hash browns and cook until golden
brown, about 10–15 minutes. Season with salt and pepper
to taste. Spread the cooked hash browns evenly in the bottom of the greased baking dish.

In the same skillet, cook the breakfast sausage over medium heat until browned and cooked through, about 8–10
minutes. Add the onion and bell pepper, and cook until
softened, about 5 minutes. Season with the garlic powder
and paprika. Spread the sausage mixture evenly over the
hash brown layer in the baking dish.

In a large mixing bowl, whisk together the eggs, heavy
cream, and 1 teaspoon each salt and pepper. Stir in the
shredded cheddar cheese and mozzarella cheese. Pour the
egg mixture evenly over the sausage and hash brown layers
in the baking dish. Bake for 35–40 minutes, or until the
egg is set and the top is golden brown. Allow the break-

fast lasagna to cool for a few minutes before slicing into squares. Serve warm.

## Peach Cobbler Muffins

**Ingredients:**
2 cups unsalted butter, softened
1½ cups sugar
2 teaspoons vanilla extract
2 large eggs
1 cup buttermilk
2½ cups flour
1 teaspoon salt
1 tablespoon baking powder
2 cups peeled, chopped fresh peaches
1 teaspoon cinnamon
¼ cup butter, chilled and cut into small squares

**Directions:**
Preheat the oven to 375°F. Line a muffin tin with paper liners or grease the muffin cups. In a large mixing bowl, cream the softened butter and 1 cup of the sugar together. Beat in the vanilla extract and eggs one at a time, mixing well after each addition. Gradually add the buttermilk, mixing until the batter is smooth and well combined. Sift 2 cups of the flour, the salt, and baking powder into a separate bowl. Gradually add the dry ingredients to the wet mixture, mixing until a batter forms. Gently fold in the chopped fresh peaches.

Make the crumble topping in a new bowl by combining the remaining ½ cup each flour and sugar with the cinnamon. Add the cold butter squares and use a fork to incorporate the butter into the dry ingredients until the mixture resembles coarse crumbs. Divide the batter evenly among the prepared muffin cups, filling each about ¾ full. Sprinkle the crumble topping evenly over each muffin. Bake for 20–25 minutes, or until a toothpick inserted into the center of a muffin comes out clean. Allow the muffins to cool in the tin for a few minutes before transferring to a wire rack to cool completely. Serve warm.

### Chocolate Soufflé

**Ingredients:**
½ cup unsalted butter, plus extra for greasing
3 tablespoons cocoa powder, plus extra for dusting
½ cup granulated sugar, plus 2 tablespoons extra for coating
6 ounces dark chocolate, chopped
4 large egg yolks
1 teaspoon vanilla extract
½ teaspoon salt
6 large egg whites
¼ teaspoon cream of tartar
Powdered sugar, for dusting

**Directions:**
Preheat your oven to 375°F. Grease six 6-ounce ramekins with butter and dust with cocoa powder, tapping out the

excess. Coat the inside of each ramekin with a thin layer of granulated sugar. Place the prepared ramekins on a baking sheet.

In a heatproof bowl set over a pot of simmering water, melt the dark chocolate and ½ cup of butter, stirring occasionally until smooth. Remove from heat and let cool slightly. In a large mixing bowl, whisk together the egg yolks, ½ cup of the granulated sugar, the vanilla extract, and salt until the mixture is pale and thick. Gradually add the melted chocolate mixture and whisk until well combined.

Beat the egg whites with the cream of tartar using an electric mixer on medium speed until soft peaks form. Gradually add the remaining 2 tablespoons of granulated sugar and continue to beat until stiff peaks form. Gently fold the beaten egg whites into the chocolate mixture in three additions, being careful not to deflate the mixture. Divide the soufflé mixture evenly among the prepared ramekins, filling each about ¾ full. Smooth the tops with a spatula and then run it around the rim of each ramekin. Bake for 12–15 minutes, or until the soufflés have risen and the tops are set. Do not open the oven door during baking. Remove the soufflés from the oven and dust with powdered sugar. Serve immediately.

### Andy's Decaf Chocolate Cherry on Top Latte

Andy's special decaf blend is his love language for Jules. It's the cherry on top for her pregnancy cravings and a cozy warm hug in a cup.

**Ingredients:**
2 shots of decaf (or regular) espresso
1 teaspoon rose water
2 tablespoons cherry syrup
2 tablespoons dark chocolate syrup
1 cup milk
Whipped cream
Dark chocolate shavings
Whole stemmed cherry

**Directions:**
Brew 2 shots of espresso. In a mug, combine the espresso
with the rose water, cherry syrup, and chocolate syrup.
Stir well. Heat the milk in a small saucepan. Pour the hot
milk over the espresso mixture and stir to combine. Top
with whipped cream, chocolate shavings, and a cherry.

**Read on for a look ahead to
LAYING DOWN THE LATTE—
the next Bakeshop mystery from Ellie Alexander
and St. Martin's Paperbacks!**

They say that you have to travel the world to find home. I had certainly found that to be true. After spending a decade sailing from one romantic port of call to another on a boutique cruise ship, I found my way back to my hometown of Ashland, Oregon, where I had been about as close to blissfully happy as one could be ever since. It was fairly impossible not to be swept up in Ashland's charms—the bustling plaza with its locally owned shops and restaurants, the Siskiyou Mountains nestling us in with a cozy evergreen hug, the creative energy that pulsed through town and the artists who also called this place home, the warm and welcoming spirit of community that connected each of us.

This morning, my beloved Ashland was washed in an early morning golden glow as I walked to Torte, my family bakeshop. Sunlight kissed the top of Grizzly Peak, lighting up the flaxen hillside like fire, though the thought of fire made me shudder.

Recent summers had seen a swath of wildfires that tore through Southern Oregon's dense forests and cocooned Ashland in a thick, unrelenting blanket of smoke. This summer felt like the days of old, with brilliant, blue, cloud-less skies that seemed to stretch out for miles, hot afternoons perfect for a refreshing iced coffee, and cool evenings punctuated by a symphony of stars. Fortunately, this summer had been smoke-free. I stopped and looked around for something to knock on. The bark of one of the towering pines would do. I rapped on the wood, not wanting to jinx the clear blue skies.

I turned off Mountain Avenue onto Main Street and breathed in the crisp, clean air. Bungalows and Victorians lined the two-way road, each with lush grassy lawns, flower beds overflowing with cranberry red and canary yellow geraniums, and front porches adorned with bird feeders and colorful windsocks. I loved the eclectic nature of the neighborhood and the fact that wild deer nibbled on climbing roses and bedded in groups beneath clumps of grapevines. It was me and the deer at this hour. Downtown wouldn't be alive with activity for another few hours. As a baker, I was used to greeting the dawn alone, and to be honest, it was my favorite part of the day.

I breathed slowly as the houses transitioned into old Elizabethan facades, and the Carnegie Library came into view. My morning walks were a time to clear my head and center myself for the day. I'd always loved the quiet meditation of a sleepy town, but now that I was pregnant with twins, my morning solace felt especially important—the calm before the storm of the coffee and pastry rush.

Instinctively, my hand went to my little bump. I couldn't quite believe Carlos and I were having twins. Twins. It had taken some getting used to, but now that my belly was starting to swell and my feet ached by the end of a long day running up and down the stairs with heavy trays ladened with sticky orange morning buns and custard tarts, it was impossible to ignore my changing body and the reality that in a few months our little family was going to double in size.

I continued along Main Street, where royal banners in eggplant and gold announced upcoming performances at the Oregon Shakespeare Festival (affectionately known as OSF to locals). My best friend Lance was the artistic director at the world-renowned theater company that attracted actors and patrons from around the globe. There was nothing like taking in a show at the outdoor Elizabethan theater on a warm summer night, guided by constellations above. Lance drew in audiences for his outrageous and whimsical production of Shakespeare's comedies, his heart-moving renditions of the tragedies that left not a single dry eye in the house, and his slant toward showcasing new and upcoming playwrights and making his stage a place where every actor regardless of age, color, disability, or sexual identity had a home. His productions received critical acclaim and a litany of awards. His penchant for playing into the stereotype of a diva director only endeared him more to tourists. He could often be found casually strolling through the plaza in a well-cut suit, stopping to pose for photos with his adoring fans. He deserved the praise, and those of us lucky enough to know the real Lance understood that behind his demure, coy smile was a man deeply attached to Ashland and those he loved.

Recently, he added to his ever-growing accolades by launching a new endeavor—the Fair Verona Players, a theater troupe hosting small, intimate productions at vineyards and Lithia Park. We'd opened the season at Uva, the winery on the outskirts of town that Carlos and I owned and managed. I was curious to see if one of his passions would take hold over the other. Thus far, he seemed to be balancing both with ease. However, he and his longtime partner had recently gotten engaged, and wedding plans were about the only thing we discussed these days.

I was thrilled for Lance and Arlo. Lance had taken a knee and popped the question at a beachside bonfire a few weeks ago. The spontaneous act shocked all of us. He proposed with a Ring Pop and the sweetest profession of his love. For someone who tended to curate every aspect of his life, watching him lean into love, even the messy, sandy, unpolished parts, had been a delight.

Ever since, not a minute has gone by without a wedding text.

Case in point: Before I turned off the lights last night, he texted me asking how I felt about doves.

I responded: Doves?

He immediately shot back, "Forget it. You're right. Too cliché. Too pedestrian. Forget I ever mentioned it."

My thoughts started to swirl as I passed the bookstore and the Crown Jewel, with collections of silky summer scarves and glittery earrings on display. Summers are typically our busy season at Torte, Uva, and our seasonal ice cream shop—Scoops. There was never a dull minute between all the baking, wedding cake construction, catering private events, mapping out staff schedules, ordering inventory, and, believe it or not, thinking ahead to plans for fall and the holiday season. But this week, there was even more than usual to do. Two of my senior staff, Sterling and Steph, recently departed to take on head chef roles at an ailing restaurant on the Southern

Oregon Coast. We'd hired their replacements, who were getting up to speed, but it was still an adjustment. Additionally, a fortuitous invitation from Valentina, one of our former colleagues from the *Amour of the Seas*, the cruise ship where we had met, had me preparing to venture to the coffee capital of the world for a tasting tour and an immersive weekend at her organic family coffee farm in Costa Rica.

Valentina had managed the espresso bars on the cruise ship. She was an aficionado when it came to not only pouring a perfect shot or crafting exquisite latte art but also about every aspect of coffee growing, production, and roasting. We had been good friends during our time at sea and kept in relatively good contact. Like me, she decided to give up her vagabond lifestyle to return to help grow and expand her family's offerings on their coffee farm tucked high in the Costa Rican mountains.

Unbeknownst to Andy, our resident barista, Carlos, and I had a little secret up our sleeves. With the changes brewing at Torte and in our personal lives, we'd decided to bring him along on our Costa Rican adventure. Andy dropped out of college at Southern Oregon University to explore his passion—coffee roasting. He'd spent the last year tinkering with roasts and perfecting his talents on roasting equipment housed on his grandmother's property. His coffees were a true art form and had grown a cult-like following. Carlos and I were ready to invest in Andy. We'd priced out commercial roasting machines and intended to offer Andy a promotion to coffee manager and head roaster. It was a win-win for all of us. We'd be able to bring our roasting in-house instead of procuring beans from other coffee roasters, and Andy would lead the charge of flavors, combinations, and our growing team of baristas. He was ready for more responsibility, and hopefully, the weekend in Costa Rica would be an intensive coffee education that would give him an extra boost of confidence and some new tools to level up his roasting game.

I couldn't wait to tell him. He was always the first to arrive, so we should have a few minutes to chat before the rest of the team showed up.

Torte came into view as I passed through the center plaza past the Lithia Bubblers and the information kiosk covered with posters and fliers for summer jams at the park, acting classes, book club meet-ups, and white-water rafting tours on the nearby Rogue River. The candy apple red and teal blue awnings greeted me, along with the current front window display. It was an ode-to-summer theme. Bethany, our lead baker, and Rosa, our front-of-house manager, had teamed up to create the luscious and delectable window set. Marzipan grapes, strawberries, and peaches filled tiered cake stands intermixed with lacquered tarts, pots of honey, tea cakes, bite-sized sand-wiches, and chocolates. Filmy gauze in pale and forest green was draped from the rafters and fluttered down like willowy branches. Strings of honeybee lights gave the window a buzzing glow. Vases with fresh-cut wildflowers and floral teapots finished off the scene.

I was blown away by their creativity and artistic eye. Everything in the window was so tempting that I wanted to reach inside and swipe a glossy marzipan berry. I re-sisted the urge and headed down the brick stairwell instead.

When I reached the bottom, I unlocked the door and flipped on the lights. Our commercial kitchen and baking stations were located in the basement. Shortly after I moved back home, Mom and I took on a massive remodeling project—moving our entire operation downstairs. It had been a bigger undertaking than either of us had initially imagined, but the final result was worth it.

The basement was naturally cool, a welcome gift, especially on days like this when temps would rise in the afternoon, flirting with triple digits. I ran my fingers along the exposed brick walls and fluffed up a pillow on the couch as I passed the comfy seating area in front of the atomic fireplace. There was no need to light the gas fireplace today. Mother Nature would be our natural heat source.

Along with the couch, there was a collection of chairs, a coffee table, and bookshelves filled with books and games for customers to enjoy while they lingered with iced cinnamon spice mochas and slices of bourbon pound cake.

The open-concept kitchen was my favorite spot in the bakeshop. It was light and bright, with ample counter space for rolling out sheets of puff pastry dough. The space was meticulously organized, with a cooking station near the gas stove and a pastry decorating counter with extra overhead lighting for those fine piping details. We designed special drawers to house our extensive collection of sprinkles, edible glitter, and pastry knives. The piece de resistance, as Lance would say, was our wood-fired pizza oven that consumed the far back wall. Neither Mom nor I had any idea a rustic oven had been hiding behind old sheetrock. The construction crew had discovered it during renovations—like a gift from the pastry gods. We baked our breads, pizzas, and hand-rolled pretzels in the oven, giving everything a beautiful smoky finish.

I started the opening checklist by lighting a bundle of applewood in the fire and heating the main ovens. Then, I brewed a pot of decaf and grabbed the custom order sheets. We kept our pastry cases stocked with a selection of signature baked goods and offered daily specials based on whatever was in season. We also baked bread for a variety of wholesale accounts, predominantly restaurants and hotels in town, who used it in their sandwiches and to accompany warm bowls of soup.

While the coffee brewed, I printed out Andy's plane ticket and quickly assessed the inventory in the walk-through fridge. For today's specials, I wanted to bake something quintessentially summer and settled on a peach cobbler with a bit of a twist. Peaches were ripe and juicy, picked from the nearby orchards, and hand-delivered to our door.

I washed my hands with lemon and lavender soap, poured myself a cup of decaf with a splash of heavy cream, and got to work by peeling, coring, and dicing the peaches. Soon, my hands dipped with the sweet juice. I mixed the peaches with cinnamon, brown sugar, a touch of salt, and lemon juice. I scooped cornstarch into a small Tupperware, added water, and shook it with the lid on until the cornstarch had dissolved. The mixture would ensure that my cobbler didn't end up runny. There was nothing worse than a runny cobbler or soggy pastry crust.

I incorporated it with the peaches to thicken the mixture. I set them to the side and cut cold butter into cubes. Then I forked it with flour, brown sugar, and oats. Once it formed a crumbly, sand-like texture, I pressed it into greased baking dishes and slid them into the oven to bake for ten minutes.

I sipped my coffee and leafed through the custom orders. There were requests for birthday cakes, baby showers, a retirement cake, and three wedding cakes. The wedding cakes took top priority because they required extra time to cool in the fridge for the crumb coat (or first layer of frosting) to set before they could be assembled and finished to the happy couple's specifications.

My phone buzzed with a text.

*Lance.*

*Of course.*

It was like he was in my head.

"We must discuss cake. Square? Round? Tiers? Individual? I will only admit this to you, but I can't keep up with the trends."

I chuckled as I gave him the advice I gave every one of our wedding clients, which was to pick a style and flavors that were meaningful to him and Arlo. Trends in cakes came and went like the rise and fall of dough in the oven—puffing up with excitement and sinking back into obscurity. The only thing that mattered was whether or not Lance and Arlo were pleased with the cake design.

"Fine. Way to be practical. Sending you inspiration pics now.

He proceeded to bombard me with dozens of radically unique designs. We'd bake whatever they wanted, but I knew it was a losing battle to attempt to reign Lance in. He loved the drama.

My timer dinged, but I didn't need it. As I teach every new baker, a chef's nose is their best guide for "doneness." Without fail, I could always smell when a batch of cookies or a cake was ready. The base of the peach cobbler was no exception. Its buttery aroma with hints of cinnamon wafted through the kitchen as I walked to the oven to remove the pans. I spread a thickened peach layer and finished it with a final layer of the oat crumble—this time sprinkled loosely over the top.

The door jingled. Andy burst inside carrying a re-usable grocery bag filled with containers of beans. His exuberant energy was magnetic. Andy was like Torte's personal golden retriever. He could brighten any room with his wholesome, genuine smile and contagious enthu-siasm. He was tall and muscular with shaggy hair. Today, he wore a pair of board shorts and a T-shirt. "Morning, boss. It's already heating up out there." He hoisted the bag on the island and lifted the first tub. A piece of mask-ing tape secured the lid and had the words TEST BATCH 24 written across the top. "Since I had the weekend off, I did some more testing, and it sort of got out of hand."

"You roasted twenty-four different batches?" I stared at the shopping bag, impressed by Andy's commitment to creating new blends and recognizing that he might be prone to perfectionist tendencies like me.

"Yeah, I think my grandma is going to kick me out soon. She said she can't smell anything other than coffee beans and that even her sheets are infused with the aroma of my roasts." He lifted his hand to his nose as if to check whether his pores were oozing with the heavenly scent of freshly roasted beans.

"There could be worse things." I tried to wink but managed to contort my face into a weird half-grin.

"That's exactly what I said." He balled his hand into a fist and pumped it against mine. "Who doesn't want to smell like coffee twenty-four/seven?"

"Well, that might be taking it a bit too far," I admitted,

although my coffee addiction was legendary, and thanks to Andy, even though I'd given the caffeine content with my pregnancy, I didn't have sacrifice flavor. He'd put countless hours into creating mouthwatering decaf options for me. I was forever in his debt. There weren't many things I cared about giving up during my pregnancy, but coffee was non-negotiable. It was so much more than just the caffeine for me. It was ritual, comfort, and an integral part of my daily routine.

"We're talking about beans." He ran his hand over the bag. "Nectar of the Gods. Java juice. Should I keep going?"

"No." I chuckled. "Although I do have some news that, in a roundabout way, involves your grandma."

Andy raised his thick eyebrows and stared at me skeptically. "My grandma?"

"Yep. Give me one minute." I held up my index finger and hurried to grab the plane ticket from the counter. "As you know, Carlos and I are going to Costa Rica next weekend for a coffee farm excursion, and we decided we needed a stowaway." I pressed the folded sheet of paper into his hand. "Go ahead, open it."

His brow scrunched tight in confusion as he studied the ticket. "This is a plane ticket, Jules. A ticket to Costa Rica with my name on it." Realization dawned on him. His freckles popped like sunbursts as his smile stretched across his boyish cheeks. "Me?" He tapped his chest. "I'm going? What? Really? No way. Are you serious?"

"Dead serious." I nodded solemnly. "Carlos and I have some big plans and ideas in store for you that we can discuss on the flight. Valentia is thrilled that you're coming—I mean, assuming you want to come."

He cut me off, bouncing up and down on his toes. "I want to come. I want to come."

"I figured," I laughed. "Anyway, Valentia will walk you through the entire process, from how they monitor the flowering cherries to harvesting, washing, drying, roasting, and everything in between. It's a good time of year to visit because they're preparing for the harvest later this fall, so things are slow on the farm. Valentina has asked for our help and ideas for the new espresso bar and pastry counter they're going to open in a converted barn, and in exchange, she's going to share her coffee expertise with you."

"This is amazing. I can't believe it." Andy's mouth hung open in awe as he read and re-read the ticket like it was a figment of his imagination. "I've always wanted to go to Costa Rica. It's the coffee heartland." He pressed his hand over his chest with reverence. "Thank you so much for this opportunity. Seriously, Jules. This is my dream."

"We're over the moon to have you accompany us, and I'm eager to learn and refresh my memory right along with you. It's been years since I've visited a coffee farm. I think the last time was when Carlos and I stopped in Costa Rica for one night on the ship."

It was fun to watch him spring around the kitchen like a bouncy ball.

"I have so much to do. Pack. Study." He froze. "Oh no, what about coverage here? The new staff are just finally in the zone. Is that going to throw everything off?"

"We've got that covered. In fact, that's the only reason I waited to tell you. I wanted to make sure we were set, and I'm happy to report that we are. Mom and the Professor are going to help, as will Wendy, Mom's good friend who used to assist my parents back in the day when they needed an extra hand. Wendy will cover the pastry counter and dining room, which frees up Sequoia, Bethany, Rosa, Marty, and the new staff to focus on baking and managing the espresso bar. The Professor even volunteered to help with wholesale deliveries. I've tweaked the schedule at Scoops, so if needed, some of those team members can rotate here, and we're going to close Uva for the weekend. We're only going to be gone for four days, so it's no big deal."

"Wow, you've gone to a lot of trouble. You might even say a *latte* of trouble for me." He winked and ran his hand over the Tupperware containers.

I groaned and tossed a dish towel at him. "You've been spending too much time around Bethany." Running a bakeshop naturally lent itself to baking puns, and Bethany was our queen of clever catchphrases. She was notorious for wearing T-shirts and hoodies with sayings like BAKE MY DAY, and I'M A WHISK TAKER.

"They get in your head, man." He made a face and tucked the ticket in the bag with his assorted roasts. "Thanks for all of this, Jules. I'm going to make you proud. I'll be sure to thank your mom, Wendy, and the Professor, too. It's so cool of them to step in and help."

"That's what we do at Torte." I checked the peach crumble, which was bubbling and juicy. It still needed another minute or two. "Plus, we get the benefit of your creations, so really it's about that—hook us up with coffee."

"Consider it done." He grabbed his things and started toward the stairs. "I'm already dreaming up a Costa Rica special for today. I'll make yours unleaded." He took the stairs two at a time, repeating, "We're going to Costa Rica. We're going to Costa Rica."

I finished my first cup of decaf while I waited for my bake. Andy's reaction was exactly what I was hoping for. I couldn't wait to fill him in on our other plans, but I wanted Carlos to be part of that discussion.

Soon, the kitchen was humming with activities as the rest of the team trickled in. I cut slices of my peach cobbler for everyone to taste, and as promised, Andy returned with a tray of sample coffee. "Try these, you all. It's my Pura Vida Latte," he said, passing around mugs after sharing the news of our upcoming research trip. "It's a classic latte with a medium roast espresso, coconut milk, sugarcane, and topped with cinnamon and nutmeg. Hopefully, it evokes the tropics. I'll improve it after we return, and I'll have a chance to apply what I learned."

His baseline was already high. I didn't see much room for improvement, but I was eager for our getaway and to watch Andy immerse himself in his passion. After all, Torte and baking were my passion and getting to pass on the same to my staff was the best gift I could ask for.